VENATUS

Book Three of the Unforgettable Series

Autumn Archer

DEDICATION

To everyone who has read my books thus far – thank you from the bottom of my heart.

ACKNOWLEDGMENTS

This is book three of the Unforgettable Series by Autumn Archer, which introduces Jamie McGrath and Shannon.

Content Editing: Allison Irwin (ExcessiveReader)

Copy Editing & Proofing: Pamela Gonzales (Love2readromance)

Cover Design: Wickedly Designed by Becca

The Unforgettable Series:

VERTO VENERI, Book One of The Unforgettable Series

VERITAS, Book Two of The Unforgettable Series

VENATUS, Book Three of The Unforgettable Series

Sign up to Autumn Archer's Newsletter for more details on upcoming releases.

VENATUS
Hunt

~

Chapter 1

There were sounds of shrill whinnies, powerful snorts and metal horse shoes thudding the earth, all fighting against the temper of Niall Ross. Startled crows took to the air, squawking with disapproval.

Shannon's flat boots pounded the dirt, until she witnessed the attack along the mucky track leading to the pasture.

Every muscle in her body tightened when Niall's deep voice yelled with spine chilling venom, "You, stupid animal. I hate you. I'm the boss around here, not you."

His leg shot up, the toe of his boot met the wide ribs of a hefty chestnut coloured gelding. The horse scooted to the side, restricted in movement by the leather head collar hooked to the lead rope wrapped around his gloved hand. His free hand whirled the end of the rope around like the blades of a helicopter, threatening to strike again. The flighty horse's hind quarters bounced, fighting against his merciless control.

Shannon flew up behind him, steadying herself to a standstill. "What the hell are you doing?" she gritted out.

Her quick breathing matched the tempo of her heartbeat when he wrenched the horse's head lower, countering its struggle.

With his legs planted wide, a manic scowl flashed across the mottled skin on his face. "Trust you to stick your fucking nose in where it doesn't belong," he snarled. "Back the fuck off, Shannon. This horse needs to know who's the boss around here." Niall's stormy eyes flicked to meet hers. "And so do you, apparently."

Unable to help, her short fingernails scraped down the lengths of her ebony ponytail that had bounced to the front opening of her padded jacket. The horse's nostrils flared with rapid pants, and its beautiful black eyes protruded with fear. Shannon gulped back the lump swelling in her throat, feeling her heart pinch with both anger and pity.

"We all know you're the boss, Niall, now let me take him," she lied straight to his face. The guy was an asshole, and she despised everything he stood for, which was being an entitled bully. Thankfully they weren't together anymore.

"What the hell is going on in here?" a deep gravelly voice boomed from behind.

The head stable hand, Bucky, appeared. His fists contracted the closer he got to the distressed horse. Jabbing a callused finger in Niall's face, Bucky hissed, "You beat that horse again, boy, and I'll shove my fist so far down your throat it'll meet your ass."

Bucky's weathered face bore the brunt of outdoor work with deep creases aging his heavy brow. White whiskers scattered his square jaw, leading to the black beanie on top of his head.

Niall staggered forward, pulling against the horse's strength. "I'll fire you, Bucky," he announced loudly with a smirk teasing his tight lips. The bastard was playing a game and enjoying it.

"Fuck you, Niall. I've worked with Harry for over thirty years, well before you were even born. Your *Daddy,"* Bucky mocked, "will cut off your allowance if he hears about this. Now, give me the fucking horse."

Shannon's hands twitched, eager to grab the lead rope and string Niall up by the balls. Adrenaline powered through her body, making her pulse race with an edgy thrum.

"Come on, Niall. Harry will go ballistic." Her voice was shaky but firm. She couldn't care less if Harry went off on him, her concern was solely for the frightened horse.

"Like I give a fuck what he thinks." Niall cracked his

neck from side to side.

Losing his patience, Bucky shunted him to the side and snatched the rope, tugging it free. "Go on, get the fuck out of here, Niall," he spat.

Niall staggered back just as the horse rushed forward, scattering the group to the side. "You see what I mean," he sneered. "It's not so funny when the fucker is trying to hurt *you*, Bucky." Niall's tone was riddled with superiority, and he almost chuckled. He tilted into Shannon's face, hovering his gloved finger close to her cheek. "If that thing kicks me again, I'll shoot it between the eyes."

Rocking back on his heels, he glared at Bucky before swaggering past Shannon like she was mist on the morning hills.

Her hands trembled with resentment, watching helplessly as Bucky wrestled with the terrified horse, trying his hardest to settle it with soothing tones.

"Easssssssy," he drawled. "I'm gonna beat the shit out of that wee prick one of these days. Get the sedatives, Shan," he called out.

This wasn't Bucky's first rodeo, he'd sedated more than enough horses in his days, and while Niall was on the yard, it wouldn't be the last.

"I need the key to the cabinet!" Bucky always wore a set of keys, attached to his belt loop. Only Harry and Bucky had keys. They were responsible for monitoring the veterinary supplies and right now, there was no time to find Harry.

"Shit." He shook his head. "You'll have to come up here behind me and remove it yourself. I can't let go of him. We need to get him into the paddock."

Awash with sweat, the horse panted heavily. Its ears pinned back, and the whites of its eyes were visible. "I can't let go of him. If he bolts, the chances are he'll get damaged, and this one isn't even ours." Front hooves lifted, raising dangerously close to Bucky's chest. "Quick, Shan. Grab my keys. He's too wild for pills in a feed bucket. I'll have to jab him in the muscle."

Steady steps brought her to his side. A thin silver chain hung loosely on his hips, and the keys were tucked deep in his pocket. His hips angled, baring down on the spot, making it easier for her to free the clanking metal and unhook the strong clip.

Backing away slowly, Shannon waited until she was out of sight and then darted across the cobbled yard. The tall white cabinet, at the back of the staff tea room was crammed with emergency veterinary supplies, from sedatives to purple antiseptic spray.

Shannon cursed Niall and his bullshit deception, allowing herself to imagine what line of deflection he would fabricate this time.

'The horse spooked, Dad'... 'It kicked me, Dad'... 'It's dangerous, Dad'... 'I was trying to help, Dad.'

You just know when someone is a little unhinged, there's a hint of a twist behind the eyes, a glimmer of disparity in their ways and a not so transparent veil of malice drapes their character... and Niall Ross displayed them all.

Chapter 2

"Yes, I'm nearly there. The bus got stuck in traffic. Don't panic." Shannon sighed into the mobile phone wedged between her ear and shoulder.

She'd been riding Trixie in the sand paddock when the first call came. One of the waitresses covering the afternoon shift threw up in the store room and was sent home.

Working in the city cafe helped to pay the bills and added a few extra pounds to her modest savings account. She had plans, big plans. So when the manager asked her to help out at the last minute, she agreed.

Thankfully, Niall hadn't noticed that she ended her training session early, leaving the horse half exercised with a kiss and a promise to finish their lesson later. He took pride in barking out the orders at Meadow Dawn, the horse yard where she lived, trained and worked. Niall was a mega asshole with a weighty chip on his shoulder, who also happened to be her ex-boyfriend, and the yard owner's son.

With the Equine Competitions coming up, she had to ride consistently. Every single day. Rain, hail or sunshine. Her schedule was whacked out with riding and shifts. Practice makes perfect after all. And this afternoon she traded her black velvet riding helmet with a baseball cap.

Ending the call, she slipped the phone into her back pocket. The bus driver slammed on the brakes seconds after she dinged the bell. Her slouched bag crashed off the seats as she navigated the narrow isle. With a subtle chin flick aimed at the driver, she jumped down onto the footpath and inhaled the city air. A salty sea breeze reminded her that she was miles from home. The squall of seagulls gathering overhead competed with growling car engines. Her gaze was drawn to the wide depths of Belfast Lough that journeyed into the choppy Irish Sea, framed by modern high-rise offices and towering cranes. It was a far contrast from the lush green fields at Meadow Dawn Stables.

Jogging to the pedestrian crossing, she checked her watch. It was almost half past four in the afternoon, and the crowds of homeward bound office workers hadn't quite peaked. Poking the cross-walk button, she waited for the red light.

"Jamie?" a shaky male voice called, just in earshot. "Jamie?" His voice cracked.

Shannon looked back over her shoulder. A smartly dressed man, possibly in his sixties, with cropped white hair and a look of terror on his pale face, paced back and forth. He didn't appear drunk, nor dangerous – more confused.

The traffic crossing beeped. She paused, hoping someone else would usher him to safety. They didn't. No one stopped. Every passing stranger made their own assessment and decided he wasn't worth the trouble. There was something about him that reached out to her. She couldn't say what it was, other than he looked like a wounded animal at the kerbside. Helping an injured animal was a given, she wouldn't think twice about it.

Shannon sucked in a breath of cool air, releasing it from her nose with a loud sigh. The elderly man dragged both palms down his cheeks. Her heart twanged, instinctively wanting to comfort him. She jogged closer, meeting him face on. "Sir, can I help you?" Her hand brushed his shoulder.

The lines around his mouth depended, and his wiry brows pulled together. "Oh, my dear. I need Jamie. My son, Jamie. I was with him, and then I…" His words trailed off.

Shannon scanned the street, searching for someone else who looked lost. "Where did you last see him?" She kept her tone soft like she was talking to a flighty colt.

His forearms hugged his chest in a self-like hug, and he suddenly stopped pacing. A blank look glazed his eyes, and he stared up at the hotel shading them from the low afternoon sun. His hand swept over his neat buzz cut. The thick golden ring on his left hand twinkled and his suit jacket splayed open. A royal blue lining peeked out at his sides and a mobile phone filled his inner pocket.

"I don't know." His expression tightened like his memory had been erased with the flick of a switch. "My eldest son, Marcus, he's flying home today. He told me he would be here." His tone was a little frosty as he clenched his fists.

Shannon made a quick mental note - his sons were old enough to take care of themselves. The man himself was lost, not his son, Jamie.

"Is that your phone?" She pointed to his jacket. "In your pocket."

He patted his jacket roughly and slipped a shaky hand inside. Pulling the phone into the open, he scrutinized the device like it had magically appeared.

"Jamie, where is he?" he whispered.

"May I see your phone, sir?" She inched out her palm and waited.

A flash of fear rippled through his glassy grey eyes. His knuckles whitened, and his lips pressed into a firm line. Warily, his tight grip released. Her fingers grazed his ice-cold palm. Instantly, his hands curled, his feet drew together, and his frail shoulders sagged.

Scrolling through the contacts, she found the only Jamie listed and hit dial. Seconds later, a harsh male voice masking desperation answered, "Dad! Where the hell are you?" The deep voice scattered chills down her spine and even the shortest hairs on her neck pricked.

"Oh, hi, he's okay. I found him outside The Fitz Hotel, in Belfast. He's a bit confused and looking for his son, Jamie – so I'm guessing that's you?" She tapped her foot.

"Is he still outside the hotel?" the man replied sharply.

"Yes, he's very…" she began.

"Don't let him out of your sight. I'm coming down now." The line disconnected.

The elderly man shuffled his feet, and his fingertips twiddled with his gold cuff links. "Was that my son, Jamie? Where is he?" His sudden bright tone was laced with hope.

Shannon rubbed his arm gently, feeling the smooth luxurious fabric of his sleeve. "Yes, sir, he's coming for you now."

A flow of air blasted from his lungs. "Oh, thank you, my dear. Do you know my son?"

Warmth thawed his fretful features when he glanced over her shoulder. Shannon turned towards the rotating doors of the grand hotel, inhaling a gust of 'holy fuck' deep into her lungs. With dazed fascination, she shamelessly gawked at the tall man running towards them like fire was biting his ass. The perfect, handsome man was squeezed into tailor-made slate coloured trousers that clung to his taut thighs, with an unbuttoned jacket flapping in the breeze. A neat grey shirt parted at the neck where a couple of buttons were left open, and he didn't wear a tie.

The soles of his expensive leather shoes clattered the tarmac until he halted, wrapping his arms around the elderly man like he'd been lost for a year. There was a definite family resemblance, only this guy was in his early thirties and stuck out in the crowd like a flashing beacon of pure sex.

His strong jawline was shadowed like he hadn't shaved in a day or two. The odd flip of her stomach came from the ridiculous thoughts of prickly scratch marks left between her thighs.

He was breath-taking but such perfection had to be flawed.

Shannon stood in silence, drawn to the most curious set of intense eyes. They were dark like molasses with a halo of glowing amber. There was no doubt this guy knew how to imprison any woman with just one look. He had that look about him, with an irresistible confidence that poured from his fluid movements. Rubbing his father's arm, he straightened his back.

"You have to stop doing this, Dad," he scolded.

Her greedy gaze trailed the length of his legs, all the way up to his broad muscular shoulders. Sucking in her left cheek, Shannon nibbled the soft inner flesh and watched the interaction between father and son. She stared shamelessly, drawing her inspection to his captivating lips that were pressed into a tight line. There was an unknown pull like the hand of a compass, twitching in the direction of the earth's magnetic field. Being so close to this guy had jolted awake all sorts of sensations buzzing through her body with no way to escape.

"Why did you wander off this time?" His deep, masculine voice was hoarse yet smooth, silky yet abrasive.

His arm snaked the man's shoulders letting the tailored material of his suit tighten around the wide curve of his bicep. The fascination trance quickly evaporated into the city air when a young, attractive woman burst out from The Fitz Hotel. She half ran, half walked to their group with makeup free skin that glowed naturally, and a strained smile that reached her sparkly eyes. She looked like one of those beautiful women who woke up looking amazing – the type of sexy woman you would expect a man like him to have.

"Oh God, George, you scared the hell out of us. Next time I visit the ladies, please stay put. Understand?" she pleaded with both authority and melancholy.

George smiled sheepishly. The darker skin under his eyes sagged with exhaustion, and his hands trembled. "Where is Marcus. I told him to be here," he snapped.

Jamie sighed. "I told you, Dad, he's flying home from America. He won't be home until tomorrow."

"Why are we outside in the cold, Jamie. Can we please go inside?" George's arms wrapped his chest, and he blew out a short puff of air like he was fed up.

All of a sudden Jamie's dark eyes were on her. The heat of the silent exchange ignited beneath her skin. The strangers handsome chiselled features were striking enough

17

to be a model, and his dark sandy, choppy hair lifted from the scalp at the front in a sexy sweep. His expression was stern, bordering on unfriendly.

Without blinking, he shoved a hand inside his jacket, pulled out a wad of folded money and flicked over a few hundred-pound notes. He wafted a bundle in the space between them, nudging her arm with the cash. "Take that for your trouble." And there it was - the flaw. He half turned back to George, anticipating her acceptance of the reward.

Typical. Just another rich asshole. A simple thank you would have been enough.

"I don't need your money," she said coolly.

A few hundred pounds was exactly what she needed right now, but the sun would have to drop into the Irish Sea before she accepted another pay off… from a man.

Latching the strap of her shoulder bag, she swung around and lifted her jaw in the air. "What a jerk," she whispered under breath.

Shannon stomped across the road as the traffic came to a timely standstill. Daring to glance back, she witnessed the gorgeous stranger usher his father towards the hotel with the pretty brunette in tow. Weird flutters hinting jealousy, wrapped around her ribs. A completely irrational reaction to a man she would never see again.

Anyway, he was an arrogant ass with the social skills of a pig. Just another Niall Ross.

Chapter 3

Jamie marched into the hotel lobby with a look of thunder darkening his tanned skin. His head flicked back to Rebecca, who hurried behind him, clutching his father's hand like he was a naughty school boy. "Take him upstairs and don't leave him alone," he said sharply.

Rebecca's lashes fluttered as if staving a mist of guilt. "Sorry, Jamie," she barely whispered.

He reached out for her free wrist, holding it firmly. "Look, love, it's not your fault. I need to put a fucking tracking device on him now. This can't continue."

Her head lowered. "I was only away for a few minutes, Jamie."

George shook out of her tight grip, resting his palms on his hips like a grumpy old man. "Stop talking about me like I'm not here, Rebecca!" He scowled.

A gust of air puffed out Jamie's cheeks as he exhaled. "Order me a drink, Dad. I'll be up in an hour, after I've finished up down here. I had to leave my business meeting to find you."

George's brow scrunched. "Where the hell is that boy? I told him to meet us here."

Jamie sucked in through gritted teeth and rolled his eyes to the twinkly crystals hanging overhead. "He'll be here soon, Dad. Just go upstairs with Becks."

He watched Rebecca escort his father to the elevator. The bustle of the busy lobby was muffled by his thumping heart. His father had become a liability, and with his new financial situation, he needed to ensure his family's safety.

Rebecca was the perfect live in caretaker for his father, and good looking too. But that was an ass he would never tap. She was attentive, caring and worth her weight in gold. There was no way he would fuck up the relationship she had with his father – not even for a messy roll in the sheets.

As the elevator doors slid shut, he released a slow breath. It was relief to know that his father was being whisked to the private bar at the top of the hotel, out of harm's way. He had to suck in his worry and return to the abandoned meeting as the legendary, ruthless asshole who had earned the highest respect of his peers and those beneath him. But a shitty fog of worry weighed him down like a concrete necklace. His elder brother Marcus had recently signed a deal that made them rich beyond their wildest expectations. With a hefty bank balance, came a flow of needy and greedy motherfuckers - assholes who wanted to beg, borrow and steel. He didn't trust a single sole out there.

He had grown up in a family of men, the youngest and most carefree. His father worked long hours to keep a roof over their heads. Marcus practically raised him. Male company was the norm until he was old enough to get his dick sucked. That was both elating and a huge fucking let down. His very first female was with Kristy Malone who had matched his age of sixteen at the time, with long blond hair that reached her school girl tight ass and pouty lips that were always covered in sticky gloss.

Jamie had always attracted female attention. Girls giggled with sexy little gasps and flaunted their perky boobs in his face. He lapped up every touch and promise. But Kristy, shit, she pulled his dick in all sorts of directions when she unzipped his jeans. The sweet, wet sensation was pure heaven, but the aftermath was fucking hell. The girl was empty inside. She had zero conversation, or soul, and even splatted a spider on the wall with her fist. There was no connection, other than she inhaled his dick.

From that day on, he quickly realised that it didn't matter if the girls didn't have a personality - they would chase, and he would satisfy. He learned that with just a quirk of his lips, they would suck his dick and jump on his boner like rodeo queens.

Marcus was his best friend and mentor. From a young age, he idolised the guy. He was the master of female attention, never having the same woman twice because he couldn't be bothered with commitment – business was everything. His brother had the act of loving and leaving the ladies down to a fine art until he met the love of his life.

Now Jamie's relationship with women was simple. They came to him. Perfect.

He sauntered across the lobby to the extensive windows that reached from the floor to the ceiling and peered across the street to the quirky coffee shop at the corner. On this occasion, his father's disappearing act unearthed something unexpected. A heightened awareness had flurried in his chest when the unknown female voice reached down the phone line. He'd instantly found her standing close to his father - protecting him.

She was stunning.

Absolutely gorgeous.

Messy black tendrils poured out from under a baseball cap, cascading over her shoulders like a wild stormy ocean. The purple cap with the logo Coffee Kicks embroidered on the front, shaded piercing blue eyes. He was staring at the very same cafe right this second, wondering if the strand of hay nestled in her hair and the dusty worn out boots meant she was actually a cowgirl in disguise.

Coffee Kicks serviced the offices lined up and down the corporate sidewalk. He decided to give their coffee a chance, a taste test to see if it met the same high standard as the coffee he sold in his hotel. Perhaps he could taste the barista too. She'd be easy to persuade.

If he hadn't been so riled at his father's little escapade, then he wouldn't have thought twice about teasing her to a sexplosion in her panties earlier. The women loved it when he toyed with them. Fuck, it was almost a sport, watching them squirm and timing how quickly he could ramp up the heat between their legs.

He noticed that when he recalled the gorgeous girl, his

anger shrivelled, and his dick geared up for action. A hot fantasy flooded his mind. The unruly little barista was gazing up at him with those big baby blues, hunkered down on her knees, ready to suck him off – shit, the blood was pumping to his dick so fast that his head felt light. He reshuffled the hardness in his trousers, wondering if she would still be working when he finished up.

Breathing deeply into his lungs and closing his eyes briefly, he let go of the arousing image. He quickly reminded himself that his father was safely tucked away upstairs, and it was time to get his head back into business matters.

A hand brushed his arm. "Mr. McGrath, I'm glad I found you," purred a sexy, husky voice.

His eyes cut to the woman in a pressed suit with his hotel name on the breast pocket. She had bold pink lips spread across pale cheeks and earthy bobbed hair that skimmed her shoulders like a set of satin curtains.

"It's Jamie, and I'm glad you found me too." He flashed a grin, knowing his showcase dimple would dent his cheek to perfection. "You're new. What's your name?"

"Tabitha." Her eyes dawdled over his mouth, and her lower lip became the victim of her front teeth.

Hmm, that was sexy.

"I've tended to the men in the conference room as instructed. They have refreshments… but they're asking for you."

She was pretty, and sweet, with a Dublin lilt to her raspy voice. He wasn't sure if she would be the dirty, hot fuck he enjoyed, or if she would be the 'hug me after' type. The woman looked like a romance junky who watched reruns of romcoms, wearing fluffy slippers and cotton pyjamas. Her big brown eyes trailed down his jacket and rested at the zipper on his suit trousers.

Gotcha!

Cocking a brow at her inspection, a fast fuck was quickly becoming a good idea. A blush of pink warmed her complexion, and her lashes fanned her eyelids as the seconds ticked by. The plan to make her squirm was in full swing. His assessment held them both in a palpable silence. Tabitha wavered, unintentionally leaning closer.

"Walk with me." He turned away from the barista's coffee shop and slotted his hands into his pockets. "You did well, thanks."

Tabitha smiled coyly, titling her chin and looking sideward with a come-hither glance. "It's nothing." Her voice was timid and low, but her body was vibrating like she wanted him to touch her.

Jamie sauntered ahead, expecting her to follow, and she did without question. "Are they content for a few more minutes?"

"They've been given sandwiches and coffee, so they should be satisfied for a while." Her brows lifted.

'Satisfied', that word left her lips like a provocative sigh, making his dick nudge against his zipper. Damn, he was horny, more fucking stimulated than normal. "Have you got a boyfriend?"

Trotting beside his quick pace, she replied, "No. I'm single at the minute."

The corridor leading to the conference suite was empty. Tabitha's kitten heels prodded the carpet, and the sound of her breathless pants became louder in the silence. Flicking his head over his shoulder, Jamie assessed her giddy steps and foxy face. She was melting like ice cream, and he wanted to lick up the puddle.

Marcus had always told him to keep business separate from pleasure, but his dick was on high alert. Although, oddly enough, he knew it wasn't Tabitha who incited the thrill. The chance meeting earlier had his boxer briefs in a twist. It would be a bad idea to play with his staff, he knew that, but a little fun would give him the satisfaction he needed and help him to think clearly in the meeting. Two birds, one stone.

Stopping abruptly, he turned to face her. "How can I show you my gratitude…" He held her gaze. "For keeping the dogs away from my throat?"

A loud gasp filled her lungs like his dick wanted to fill her mouth – full and fast. Tabitha's dainty fingertips pressed against her smile. "Kiss me."

Teasing the pads of his thumb along her jaw, he noted a subtle flare of desire behind her eyes and mentally patted himself on the back. He hummed low in his throat. "I don't make a habit of kissing my employees."

"I need this job. It will be our little secret."

Jamie puffed out through his nose and tilted into the lengths of her hair, barely touching the shell of her ear with his lips. "I wouldn't fire you, Tabitha. I mean, it's not like you're gonna get all clingy and follow me to the fucking toilet. It's just a bit of fun, right?" he rasped, biting back the desire to rip her panties off. "We're grown-ups."

The ball in her throat bobbed when she gulped, and her silky strands swished when she nodded. "I'd like to… this room behind us is free." Her voice trembled as she pushed open the door to a vacant suite.

Using his hands, he propelled her trembling body into the room. Slamming the door shut, he crooked his finger. "Get over here."

In two strides, Tabitha's hands were on his chest and her lips mushing all over his. Guiding her backwards, one hand grabbed her ass and the other threaded the neat strands at her nape. He wanted it messy, to rough it up like the barista's natural untamed lengths.

With a forceful nudge, Tabitha's shoulders hit the wall. Sliding a hand over her hips, he popped open the stiff buttons on her jacket while his other hand drifted to the delicate curve of her throat. Wrapping his fingers lightly around her neck, he growled.

Bracing his hand on the wall by her head, he kept the other hand under her jaw, lifting her chin high. "You ready?" He dragged his tongue over her lips.

"Yes," she panted.

Tabitha reached out for his zipper with fumbling fingers, as the light pressure teased the fabric, his mind darted to the men waiting for him along the corridor.

Marcus's cock blocking voice in his head challenged his libido, warning him about mixing business with pleasure. The massive hard-on in his trousers needed immediate action, but he'd kept his guests waiting long enough. Marcus would trail his ass over hot coals if he found out that he was getting down and dirty instead of prioritising.

"Hitch up your skirt, Tabby cat."

She obeyed. Spreading her thighs wide, he teased the edges of her panties with gentle swipes, and when he was satisfied that she was wet enough and begging to be fucked, he snapped his hand away.

"Right then, Tabby cat. You know where to find me."

Her gasp was a strangled moan with frustration hot on her lips. She fiddled with her lapel, panting breathlessly. "But…"

"Later." He shifted his zipper to make room for his visible hardness with a teasing smirk on his face. The game was on, she'd be wet and beyond needy by the time she came knocking on his door.

"Okay, sir." Her eyes were wide and pleading.

"It's Jamie," he affirmed, checking to make sure the tails of his shirt were tucked in. "You can call me, sir, later."

Jamie waved his arm, gesturing her exit from the room and into the hallway. Tabitha was eager, but her eyes were bland compared to the woman who saved his father. The barista's glacier eyes were like a frozen ocean, ready to drown any man who cracked through the surface, but he had the skills to make sure he floated unscathed.

He quickly shook off the image of her face and sauntered down the corridor. Tabitha was hot on his heels, scurrying behind with the scent of lust oozing from her pores. A raucous chatter came from inside the occupied conference room. It was only a matter of time before the men became impatient, and in fairness, he would have left by now.

Swinging the door open, he shouted, "Gentlemen!" Then he looked back at Tabitha who stood in the hallway like she needed a hug, or a hard dick. "I'm staying in the Lagan penthouse suite. I like red lace and black leather." His voice reverberated with a low rumble.

"McGrath! You gonna keep us waiting any longer?" shouted one of the men who sat around a long rectangular table.

Jamie nodded curtly at Tabitha, then turned back to face the group. Marching into the room, he slammed the door shut behind him. "I had something important to take care of. My apologies for the interruption, gentlemen."

"You think we have all day to wait around for you, McGrath?" jeered a balding male with ears like the handles of a trophy. "I've got other business to attend to."

Clearing his throat, Jamie sauntered towards the table. "If you're gonna be a dick about it, then why don't you leave? You'll be one less name on the list, Patrick, and you can forget about VIP entrance to the winner's circle. Now get the fuck out of my meeting."

"I only meant to point out the length of time we've been waiting. I have other meetings scheduled today, and this is eating into my time. Sorry, Jamie."

"Yeah, you're sorry. I'm sorry. We're all fucking sorry. Now let's build a fucking bridge and get over it already. Unity isn't for sale. But I'm willing to take on new partners if you bring winners to the game."

Chapter 4

The next shift at Coffee Kicks was the following morning. Jess, another student barista, conveniently sauntered in after the morning rush had ended.

"Sorry I'm late, Shan." She wasn't sorry. Jess was always late.

"Yeah, sure. What happened this time?"

"Eh... I..." Jess stuttered.

"I needed your help. It was really busy."

"Sorry, Shan. I'll be on time tomorrow. I hate the early starts when I have to study for exams the night before."

Try horse riding for hours, scooping up horse shit, chasing horses around fields bigger than a football stadium and cleaning out horse lorries. "There's a support group for that, Jess. You want in? It's called 'Everybody has to work', and we'll be meeting here tomorrow at 7 a.m."

"Very funny, Shannon." Jess stretched her lips, but she wasn't amused.

Jess was slender and tall like a beanpole with weensy boobs, padded and pushed up like two ripe mini melons. Her wispy dyed white hair tightened in a knot at the crown of her head. Thick black eyeliner winged at the outer corners of her pale grey eyes like a sexy cool kitten. She was pretty - in a made-up way, but her chattiness grew tiresome when she talked and pouted more than she poured.

Shannon, on the other hand, was petite in stature and loved food. The tee she squeezed into today emphasised her narrow waist and hugged her breasts. She had thrown on an old pair of trousers that hugged her muscular thighs and firm round ass, both earned from all the physical work she took on at the stable yard.

27

The rest of her day was usually spent in a worn out hoody and scruffy leather boots, but working in the city meant she had to polish herself up to a respectable standard. The primary focus was her riding career, with the goal of making a name for herself in the winner's circle.

"Damn it." She stared at her feet, eying the same dirty boots - not her work sneakers.

"This day is going to drag. I'm so tired." Jess held her chin up on the counter with her knuckles.

Shannon arched an eyebrow, slamming the fridge shut after counting the cartons of milk in the fridge. "Maybe you could clean up those tables?" She nodded to the empty chairs.

Jess pursed her lips. "Ugh! If I must," she moaned, trudging away to the coffee cup devastation that lay waiting.

"I need to go out the back and check if a milk delivery was put through yesterday. I don't think Connie got around to it before sharing the contents of her stomach with the store room," Shannon hollered, vanishing from sight.

After a few moments, she returned from the office with a pen wedged behind her ear. Jess was entertaining the male customers with her cheeky giggle. Her elbows rested on the counter, pushing up her breasts like a peacock spreading its feathers. A sweet laugh held a teasing rasp that was intentionally flirtatious. Shannon wasn't interested in making the same effort with men. They were a no go for now, in a cordoned off zone after Niall left a bitter taste of iron in her mouth.

Ignoring the flirty side show, Shannon cleared the tables that Jess accidentally on purpose, missed out. A sudden shiver scattered her scalp. With a tray piled high, she looked up to meet dark amber eyes that watched her every move.

It was him. The sexy as fuck guy from the day before. The same irresistible ass who didn't think it was important to say thank you for helping his father, rather shove money in her face. Did she actually think he was irresistible? He was unquestionably gorgeous with his broody, moody looking gaze and knowing smirk, but she could resist him. No problem.

He just stood there, with those dark intense eyes narrowed and his arms folded across his chest. Jess cleared her throat, ready to take his order, but his gaze never wavered, holding Shannon in a lustful spell.

"So, you do need money after all?"

Her mouth snapped shut, stung by his observation. "Not that it's any of your business, but I didn't help your dad to get a payoff. Having money thrust in my face like that was insulting. A simple thank you would have been fine." She gathered the courage to walk, even though her knees had weakened.

"I was strung out yesterday because my dad went missing. I'm sorry, I didn't thank you properly. I was an asshole. Can you forgive me?" His beautiful lips rose at the corners. Perfect white teeth peeked through his impish grin and a dimple on his right cheek added to his effortless sex appeal. A tsunami of heat rushed straight to her core.

"Suppose so." Her composure was hanging in the balance.

He shifted the knot in his tie. "You have amazing blue eyes."

Regain control.

Do not let this guy get the better of you, Shannon.

Put the tray down and walk away.

Where to?

I've never noticed how small this place is.

Claustrophobic in fact.

His woodsy aftershave smells amazing, and his bronzed skin looks so smooth...

Just breathe.

Deep breaths.

In and out.

"Oh, that's original," she added, forcing up an eyebrow in a bid to appear unimpressed. "You have a great... ear!"

The right side of his mouth quirked, dimpling his cheek

again.

Sweet Jesus!

"Well, at least, there's one thing you like about me."

She inhaled sharply. "I wouldn't say like, as far as ears go, they're pretty standard." She bit her lip, stifling a smirk.

He slipped his hands into his tight trouser pockets. "How about I take you out for lunch, to say thank you for helping my dad yesterday?"

Damn, this guy was smooth with a capital S. Any girl in her right (not so right mind) would jump at the offer, but she couldn't accept. There weren't enough hours in the day. Her routine was strict, and there was also the small matter of rule number one. No men. Especially fascinating charming men who threw around money like sugar coated candy.

She stepped back, lessening the gravitational pull tugging her towards his tall, brawny physique.

"Look, I'm too busy. I have enough on my plate right now," she replied, steadying the tray as a paper cup tumbled to the floor.

His brows furrowed, in one swoop he collected the empty cup. "I don't want to compete with the shit stacked on your plate, love. Think of me as a distraction. Something pleasurable that you can get a whole lot of satisfaction from." He smirked. "Someone to help you relax after a long shift."

As he spoke, her eyes traced the fullness of his lips, and her ears absorbed each syllable that was perfectly enunciated in a sultry timbre.

An unfamiliar feeling resided in her gut. She wanted to indulge in his wickedness and lose herself in those rich amber eyes that were clearly undressing her, leaving her vulnerable and dizzy. It was a bad idea, she didn't need a distraction. Her life was working out as planned without any complications.

Moving behind the counter, Shannon put a necessary barrier between them. "Thanks. But no thanks. I have a life outside of this place, and there isn't any room for a social life." She turned away, set down the tray and pretended to clean the coffee machine.

A few seconds later, the door chimed. She glanced back, and he was gone, with only the empty cup on the counter in sight. Her stomached roiled.

It was for the best.

Chapter 5

Shannon gathered her bag from the locker in the staff room. "Alright, that's me finished up, Jess. Hopefully you'll be on time tomorrow." She shrugged into her coat.

"I'll try."

The morning shift was finally over. Even though it had only been a few hours, every second dragged at a snail's pace. During quiet periods she let herself day dream about the exceptionally striking man who she turned away earlier in the morning. He'd left her restless and a little unbalanced.

A gurgle in her belly signalled lunch time. The night before she threw a packet of salty potatoes chips into her bag and a bottle of water for the bus journey home. Breaking free from the cafe, she checked her phone.

Harry:
The farrier is here. No need to rush back.

The winter sun eclipsed. A shadow blanketed her with a familiarity that was both terrifying and exhilarating. It was him, again, wearing the same tailored suit, only this time his tie had been loosened and the top button was open, drawing her greedy gaze to the golden skin beneath.

His arresting dark eyes glistened and his mouth curved to a lopsided grin. "Hey. Would you like to join me for lunch, now that your shift is over?"

The sound of his voice was both husky and caressing, chilling every follicle so the hairs stood up and listened. Her feet shifted bringing her a fraction closer without thought. Dropping her gaze to his extended hand, she debated the contact. There was a danger to his charm that reached far beyond anything she had ever encountered.

Inhaling deeply, her small palm met his large hand that enveloped with a firm squeeze.

"It's a pleasure to meet you. I'm Jamie."

The immediate sensation sparked a volt of electricity that sizzled up her arm, searing her blood and warming her entire body from head to toe.

Holy shit.

The mix of his intoxicating woodsy smell combined with their skin on skin connection, was enough to gift her mind with a shadow of dark indecent images, as if oozing from his soul to hers. Her heart thundered in her chest like Trixie's hooves on the gallops.

Walk away. Say no.

She looked up under her lashes feeling absurdly nervous. "Shannon Colter," she replied with a shy smile. "Have you been lingering outside long, Jamie?"

Their contact slipped away as his warm hand released her palm. An unexpected shiver prickled her scalp. He casually slid his hands into his trouser pockets, relaxing his shoulders as if the sound of her voice comforted him.

"I just got here, Shannon. Will you join me for lunch? My treat." His intense stare lingered on her lips. "There's a million ways I'd like to thank you, but lunch is a good starting point." A playful grin spread across his handsome face.

Her racing heart gave her mouth permission to open before her brain could disagree. "Well, I am really hungry."

"So that's a yes?" he asked without surprise.

"Uh-huh." She nodded while her chest fluttered with erratic palpitations.

He pulled his hand from his pocket and snaked her waist. "I knew you'd agree, sooner or later."

"Are you serious?" She dished out a look of disbelief. "You really did have this planned?"

"Sure, I did. You work across the road. It wasn't hard to find out when your shift ended." A faint smug smile teased his lips.

It wouldn't be a hardship to eat out with this particular

handsome man, but damn if he wasn't a cocky ass. He had bad news stitched into the lining of his designer suit.

"Let's get you fed. I know a nice place across the road."

Jamie guided her into the revolving doorway of The Fitz Hotel and through the lavish lobby, all the time holding her to his side like he was afraid she would run away. Shannon absorbed the warmth from his body, internally chanting to herself that she'd made another bad decision.

"Do you work in the cafe every day?" he asked.

The suave rhythm of his voice held a certain deep rasp that made her temperature surge. A strangled sound, resembling a grunt left her throat before she replied, "Not every day. I do rotational shifts. I have two jobs."

His protective arm slackened but the welcomed contact remained. Tipping his jaw, he looked down at her face, making her rib cage expand with a quick inhalation. Shards of light danced across every surface in the lobby, refracting tiny sparkles in his eyes, making them blaze. "What's the second job?"

"I help out a friend." She half shrugged with a tight smile.

"With?"

"You ask a lot of questions." She leaned back, purposefully distancing herself.

He stood still, pausing at the entrance of the restaurant. A low chuckle followed his fingers as they tucked a lose strand of hair behind her ear. "Just making conversation."

Peppermint laced his breath, and she wondered how good those lips of his would feel. The sensation of his finger brushing across her cheek startled her heart into thinking he cared.

The restaurant was busy with soft romantic lighting that was kind enough to filter her make-up free face. Mellow jazz tones blended with chatter. All the waiting staff nodded respectfully as they weaved through the room like Jamie was king of the kingdom. Did everyone fancy the guy as much as she did?

His palm pressed into her lower back with a firm pressure. He ushered her towards the farthest booth, set for two. A pretty waitress with hungry green eyes hurried to their table.

"I reserved that one for you, Mr. McGrath, if you'd prefer it?" She pointed across the room, to a table near the bar.

"This one is fine. We'd like some privacy."

Taking a step back, the waitress hinted disappointment on her freckly face but widened her smile regardless. "Of course, I'll let you get settled before I take your order." She stood to the side and stared, parting her lips when he helped Shannon shrug free from her puffy coat like the perfect gentleman.

"The usual, Vicki." His eyes drilled in on Shannon who bounced onto the leather seat. "What do you want to drink?" Jamie flipped open the long black drinks menu and set it on the table before her.

After bundling her jacket in the corner, she scanned the fancy drink options, noting the extortionately priced cocktails. "Uhhh...." She found Vicki's green eyes blazing, suggesting she was battling a bad dose of envy. The dainty young thing wasn't jealous of her looks, the only other plausible option was Jamie. It was clearer than a starry night sky that the waitress fancied the pants off him, and for some reason, that fact bothered her.

"Sparkling water, please." Shannon half smiled in solidarity.

"Of course." The waitress cut back to Jamie. She almost curtsied. "I'll be right back to take your food order."

Jamie flashed that waitress an innocent pantie melting grin. It wasn't meant as a flirty gesture, more of an acknowledgment of service, but that natural act was her demise. Her shy retreat resulted in an awkward bang, bumping into the unoccupied chair behind her as she dared to slip him a cheeky smile of her own. What made the whole situation even more embarrassing was the fact Jamie hadn't even noticed her leave.

So this is how it was for the charming, Jamie McGrath.

While he slipped off his suit jacket, Shannon found herself gazing greedily at his torso. On very close inspection it was obvious he worked out. The fabric of his shirt clung to every curve of every muscle, and she began to wonder what he looked like naked. Her fingers found her mouth, and her teeth gnawed her short nails. She noticed things about him that normally didn't faze her, like the size of his strong hands and the way he moved with confidence and grace. He was fluid and powerful in one mega hot package.

"That's better," he said, dropping down to face her in the booth. "I hate wearing suits, but it has to be done."

Unbuttoning his cuffs, he rolled each sleeve to his elbows, revealing a hefty gold Longine watch. There was nowhere to run and nowhere to hide. Jamie was slap bang in front of her. So close she could reach out and run her fingertips over his lips. His undivided attention was all hers, and she loved it, even if her heart rate was out of control.

Repositioning the cutlery, his eyes gleamed. "So, Shannon. About yesterday. I owe you a massive thanks."

"Accepted." She smiled triumphantly. "That wasn't hard, now was it?"

He rubbed his chin and laughed quietly. "*It* wasn't hard, but *it* is now."

She rolled her eyes upwards faking nonchalance, just as her cheeks turned a pale shade of crimson and her skin broke out in goose bumps. "Is this your usual line of conversation? Sexual references over lunch. Classy guy," she simpered.

"To be honest, I don't usually have to work this hard to impress." A low chuckle rumbled in his chest, and his head shook subtly from side to side like he was bemused.

Parts of her body that hadn't been awake in years, or ever, tightened. Her brows snapped together. "You're trying to impress me? What about the woman you were with yesterday?"

The waitress lent in and set the drinks on black and gold McGrath coasters. "Ready to order?" She whipped out her notepad and tapped the pen, all the while smiling at him like a deranged stalker.

Jamie nodded to Shannon. "Go ahead."

Her heart leapt at the mannerly gesture. Maybe he wasn't that bad after all. She drew in a light breath, browsing the menu. "Ummm...I'll just have the house burger and skinny fries, please."

Without looking at his menu, he hummed with approval. "Good choice. Make that two, Vicki." This time the waitress trudged away from the table without a reward.

He sat back in silence. When she looked up, his eyes were on her. Automatically, her finger slipped into her mouth so she could nibble the side of her nail again. Biting her nails was a disgusting habit. It certainly wasn't something she did after shovelling shit all day, but right this very second, she was nervous as hell. Those intense eyes of his were turning her into a wet, hot mess.

After a few seconds, he said, "Would you be happy to know the woman I was with yesterday is my father's caretaker, not my girlfriend?"

A twinge of relief flipped for joy in her stomach. "Right. And I'm sure you haven't put the moves on her yet." She batted her eyelashes, angling her head to the side playfully. The statement didn't require an answer, although she desperately wanted to know.

He tapped the coaster underneath his whiskey. "My dad and Rebecca have a really good relationship. I wouldn't ruin it by having sex with her," he replied with sincerity. Oddly enough she believed him. "Although, it's pretty rare for a woman to resist me. I have to be careful. I couldn't break the poor girl's heart, now could I?" His tone was playful.

Shannon flicked her eyes to the bar and back, then ducked forward, meeting his gaze. "Oh my god, do you hear that?" she whispered.

His brows pulled together, and he lowered his head closer. "Hear what?"

"The sound of your ego landing." She sank her teeth into her bottom lip to stifle a giggle.

What was even better than his ego falling on her lap, was the rumble of his laughter, a deep delightful sound that made her smile widely.

"Witty and sexy." After a heartbeat his smile faded. "Do you have a boyfriend, Shannon?"

There was something about the way he said her name, how he drawled the first few letters and stared right at her.

"Nope," she said with a shy smile. "Do you have a girlfriend?"

His elbows rested on the table, and his fingers clasped under his chin. "Not my thing. I like women, don't get me wrong. I just don't think I'm capable of settling down. There's too much choice out there."

"It's called FOMO," she said through a laugh, even though his confession oddly pinched her heart.

"Fear of missing out? Believe me, Shannon, I never miss out." His chuckle was dirty and deep. "I'm surprised you don't have a guy."

"I don't want one. My sights are set on my career. They're just a hassle. I'm only twenty-four, there's plenty of time for that in the future." It was true. There was no time in her busy schedule for pointless dates and fluffy romance nonsense.

Her phone vibrated on the table beside her drink, ending her dreamy daze. Glancing down to the illuminated screen, she read the message.

Niall:

Where the hell are you? Why aren't you at the yard?

She grunted loudly. Niall was a fly in the ointment who turned everything septic. She used to be in a relationship with the guy, back when they were teenagers. Perhaps she should have seen the warning signs sooner. As he got used to the steady flow of cash his father handed him, he also got used to the influence that money brought with it. Niall morphed into an arrogant, spoiled brat who got whatever he wanted. After three years of a rocky affiliation – the latter year being more turbulent than the rest, she finally reached her limit and dropped him like a herpes scab.

"Problem?" Jamie's soothing voice broke her anger fuelled trance.

"Eh, no," she lied, forcing a smile. She had no intention of talking about her ex, and she most definitely didn't want to think about his ugly twisted personality for a second longer. "I just have stuff to do back home. I'll need to leave straight after we eat."

His long fingers reached across the table, stopping millimetres from her own. "No dessert, Shannon?" The raspy masculine tone of his voice rippled through her core and shook up the knots in her stomach.

She inhaled sharply, taking a second to play out the deed of smothering him in warm custard and licking him clean. "Nope." Her thighs clenched together.

Her phone glowed again.

Niall:

I'll take Trixie out if you can't be bothered.

Her nostrils flared. "Asshole," she muttered under her breath.

A rush of anger tightened the muscles in her back, creating an unbearable edgy and fractious feeling. If she sent a reply, the onslaught of text messages would ruin their lunch, and she was enjoying this guy's company, if not falling for his devilish dimple. She quickly decided it was best to eat and run.

Jamie's fingers covered hers, instantly soothing, calming and kindling a warmth that crept from his touch and scattered into her tight muscles.

His eyes burned hotly as his fingers stroked the rough skin on her hands. "Something I can help with, Shannon?" he asked, surveying her simmering temper.

She pulled back, his fingers slid off hers onto the table. The powerful connection was broken. Jamie was fogging her brain and making her lose sight of the end goal.

"Nah. I've got it sorted." She smiled tightly.

"I'm sure you do." He strummed the table with his fingers like he needed something to do with his hands. "You seem very capable."

Her brow scrunched. "Capable?"

"Yeah, capable. Feisty."

"I can look after myself, if that's what you mean."

And yeah, she could take care of herself. It had more or less been that way since she moved into the loft at Meadow Dawn. But she had other needs – a new sexual hunger that was begging to be fed. The prospect of using a man like Jamie to quench her sex drought was getting her hot and bothered in the pantie department. But today just wasn't a good day. If Niall rode Trixie, he would hurt her, setting their training back weeks, if not months. No one other than Shannon was supposed to ride her, although she was under no illusion that Harry would let the spiteful git saddle up anyway, just in the name of 'helping out'. The ride would quickly turn into a whipping session because Niall couldn't ride for shit.

Sitting upright, Shannon created an invisible boundary between them when the mammoth sized burgers arrived. Jamie sat back in the booth, relaxed and oozing masculinity.

"It's huge!" she gasped. "I can't wait to tuck into this bad boy."

Jamie laughed in a quick burst. "All the girls say that." He smirked.

Her lips pouted and her eyes rolled. "You're so full of yourself."

He shrugged casually. "It's not my fault if that's what they all say."

"Ah, but do they mean it?"

"You can make up your own mind."

Her mouth quirked, and she lifted the burger to her lips. "It's okay, Jamie, I'll take the word of the hundreds of women who have already seen it."

"I'm always happy for you to make your own

assessment. I promise, you won't be disappointed." The heat from his blistering smile sizzled across her skin.

Shannon opened her mouth and sank her teeth into the fresh brioche bun. A soft moan hummed in the back of her throat as the beefy flavours exploded in her mouth. She chewed happily as the food made its passage to her hungry stomach and settled with resounding thanks. She licked her lips and flicked her eyes up to his - he wasn't eating. His back was straight, his hands were fisted. His dark eyes were lit with a blazing fire that shadowed a darkness, like sordid thoughts were out of control.

"Not hungry?" She dabbed the corners of her mouth with a napkin, so she could hide her embarrassment behind the black linen material.

He cleared his throat. "I didn't realise I could get so turned on by watching someone eat a burger."

She inhaled sharply, and her wide-open mouth locked.

His cheek dimpled. "Please, do continue."

Shannon set the napkin back on her lap and smoothed it across her jeans. "I wasn't trying to put on a show." She kept her eyes low.

He tipped forward. "Sorry. I'm being unfair. I asked you to lunch so we could get to know each other. Please, finish your meal." He collected his burger in his long fingers and grinned wickedly as she dared to peek up at him through her lowered lashes.

A soft laugh bubbled in her throat. "I thought you invited me to lunch as a thank you?"

Chewing happily, he swallowed. "The food is the thank you, however, I'd like to see you again. Maybe we could get to know each other under the sheets? If you'd really like to check out the size of my dick we can forget about the food and get a room?"

Her brows flew up and her lips parted.

"I'm joking, Shannon. Well, half joking." He gifted her with a wolfish grin that reached across the table and squeezed her insides. "Your face is so pretty, especially when you blush."

She looked everywhere and anywhere that wasn't in the direction of his face.

"Shannon…" He bobbed his head to catch her eye while he chewed. "I'd like to take you out to dinner some time?" he said between bites.

"Oh really?" She raised a sceptical brow.

"I'm being serious." He looked straight at her.

Her gaze dropped when her heartbeat skyrocketed through her chest. A warning bell reverberated in her mind. "Look, I meant what I said, Jamie. I don't have any free time at the minute."

His eyes narrowed. "I'm a bit tight on free time myself, love, but everyone needs some fun. Right?"

"I have fun," she fibbed.

Circumstances had presented her with the possibility of Jamie, but reality overtook the wicked daydream, and the face of Niall and his trigger-happy tendencies bounced around in her brain like a jagged ball. Mistakes were meant as lessons, not to be repeated by fools. Niall was one of those mistakes, and she knew the wealthy man in front of her would be an even bigger mistake.

"What, or who takes up all your time? Who do you have fun with?" Jamie popped a few fries into his mouth.

There was no way she would tell this mega hot guy that she rode horses. Shannon had been one of the few country girls at school. All the city kids thought she was a strange country weirdo. They constantly poked fun at her, inventing silly horsey names and taunting her in the corridors. None of them understood the drive and determination that burned in her belly.

Horse riding wasn't just a hobby – it was her passion. A passion she'd kindled since she saw her first pony at the country festival at the age of five. Not even her friends knew the level of devotion required to train a horse from wild animal to well-trained, first place rosette winner – on a horse that wasn't even her own. No one believed she could do it. Even her parents had been sceptical, which only fuelled her determination to succeed. If Shannon was told she couldn't do something, then she damn well did it twice to prove them wrong.

She shrugged. "I just help out a friend with his pets." It was more of a loose truth than a lie, there was just no point in elaborating.

His forehead creased. "Pets?"

"Yeah," she replied causally, hoping he wouldn't delve further. "And what takes up all of your time, Jamie?"

"My businesses. I dabble here and there, working pretty much twenty-four-seven," he replied with a sigh. "I'm in the property business with my brother, Marcus. It's pretty full on, so I have to make time for the fun stuff, or I'd go fucking crazy," he added. "I also have a few businesses of my own."

"And your dad, does he always walk off?"

A sadness shadowed his eyes, the charm and charisma that teased his features vanished briefly. "I have to face it every fucking day. Sometimes, I just need to get away from him, so I can remember the man he used to be."

He pushed his plate forward and chucked the napkin on the table. "He hasn't changed *that* much, but he forgets things and gets confused sometimes."

"It must be hard for you, Jamie." She dabbed a bunch of fries into a gloop of tomato ketchup and popped them into her mouth, one bite at a time.

"It's life, sweetheart. You gotta ride the highs because the lows are fucking brutal." He half smiled and folded his arms.

Her silly heart swooped up to her ribs for a better look at the honesty in his eyes. She wanted to lunge across the table and press her nose to his neck, just so she could inhale every last drop of his sexy essence.

The repeated glow of her mobile phone screen caught her attention again, but she swiped the message away before reading Niall's rant. Glancing to her plate, with just a few skinny fries left, she sighed. Under the table, her legs jiggled as her slow burning temper made her antsy. She had to leave. Pronto.

"I'm finished. Thanks for the food. I've got to go now. I'll nip to the ladies before I leave. It's a long bus journey home."

He nodded. "I'll drive you back?"

"Eh, no thanks, I've got a return bus ticket to use up."

"It would be my pleasure."

"No, it's okay." She held up her palm. He would have to drop her off at the yard and the awkwardness of that conversation would eat her alive.

Jamie shrugged as she slid off the booth. An odd feeling powered through every molecule in her body, pleading her to stay with him as she navigated around the tables. Trixie came first, and men came, well, they came further down the list after work, food and possibly wine, and the reality was she had to leave.

Prior to meeting Jamie, she had erected boundary lines where men weren't welcome, but this guy made her swoon every time his cheek dimpled, or their eyes met. Why did her senseless heart gallop like a wild stallion when his skin touched hers? Was this the true meaning of lust – a sensation she had never truly known.

She had fallen into a relationship with Niall because he was always around when she worked at the yard. On reflection, there had never been a spark, or any sort of chemistry between them. Which is why the feelings buzzing through her now where new and thrilling.

Shannon finished up in the ladies, trailing her fingers through her shiny black waves in an attempt to look less tousled and wild. She crossed the restaurant with a wide smile aching her cheeks. A strange stutter messed up the rhythm of her heartbeat when she reached the table.

"Thanks for lunch. It was nice to meet you, Jamie." The words caught in her throat when he dragged his nails across his jaw and stared up at her.

He stood, patiently waiting with a business-like gesture of a hand shake. Her insides turned to mush. Jamie was happy to say goodbye, with no further indication of pursuit or seductive suggestions for another date. His expression was soft, but his predatory stance remained, holding out for her shaky hand.

She unfurled her fist, and slowly grazed his palm, curling around his firm hand. Sparks catapulted through her body like lightning bolts. Her eyes widened as his beautiful full lips found their way to her cheek, placing a warm kiss just millimetres from her mouth. Her head turned a fraction, wistfully anticipating his lips, but they drifted to the shell of her ear, leaving a heat trail on her skin.

"Thank you for helping my dad, Shannon. I owe you more than lunch."

She inhaled sharply. His breath rested on her flesh like a secretive sin, igniting millions of fireworks across the surface. Fingertips teased a lock of hair that rested on her shoulder while he stood in silence with a look of amusement tugging the corners of his mouth. A soft sigh puffed from her lips, and she unwittingly dragged her tongue across the opening. He was standing so close she could swear there was a halo of energy flaring between them, like electrical charges for the whole restaurant to see.

Her eyes closed, hoping, wanting, waiting to taste him. Then bam. His lips pressed down with a seductive pressure, teasing and soft. Light leisurely licks brought their tastes together, and her insides jumped. This kiss wasn't innocent, or even friendly. It was fiery and hot and controlled. She melted into his chest with faint groans, letting his hands swoop up to cradle her head, and his fingers delved into her messy locks. The intensity deepened as his tongue dipped inside, on a mission to blow to her mind - and it was working. She let him devour her mouth like he was starved. His hand released, and his lips retreated.

"You taste like cherries. The kind of glossy red cherry that tastes sinful and sweet." The pad of his thumb dragged down her lower lip. "You'd be the perfect cherry on top of my dick, love."

Shannon slanted back, clutching the table for support as her head spun. Words tumbled and evaporated. She had to take a second to find her mind and pull it back down to earth. The entire restaurant blurred, and all she could see was him. His eyes. His angular jaw. His choppy hair, and his smirk.

The thick fog lust shrouding her brain vanished. He fucking knew she was wet for him.

"Goodbye, Shannon." His lips were lightly bruised with a just kissed redness.

Jamie grabbed his jacket, swept it over his forearm and swaggered away from the booth. Every step he took was self-assured and magnificent. He was the kind of man who silently provoked iniquitous intentions and could easily strip a woman of her ability to resist him.

And Shannon finally realised that woman, was her.

Chapter 6

What the fuck just happened?

Jamie's strides buzzed with adrenaline as he left her behind. There was an uncontrollable skip to his pulse and the whopping hard-on straining in his boxer briefs was growing painful. She was stunning. Gorgeous. Intriguing. Hot. Fuck! That kiss reached right inside him and shook up all his organs, and the gush of blood pumping in his skull was making him dizzy.

He had to see her again. If that's the rush he got from a simple kiss, then imagine the high he'd feel from having her perfect body beneath him. And damn, what a body. He loved how her tee was so tight he could make out the line of her bra and note the curve of her concealed breasts. When she took off her coat, he mentally thanked her jeans for being so skin tight to her fine perky ass. Her uniform will be a pleasant addition to his bedroom floor, and her tight naked body would be wrapped around him, sooner rather than later.

"I'll be in touch, Shannon," he muttered to himself knowing she wouldn't hear him.

He'd let her think on that kiss for a while, before hunting her down. Throughout the meal there were no references to his bank balance and even when he mentioned his businesses, she didn't ask if he was a big earner.

It wasn't obvious from his tailor-made suit that Jamie recently gained a solid foot hold in the financial big league. The McGrath brothers were newly made billionaires. The magnitude of their circumstances hadn't quite bedded in. They were learning how to deal with the reality of never having to work another day in their lives again, if they chose not to. That was an absurd revelation because they had worked their way up the food chain together, from nothing. Both men got off on power and the authority of being successful.

Now they had it all.

Aside from the joint ventures with his brother, Jamie had his own portfolio of hotels, properties, vehicles for every occasion, including a superyacht, and most importantly, thoroughbred horses. He was a sucker for a fine race horse and had just spent the previous week in Dubai, considering a new addition to his ever-growing collection.

He became used to the steady flow of women who chased him for sex. Each one hopeful to clinch the sought-after title of 'The First Mrs. Jamie McGrath', but none of them found the map to his heart, never mind the key to unlock it.

Beautiful, sexy women came, multiple times, and went. Sometimes, his interest was held, and he would let the odd one hang around for a while, but the cold hard truth of the matter was his wandering eye. Another fit woman would strut past and stir his intrigue – so he had to play with her too. Of course he did. He liked it that way, what hot blooded man wouldn't?

His father, George, had been struggling for years with dementia, a cruel and ugly creeping death that was stripping the man of his memories and robbing him of his soul. Watching him deteriorate only made Jamie's drive for fun more urgent. He made no apologies for being a man who loved pussy, and never made a promise that he would stick around.

A weird excitement fluttered in his chest. Shannon had managed to conjure the most impressive thrill, a sensation more powerful than he'd ever experienced.

Shannon Colter was a challenge.

Sure, her prefect full lips were the colour of sin, and she held a flash of seduction behind her eyes that begged him to come closer, but her words denied him access to all areas. She didn't want to hook up, and she didn't even want to have dinner. The woman didn't want to see him, period.

Shannon was a blend of shy and reserved with a hint of wildness like an untamed filly. It was completely unheard of for Jamie McGrath to get knocked back, yet it was refreshing and sexy as fuck. But he knew all too well, she'd cave in eventually, with some gentle persuasion - which is why he opted for a slightly devious approach.

During her time in the ladies, Jamie had grabbed her mobile phone, which thankfully didn't have a security code in place. He added his mobile number, and then rang his own phone to capture hers. By the time she ambled back to the table, he had taken care of the bill and ensured she was accessible for the hunt.

Her lips had curved to a sweet smile, and her bright blue pools summoned to him, begging him to rip off her clothes and impale her balls deep. She shook his hand tightly, but that simple contact hadn't been enough. The moment his lips brushed her skin, his breathing had hitched, and a bead of pre-cum nestled into the fabric of his boxers. She was a cock tease who held onto an innocent misconception that she was immune to his charm. The poor girl wouldn't stand a chance now that his sights were firmly set on her.

He reached the busy lobby and inhaled the hustle and bustle. The familiar ring tone assigned to his brother Marcus, played out in his jacket pocket.

"Well, brother, what's up?" he sang into the phone.

"Jeez, you sound happy. Don't tell me. I don't want to know the sordid details."

"Fine. Just 'cause you're all loved up, old man. And if you must know, I've only just met her. I haven't shown her the time of her life yet."

"You haven't? Do you need me to call the doctor?" Marcus mocked playfully.

"No, asshole. I've no problem getting hard. In fact, I'm still rock solid after watching her eat."

"So, what's the deal then?"

Jamie exhaled loudly but smiled with disbelief at his words. "She's too busy. Allegedly."

He pulled the phone away from his ear as Marcus roared with laughter. "You've lost your touch, little brother. I feel bad for you; all the women must be heartbroken now that I'm off the market."

"Yeah, I'm sure they're dying inside," Jamie sneered.

"Where did you meet her?"

"Dad wondered off again. She found him. I actually owe her more than lunch."

"You owe her more than your dick, mate. We need to lock him down, Jamie."

"I know. He scared the shit out of me."

"Look, don't worry about it, kid. Leave it up to me. I'm on top of the security. That means you can brush up on your charm," Marcus said through a husky chuckle.

Jamie scowled. "I guarantee you, I will have sex with her before the week is over."

"Maybe I can help you there. I was calling to remind you that Devereux is flying into Belfast this weekend. Now that the deal is sealed, we should celebrate. I've asked Freddy to do the catering."

"That will give him good publicity for his new restaurant." Jamie nodded in approval.

His hip dipped against the welcome desk. A figure outside the hotel caught his attention. Stretching his neck upwards, so he could see over the mingling guests, he found Shannon darting past the front window with the wind in her sails. An odd flutter of excitement tumbled in his chest until she vanished into the afternoon crowd. The quickened rhythm of his pulse revved. The knots in his stomach settled when he picked her out from the crowd again.

"What the fuck is happening to me?" he muttered to himself in a whisper.

What if he actually never saw her again?

"What do mean, Jamie... What's happening? Are you listening to me?" Marcus's voice snapped him away from his search.

"I'm here," he affirmed as he marched to the doors and scoured the streets, only to find her waiting at the bus stop across the road.

"Lana is planning the bash in The Fitz master suite. We considered The Gift Hotel in New York, but we need to stay close by for Dad's appointment. The party is scheduled for tomorrow night – bring a girl, maybe the one who is squeezing your nuts in her hand."

"She'll be there," Jamie drawled. "Although, Devereux always has an entourage of fuckable females. If she doesn't come with me, then I'm sure I can amuse myself."

They laughed together until Jamie terminated the call. His thumb swiped down the entries in his contacts list, finding Shannon's name. A flurry of anticipation swept down his spine. What was it about this girl that made him so jumpy? He wanted to hear her voice again, but he wanted to see her smile even more.

"Excuse me, Jamie. There is a call for you on line four. It's Ronnie Carter," chirped a perky male receptionist.

He would call her later, once he had time to concentrate on her sweet sexy voice.

Chapter 7

The long bus ride back to Meadow Dawn gave Shannon unwanted alone time because all she thought about was Jamie. Or more to the point, his hot lips and that sensational kiss. It was crazy how her brain had fogged over, and the mere touch of his lips left her speechless.

Is that supposed to happen? Are real men capable of such sorcery? And boy, was he a real man. In every possible way. From his manners right down to his boxers. She even wondered if they were fitted and tight, or loose enough to let his manhood swing freely - yeah, swing. It had to be a good size, otherwise he wouldn't be so damn cock sure of himself. The sweet agony of her arousal was mounting pressure between her thighs.

He'd paid the bill, kissed away her sanity and then left. No further contact requested. A deep sigh puffed out her cheeks. Why would a guy like him want anything to do with a girl like her anyway? He was used to skilful party girls. Unlike her, the inexperienced country girl who much preferred the company of animals over people. Sinking back into the seat, she sighed. Jamie could charm the petals off the prettiest rose, leaving it stripped bare and exposed in a winter chill yet still craving his attention. He had a certain irresistible appeal that had chipped into the massive boundary erected around her life.

It didn't matter anyway, she was too busy, and he was finished with his little game. It was obvious he felt a duty to pay off his debt after she refused to take his money. Buying lunch was an underhanded way of making her accept his financial token. Palming her brow, she groaned. Ugh! Jamie had become a huge distraction, just like he said he wanted to be.

Devilishly indecent thoughts swirled in her mind, clouding all the reasons why she was better off without men. But through the haze, Jamie had unlocked a door to her curiosity, welcoming smutty thoughts to excite her boring and mundane ones. He was super sexy, and no doubt, fully accomplished in the steamy sex department.

Acceptance sat heavy in her belly. Keeping him at arm's length was the right thing to do, even if she was missing out on the best sex ever. Back down on earth, away from thoughts of his dirty dimple, she focused on the major events planned for the weekend. The finals in the cross-country league had arrived, and she had to prove her horse-riding ability. As much as she tried, she just couldn't shake the burning heat in her core.

There was only one other traveller on the coach – six rows down, wearing ear phones that were turned up too loud. Shannon sat one seat down from the back row, hidden, alone and unusually horny. She craved a release to rid herself of Jamie and his wickedness, once and for all. The pulsating between her legs magnified, and it didn't matter one bit if she squeezed her thighs together or crossed her legs, the throbbing just wouldn't go away.

She kept her eyes above the headrest of the seat in front and slowly unzipped her jeans. Slipping her fingers inside, they teased the fabric separating her hungry, needy touch and her swollen bundle of nerves. Quick quiet breathes, from both exhilaration and desire, agitated a soft wave of hair dangling over her cheek. Her nails traced beneath the material. It was a little too tight to allow her unrestricted access, so she shunted her jeans down a fraction – just enough to let her fingertips loop the slick swollen tissue.

Jamie took a front row seat in her fantasy with his handsome face and snug work shirt. Her fingers swirled and circled furiously until the coach suddenly jerked to a stop at a set of traffic lights. No! She couldn't stop now. The burning rage of desire consumed her, she was stimulated beyond return, an intensity mounting in the hope of a glorious finish. Slapping her free hand over her mouth, she muffled a mellow groan. Punishingly rubbing her sensitive nub and provocative thoughts of Jamie, sent her rippling over the edge. Her legs extended, her spine stiffened, and she rode out the wave of her quick stimulation.

Her breathing regulated from short pants to long, deep inhalations. She scurried frantically, hoisting up her jeans. The thrill of covert masturbation, on a public bus no less, had her adrenaline pumping.

The secretive silence was ruptured when her mobile phone belted out the theme tune of Black Beauty. The screen glowed with the name of an incoming caller – Jamie.

What the hell?

She gulped, feeling her cheeks turn a million shades of humiliation. "Hello?" She held her breath.

The gruff voice of her masturbation fantasy filled her ear. "Shannon. I hope you don't mind, but I added my details in your phone, just in case you wanted to have that dinner."

The line went silent.

She shifted and peered through the seats. "Persistent aren't you." The words flew out like a flock of startled sparrows, and she glanced behind her.

"I work hard to get what I want."

"And what is it that you want, Jamie?" Shannon pressed her forehead to the smudged glass, unsure if he was watching from outside. A flicker of panic thrummed in her neck. She searched for a voyeur – for him. The bus windows were too high, and all she could see were car bonnets.

Relax.

"Why are you really calling?"

"Have I caught you at a bad time?"

If only he knew!

"No, not at all." She winced. "I'm on the coach. Alone. By myself. Not doing a single thing."

He cleared his throat. "Right. I just wanted to throw something out there. My brother and I are hosting a bash this Saturday night, at The Fitz. How about you come along as my date for some free booze, amazing food and most importantly, company with yours truly?" She could detect the smirk in his tone, hear the sexual invitation in his rasp and feel the rush of possibilities through the phone line. There was no doubt his perfectly sexy dimple was teasing his kissable cheek.

Shannon had already decided that it didn't matter if he earned a few quid more. It was more than likely that 90 percent of the population earned more than she did anyway. And he'd already weaved his way into her head, so why not into her bed for one night?

Pressing the phone to her temple, she gulped back her disappointment. "I'm really sorry, Jamie, I can't. I have an important thing to do this Saturday. Maybe another time?" It wasn't a suggestion, it was a wish and a hope and prayer.

Silence.

"No worries, Shannon. Have a great weekend, love."

The line went dead.

Damn.

It.

All.

To.

Hell.

Chapter 8

Striding down the gravel path to the large stable yard, she pulled off her cap and shoved it in her bag. She waved at Jim, the farrier, and Harry, the owner of Meadow Dawn, then roughly secured a messy bundle of hair with an elastic. The two men were reminiscing about a boisterous mare who freaked out in the stable then broke its leg. Jackson, Harry's Irish Wolfhound, was sniffing around the feed room on the hunt for rats.

She jogged up to the stall, thankfully still housing the magnificent, chestnut coloured Irish Hunter, Trixie.

"Hey girl." She patted its firm arched neck, allowing the huge animal to nuzzle her jacket and pinch the fabric between its big lips. "Looks like I got here in the nick of time before, shit head Niall, took you out."

Footsteps stomped up behind her. "Where the hell have you been?"

Without the need to face the irritated voice riddled with accusation, she continued to stroke Trixie's rounded cheekbone.

"You're paid to work in this yard, Shan, not ride at your leisure. Jim finished over half an hour ago, and the stables still need a fresh layer of bedding. The other paid stable hands are doing their job and exercising the horses."

Shannon turned to meet the furious face of Niall Ross, with his crisp white polo tucked into pale jeans and tawny hair flapping over his forehead. He was slender with a sporty physic, not muscular nor puny, just mediocre. She hadn't really given it much thought until today, after eyeing up the solid form of Jamie McGrath.

His cold grey eyes glared her down, and his lips

twitched.

"Yeah, I get paid to work here and at the coffee shop. Do you get paid to be a dick?" she retorted.

"Fuck you, Shannon," he snarled. "Get the stables sorted. I'm taking Trix into the paddock now." A glean of malice clouded his gaze.

Rage scorched up her neck, flashing across her cheeks. "I'm riding her. You can ride Merlot. He hasn't been exercised in a few days," she gritted out.

It took all her power to remain calm in the face of stupidity and evil.

Niall stepped closer, his nostrils flaring. "I'll ride whatever fucking horse I want, Shannon. That decision isn't made by the help. Got it?"

The voice of reason called from across the yard. "Hey, Shan! Bucky is going to help with the horses, so you can get Trixie back in the paddock. Carlos is on route for another grid lesson. He'll be here in half an hour."

A smirk crept over her lips. "Thanks, Harry. I'll skip out the stable first, and then I'll get her tacked up." She waved over at him in a casual two finger salute.

She looked up threw her lashes at the contorted face of Niall. "Oh, sorry, mate, but I think Harry has just asked me ride Trixie. You're out of luck this time." Her head cocked. "Looks like, Merlot, gets the pleasure of your ass bouncing on his back like a sack of spuds. Go easy on the poor thing. It's not his fault you're a shit rider." She smirked.

"Whatever," he spat. "I might compete on Trixie in the comps this weekend."

Shannon turned her back and marched across the yard towards the wheelbarrows. There was no point rising to the bait. He was talking crap and they both knew it. Niall wouldn't survive the first fence, let alone finish the show jumping course.

Absolute tool bag. I hate him. I hate him. I hate him.

She loved rolling up her sleeves, even if it meant regular trips to the dung heap. This wasn't like actual work – it was second nature. The regular chores had been part of her routine since she was sixteen. Her parents asked Harry if she could work for him over the summer, after several years of pleading to get a horse. They thought the hard work would put her off, but it spurred her on, making her even more determined.

Harry had taken Shannon under his wing, letting her work past the summer and into the eight years that followed. He helped her natural riding skills to flourish under his persistent tutelage. Then, Venatrix was born. A day that would be forever ingrained in her memory. Harry's best show jumper, Velox, had been on lock down in the barns. Shannon and Harry had split the night shifts, keeping a concerned eye on the expectant mother. It was during Shannon's late-night stint that the cutest, gangly legged foal was born – just like that. A new life joined the yard with twinkly eyes that ate her up with love. That night, Harry patted her shoulder like a proud father and told her that, Venatrix, or Trixie, as she's called in the yard would be the horse to take her riding career to the next level. That was five odd years ago now, and the pair had developed an unbreakable bond.

Scooping up sodden wood shavings, her thoughts filtered back to the lunch date with Jamie. He was naturally attractive, with a sexiness that burrowed into her mind, simmering under her flesh in a wave of lust.

This same guy asked her to a social event, with his brother. Why on earth did he choose her? A man like him must have a collection of fancy ass women in reserve for such an occasion.

The reality of hot women swarming around his damn fine body, like pesky flies, awoke a pang of jealousy that shook her mind. She stabbed the manure with gusto before flicking it into the wheelbarrow. There was something undeniably enchanting about him. If it wasn't for the finals this weekend, she might have considered his offer. Nonetheless, the competition came first. Trixie came first.

Perhaps there are a few decent rich guys out there? It's not like he's a billionaire with cash to burn and morals to disregard. The tailored suit and gold wrist watch all screamed wealth, yet his casual demeanour made him down to earth and approachable. Really rich men were usually assholes, who took liberties and held high expectations with little, to zero return.

Shannon didn't want a man for the long term, but she did yearn for a dirty night of sex - with Jamie. He was the guy who was responsible for waking her hibernating sexual beast.

The last of the afternoon sun streamed into the stable while she fluffed up the bunkers at the walls. With a flicker, the light became dull. Her gaze lifted to find Niall, propped up against the door frame with his ankle crossed over the other and his arms folded.

"You make a damn fine slave." His eyes narrowed.

"Go away, Niall." Turning her back, she returned to the job at hand.

"Nah, I'm happy to stand here and assess your work. I like watching you get hot and bothered. It's pretty sexy."

Shoving the pitch fork into the fresh bedding, Shannon rested her forearm on the wooden handle and looked over her shoulder. "What do you want, Niall."

A gust of air shot down his nostrils, and his chin raised. "Is that an invitation?"

"No," she snapped the second his lips quirked.

A sly grin nudged the right corner of his mouth, and his arms crossed over his padded jacket. "I don't need an invitation. We both know that, Shannon."

The pompous tone lacing his voice made her hands fist. "Stay the fuck away from me, or I'll tell Harry that you're up to your old tricks again."

"Like that would do any good," he scoffed, pushing off the frame to breach the gap between them. "I want to bend you over, right now, like I used to do. Remember?"

Raising the pointed prongs, she hovered the jaggy ends at his groin. "That was in the past. Now get the fuck away from me before I scream." Her pulse throbbed with her forced hesitation because it took all her might not to stab the smug asshole in the gut.

"Aw, Shannon. You're such a spoil sport. We both know a pitch fork wouldn't stop me, if I really wanted to get close to you, but I'm needed elsewhere, unlike you. No one needs you. Not even, my dad. You're easily replaced." He clicked his fingers. "Just like that." The wink that followed scattered a rush of chills over her scalp.

Shannon knew he was arrogant, but lately he'd taken his asshole-ness to a whole new level. He'd been a bully, even back when they dated, but over the course of the past year, he'd become volatile like a hidden grenade.

"See you later, Shannon." A threatening grin crept over his boyish face.

"Hopefully not," she muttered under her breath, watching him stroll into the sunlight.

Chapter 9

Knocked back again.

How many times in one day can a guy be turned down? It was unusual and a little unnerving, to say the least. He tried again by inviting her to the party - but still, a resounding no. She had some fucking event of her own to attend, or so she said. It wasn't a flat out no way, never. But nonetheless, Jamie was pissed off at the apparent rejection.

Tonight, he was flying solo. Just the way he liked it. There would be plenty of options to choose from. His single situation would be easily rectified. With a sweep of his gaze and flash of his smile, he wouldn't go home alone.

The master suite was filled with business associates and friends. It was the usual crowd of rich bastards and monied women. He loved a social event as much as the next crazy motherfucker, but tonight he was off his game. The three shots of tequila didn't help, nor did the obvious gaping ladies.

"Jamie!" Lana wrapped her arms around his neck, tugging him into her sleek dress that hugged every god damn curve on the woman's sexy body.

He swept up his brother's fiancée, twirling her in a playful embrace. The two had grown fond of each other since Lana became a permanent fixture in his brother's life. He didn't hold any resentment towards her for taking Marcus off the market, even though it dampened their drink fuelled nights. Marcus was whipped. When they partied, he usually left early, running home to Lana before midnight in case he turned into a fucking clown and lost his red nose.

Even though Jamie teased him, each and every time, he

was glad his brother finally allowed himself to be happy, to bury his demons and accept his feelings for Lana. They'd had a rocky start, which only made them stronger together. Now, Marcus laughed more than he scowled, and he spent more time on holiday than he did in the office. Did it matter – no. The guy was filthy rich, and in love.

"You look sensational, as always." He grinned, planting a brotherly wet smooch on her cheek.

Lana smiled up at him. "Did you bring a date?" she asked, her sparkling blue eyes searching his face for a clue. He had to admit, Lana was stunning and the perfect match for Marcus, although, the vivid blue eyes staring back at him didn't have the same mesmerising ice blue hold as Shannon Colter's.

He mentally shook off the image of her pretty face. "I'm guessing, Marcus, has already blabbed – and no, she's not coming." He raised his shoulders to his ears casually.

Lana brushed her palms down his fitted, olive green shirt. A knowing glint twinkled in her eyes, and a smirk pulled at her coral stained lips. "Sounds like you've met your match, Jamie."

"Pff, I'm sure I'll be able to fill the void." Looking over her shoulder, he mentally undressed a passing brunette.

The penthouse suite morphed into the perfect party pad for the rich and influential. Lana kept invitations exclusive and provided a well-stocked free bar. It was a casual affair – no suits required, yet for those who attended, dressing down meant this season's catwalk collection with an expectation of lavish luxury behind the hotel doors.

An international DJ set up decks in the master bedroom, with wireless speakers dotted throughout the grand suite. Catering staff carried shiny platters of the finest canapés, from caviar blinis to pancetta wrapped figs, all courtesy of Marcus's ex chef, Freddy. It was a well-played move for Freddy, whose new restaurant was opening in New York, with Lana's help of PR and marketing.

Multi-billionaire entrepreneur, Luke Devereux arrived with an entourage of beautiful women, all eager to impress. It appeared completely chauvinistic, yet in this social circle, it was perfectly acceptable. With a nod of his head or a flick of his wrist, Devereux had his whimsical expectations fulfilled. The roguish man didn't make any apologies for his female followers, who did so of their own free will. It was true, the women happily lapped up his attention and the additional financial benefits that were dished out like bonbons.

Suited men with earpieces scouted the room, standing with their backs to the walls to keep a strategic line of vision on the guests.

Luke held his hand towards Jamie, sliding a glance at Lana. "I'm a little disappointed that we aren't having this party in the Verto Veneri bar. I'm always up for meeting like minded people." He smirked.

Jamie stepped a little closer to Lana. "You planning on getting married soon?" His brows rose sarcastically, knowing the answer before Luke even opened his mouth in repulsion.

"Hell no, Jamie." Luke's voice cracked in laughter, aimed at the ridiculous suggestion of marriage. "I have my hands full with *that* lot." He looked back over his shoulder, acknowledging the women mingling close by. "Do you think we should modify the rules for the new clubs – an anything goes vibe? Everyone knows sex sells, so let's ramp it up."

"And turn the clubs into brothels? Never gonna happen, mate. You bought into the elitism of Verto Veneri, and with the changes, it will be even more desirable," Jamie countered, keeping his new business partner in check.

Luke patted Jamie's arm. "I know. I know. Worth throwing it out there." He chuckled, his eyes shadowed with mischief.

Inching towards Lana, Luke half smiled. "Is this your date for the hour?"

Jamie rolled his eyes for Lana's benefit. "I'd like to

introduce you to Lana, my brother's better half." Jamie nodded towards her.

Luke's eyebrows shot up. "Marcus has a ball and chain? He kept that quiet when he came out to New York to settle the deal," he scoffed as though the words burned a hole in his tongue.

"I'm his fiancée." Lana stepped forward, shaking hands with the tall, suave man who reeked of trouble and money.

"Luke." His hand held hers tightly. "It's an honour to meet the woman who can tame that son of a bitch. I'm intrigued." He gave her a not so subtle once over, nodding his head when his eyes reached her curvy hips.

Lana half laughed, obviously indifferent to his reaction, and quickly pulled her hand away. "Don't be – I just don't believe in bullshit or tolerate it. Enjoy the party, Luke." She sashayed away with her head held high.

Luke whistled with appreciation. "Gutsy. I like that. No wonder he's held on to that one for a while. What about you, Jamie?"

A waitress appeared beside the two men, balancing a duo of crystal tumblers on a tray. Jamie winked at the pretty young girl and grabbed the drinks. Her cheeks turned crimson and her eyes sparkled, but Jamie didn't gift her with a second look.

Nudging a glass forward. "I'm in no rush to get hitched anytime soon," he replied.

Luke swilled the tawny liquid. "Good, because the reason we're in business together, is down to the fact that the McGrath brothers are crazy, unpredictable assholes – much like me. Having ties makes us vulnerable and weak, like exposed soft flesh where the fuckers can stab us. At least you haven't settled." He looked almost serious. "To us!" He clinked his glass with Jamie's before sinking the contents in one gulp.

A pair of tall, attractive women pranced across the room like docile deer. They trotted to Luke's side and linked his arms. Both of the women had wavy golden locks that kissed their round protruding breasts with long lean legs that went on for miles. Jamie eyed the beauties, soaking up their flirtatious lip licking and wicked grins. As much as he appreciated a fine-looking woman, an odd feeling of uncertainty pinched his gut.

Since when did the height of a woman interfere with his intentions to fuck? Both women were tall, perhaps just a fraction smaller than Jamie and Luke, but Shannon was petite in stature, which made her appear vulnerable and all the more fascinating. He never really considered hair colour before either, it was irrelevant in the grand scheme of sexual satisfaction, yet Shannon's glossy black hair, framing her bright blue eyes, conjured darkness and mystery.

"If you see anything you like, Jamie, be my guest." Luke intercepted the ridiculous thoughts dancing through his mind.

Immediately one of the blond women stepped into his space, running her fingertips along the waistband of his jeans. Her teeth plunged into her lower lip, and a sexy soft moan left her throat.

Hell yeah. I'm still young free and most definitely single.

Chapter 10

He could avail himself of any unoccupied room in the entire hotel, but Jamie was on a mission to have sex with the eager woman who willingly skipped behind him as he ploughed through the throngs of guests. He had a sexual urge that needed to be gratified, like a fucking irritating itch that begged to be scratched. Since meeting Shannon, he was beyond horny. Blondie would fill the void and satisfy his burning sexual appetite.

Having more or less offered herself up on a plate, he was happy to accept. In a few strides they were in the large bathroom. He locked the door behind them, and by the time he turned around to face his partner in crime, she was naked. The dress puddled at her ankles, no underwear.

"My kinda girl." He smirked, unzipping his light blue jeans.

Before he uttered the command to drop to her knees, she knelt and crawled towards him like a cat. Her quick fingers released his long hard shaft from his boxer briefs, and her eyes widened as it sprang to attention.

"Like what you see?"

"Fuck yeah, Jamie. It's bigger than I expected."

This was a common occurrence in the life of Jamie McGrath. Minimal effort required to have a good time, and that's exactly what he was used to and just how he liked it. He worked hard enough in business, so why the hell would he want to work to have sex.

Her warm wet mouth engulfed the thickness. His hands fisted her hair, pushing her mouth further down his length. She gagged as it hit the back of her throat. Then he tugged her head back, angling it in a way that he could watch her stretched mouth slide up and down.

"My dick looks good in your mouth."

Pencilled eyebrows raised in appreciation, and her relentless mouth kept sucking and dragging along his erection. She hummed, heightening the pleasure, yet her average mouth was just about keeping him aroused. His mind had taken a detour, revisiting the fresh face of his lunch date the day before.

The suction came to an end. "You like my lips around your cock, Jamie?" The blond woman sat back on her knees and fluttered her false lashes.

His eyes pinged open, and he tried to disguise the shadow of disappointment when he saw the wrong face. "Keep sucking," he growled.

Grabbing a fistful of her hair, he thrust his cock into her open mouth. The pleasurable sensation of her warm lips helped him rise until his balls tightened, and he grunted with a release, spurting into her mouth. She didn't swallow his salty offering but held it in her mouth until he finished. Blondie turned to the sink and spat repeatedly, expelling all traces of him.

This was a perfunctory sexual act between two people who meant nothing to one another. A soulless joining that would normally fuel Jamie with a vigour to carry on and fuck the girl until she couldn't remember her own name, but now, now he just wanted to zip up his fly and walk away.

What the fuck was that all about?

Tucking his semi back into his jeans, he wondered why he was off his game. Blondie sidled back over to him, wiping her mouth with the back of her hand. She tweaked his nipples through the taut fabric of his shirt. "Like for like, Jamie. My turn now," she purred.

He just wasn't that into her.

If this was going to work, he needed to get in the mood, and fast. He pressed his mouth to hers, groping her breasts while she rubbed herself against his thigh. Her arousal began to build, the heat between her legs burned against him. His cock hardened. Of course it did, he was a man and she was a naked woman getting herself off on his leg.

She maneuverer his jeans lower. He grabbed her waist and heaved her onto the counter surrounding the basin. She nodded towards her sparkly clutch, close to their feet.

"In there. A condom," she rasped under her breath.

Jamie dropped down, at the same time as his phone rang.

"No way, Jamie. Don't get that, please," she whined.

His cock sprang to life when she begged and panted. Grabbing the bag, he flipped out a condom and tore the packet with his teeth. The ringing finally stopped as he covered his long hard shaft. Then a beep. A text message landed.

"Shit, I need to get that. It might be about my dad. Hold on." He crouched like a tiger scavenging for prey, finding his phone next to her bag.

One missed call from Shannon.

One text message from Shannon.

Fuck!

Shannon:

Hi. I'm back early from my event. On route to Belfast if your invitation is still open...

There was no way in hell he could bring her to the party now, not after blondie had just layered the sink with his cum. A serious case of bad timing. It was like Shannon knew he was just about to plunge balls deep into another woman.

His cock quickly became less enthused. The urge to fuck deflated like a punctured bouncy castle at a kid's party. "I have to go." He rose, ripped off the condom and hoisted up his jeans.

"What the hell, Jamie. You can't just leave me hanging like this. I let you shoot your load in my mouth for godsake!" blondie whined, shunting her breasts out.

"Sorry. The party's over." He shrugged.

Blondie nudged into him with her shoulder. "Maybe later?" She winked.

Tilting his chin, neither agreeing or disagreeing, he turned on his heels. Escaping the clutches of the unfulfilled woman, he strode out of the suite and into the hotel corridor. Once the door shut behind him, the music muffled, blessing him with much needed space and calmness.

He scrolled down the contacts list, hovering his thumb over her name, pausing before he hit dial. Why was he unsettled?

She answered on the second ring. "Hi, Jamie."

Her silky voice sent tiny arrows through the line, landing deep in his groin. He wanted to see her, but he'd blown up any chance of hooking up tonight. It wouldn't feel right to have Shannon pick up where blondie left off. Normally, those shenanigans wouldn't bother him. It was sexy as fuck watching a couple of chicks share his dick, but something about Shannon was different. He wanted to savour her, slowly, and most importantly, alone.

Her eyes were filled with honesty. So fucking pure. Pacing the carpet, he cursed the shit blow job that cost him Shannon's company for the night.

"Sorry, Shannon. I'm tied up with my brother and our business partner," he said huskily, oddly hating himself for manipulating the truth. "Another time?"

"Oh, right. No worries."

The background noise sounded like she was in a bar.

"Where are you exactly?"

"The Fitz lobby."

Shit!

Jamie took a deep breath and swallowed. "I'll be right down."

"No! It's okay, honestly. I'll just head back. I've an early start in the morning." Her voice feigned disappointment tinged with embarrassment.

"Don't move an inch. I'll be there in a minute," he ordered.

Chapter 11

Wrapped in a mustard downy coat and black knitted scarf, she perched on a low-slung chair in the hotel foyer.

Anticipation tingled up her spine. She was a simple girl, who liked simple things, and this was way out of her comfort zone. Waiting for Jamie was like waiting for the rollercoaster car to pull up, ready to take her on a bone rattling ride.

"Shannon." Jamie strolled up behind her, his sexy voice fluttered in her chest.

Flicking her head around, she eyed his swagger from across the lobby, with hands stuffed into his delightfully tight jeans. His lean muscles filled the fabric of his green shirt, and his tanned skin darkened under the low lighting. She tore her gaze away from his torso and licked her lips without thought. This guy had an abnormal effect on her body.

Jamie sauntered to the cluster of seats where she waited, gifting the air with his woodsy cologne. Heady tones of Cedarwood fired up a desire to reach out and grab him - anywhere, and everywhere.

A gulp of air stuck in her throat when she sucked in her sudden shyness and stood. "I'm sorry that I just showed up... I should've checked with you first." It was a rash decision to jump on a bus and wander into the hotel before checking to see if he still wanted to cash in on the whole date thing.

He silently stared right at her for a heartbeat. "I invited you, Shannon," he said with a sultry low growl.

A hum of excitement powered through her muscles as he reached out his large hand. "Let me take your Eskimo outfit." His mouth quirked.

Her pale cheeks had turned to a delicate pink after entering the warm hotel from the cool evening air, but now they deepened to match her awkwardness. "It was freezing at the bus stop." She felt foolish and out of place, but giggled with a quick high-pitched laughter that gave away her stupid nerves.

His cheek dimpled, pulling a lopsided smile to raise the temperature even higher. "I would've sent a car for you, love."

"The bus is fine, I prefer it," she said quickly, shaking her head gently.

His head flinched back, enough to show his surprise. "The bus? Really?"

She peeled off the padded layer and looked to the ground. "I can pay my own way and sort out my own lifts." The coat hung between them like an air bag after the rollercoaster crashed. Jamie tugged it from her curled fingers. "Thanks anyway."

What she didn't tell him was that it would be easier to leave when it suited her, without relying on anyone else.

Her skinny jeans were as dark as the night sky, and she wore a loose denim shirt with a few risky buttons left undone, revealing her silver horseshoe necklace. Lightly sucking in her lower lip, a swell of bravery gathered. She'd thought about him all day, throwing her concentration into a tail spin. It was the memory of his soft wet lips and the hint of his sexual capabilities that intrigued and excited her. Even Harry had asked why she seemed dreamy and distant. It had taken all her effort to push Jamie McGrath to the back of her mind so she could power through the jumps with Trixie. The frustrating thing was, she had broken her strict 'no men' rule - for him. She knew it, and he knew it. How could she not accept when the guy offered to take her on a date?

Jamie strolled to the reception desk and placed her coat on the counter without saying a word. He commanded authority without any effort. His smoking appearance was a visual gift, his charming personality was abundant and natural, while his pantie sizzling grin was the fucking bomb. She tightened her shy smile, trying to hide the silly crush escalating faster than wild fire on a windy day. With one glance, he had the ability to visually strip her bare, leaving a vulnerability that shocked and confused her.

"What can I get you to drink?" he asked, re-joining her at the comfy seats.

"Aren't we going to the party?" Her brows snapped together.

"Maybe later. The music up there is too loud. I'd like to chat with you." He nodded to the seat at her legs. "What would you like?"

She dropped down into the chair with her back straight and knees pressed together. "Just an orange juice please. I'm up early tomorrow morning."

He nudged his chin upwards, catching the attention of a young girl wearing a hotel uniform. Even though Shannon was sitting beside him, she trotted to his side with a pen tucked in her ponytail and bright eyes. "What can I get you, sir," she chirped with a flirty cadence.

"It's Jamie," he added with a second nature wink.

"Oh yes, sorry, sir... I mean, Jamie. What would you like to drink?" Her neck reddened.

"An orange juice and the best liquor in the house," he said playfully.

She nodded. "Certainly, that's the one thing we'll never run out of," the girl quipped, sporting a sweet grin like they had a weird secret that Shannon wasn't privy to. Her pulse jumped.

Jamie dropped into the armchair beside her, watching as she contorted herself on the chair like a poker, stuffing her hand inside her tight jeans pocket. "Let me get this round," she muttered, dragging a clump of crumpled notes out into the open.

Smoothing out the five-pound notes, she reached back into the same pocket for a few golden coins. Internally, she counted her stash, moving her lips subtly with each number. Silently totting up the pounds, she tallied twenty-four pounds and a few pence. Her tongue peeked out of her mouth, and her head bounced lightly from side to side as she stacked the coins on top of the notes.

Jamie cleared his throat with a gravelly growl. The delightful sound resounded in her belly, making her look up instantly and into his blazing eyes. They were focused on her tongue with an overwhelming intensity. His amber depths were sucking her in, fascinating every cell in her quivering body.

The young girl returned with their drinks and set them on the walnut coffee table between the two armchairs. Shannon parted her lips, ready to call the waitress back to pay for the drinks.

"It's okay. I've got a tab running," he said quickly.

"I said I would get this round."

Jamie sighed softly. "Look, this is my hotel. My staff always has a tab running for me. I pay it off every so often. My guests don't pay."

She sank back, focusing on the insignificant amount of cash on the table. "You own this place?"

He swilled the whiskey in his tumbler before taking a swig. "My brother and I own it, actually."

She expelled a puff of air from her nose and sat upright like he just punched her in the gut. The guy has more money than she first thought. He owns the damn hotel they're sitting in. That explains why everyone looks at him like he's the boss - because he is. She closed her eyes briefly, hoping Jamie wasn't one of those entitled rich guys.

He owns a hotel, it's not like he's a millionaire.

With one hand, she grabbed the tall glass filled with juice, while the other hand chucked the money on the coffee table in a quick exchange. "Well, there you go. Use that to pay your tab."

"Sure, no problem. Thanks." He held up his tumbler and nodded. "Cheers, Shan, thanks for the drink."

Did he really just call her Shan? Her toes curled inside

her boots, and she dropped her chin. "Cheers, Jamie," she said softly.

"So, why did you come tonight? I thought you had some big event to attend?" His handsome face wore a knowing smile.

The glass at her lips provided a welcomed coolness to her warmth. She took a sip. "I got finished earlier than expected." Her fingers drifted to the tousled tips of her hair.

"I'm glad you came."

"Oh, right, and why is that?"

Whiskey moistened his lips when he mirrored her movements and took a sip. "I thought I was losing my touch." His mouth quirked, and she knew right that second that he never really doubted his charm.

"How could I not show up, after all, you made it sound like so much fun. I had to see if you lived up to the hype."

"What part excited you, Shannon?"

"Free food. I'm a sucker for cocktail sausages. Those wee buggers are addictive," she said through a light giggle.

"I can guarantee you, Shannon Colter, I will most definitely live up to the hype." A smile ghosted his lips. "How did your big event go?" he asked like he was interested, stretching out his legs and crossing his ankles.

She sucked in her lower lip, embracing her recent victory. "It was actually really amazing. I won the…." Her words trailed off. She was just about to reveal a little morsel of information, carried away in the excitement of her success.

"What did you win?" He drew in his legs and angled himself closer.

"Just a silly competition. No biggy."

"Beauty pageant?" he asked with a sexy smile that invited his dimple to wink at her.

"Nooooo!" She sniggered, twirling a lock of hair around her forefinger.

"Are you gonna leave me hangin'?" he demanded. As he lifted the whiskey to take another sip, an ice-cube rattled against the glass.

"You'll think it's utterly boring and nerdy."

He hummed low in his throat. "The image of nerdy Shannon makes me hard."

"Such a charmer."

His attention was fully focused on her, just her. Not the women who walked past him, nearly breaking their necks to catch another look. "Shannon, even the sound of your voice makes my dick twitch."

"Ugh! Seriously, Jamie?" Her laugh stuttered in her throat. She was melting right in front of him.

"Tell me what you won, love."

"Okay. I won the finals in a show jumping league. Which means I've qualified for the equine championships."

His eyes widened. "You ride horses?"

"Yeah. Told you it was nerdy. I used to get hackled at school and called stupid names. Saddle Bags and Winne Weirdo was as inventive as they got."

He chuckled deep in his chest. "I would've kicked them up and down the corridor if I knew you back then."

"I would've enjoyed watching that." She grinned.

"You actually like horses?" he asked with a hint of disbelief in his tone. "You're competing in the Equine Comps?"

"Yes."

He gifted her with a boyish grin. "I fucking love horses."

She inhaled sharply and a wide smile ached her cheeks. "Really? You're not bullshitting me right now to strengthen your end game?"

"End game?" He chuckled. "Is that what all the kids are calling sex these days?"

"I'm a woman, Jamie."

"You sure as hell are, Shannon. I've loved horses ever since my dad took us on a trip to the country when I was a twelve." His eyes gleamed. "We rented in an old cottage that stank of cow shit. Right next to it was a field filled with muddy horses. Back then I thought they were fucking huge." He laughed. "There wasn't much to do, so I'd sit on the gate in the sun and just watch them. They always came over. They trusted me. It was pretty cool."

He ran a hand through his thick textured hair. "It was peaceful, just me and them. I could forget about shit – you know?" His brows popped up.

With a few words he tapped into her mind and described a sensation she had enjoyed a hundred times over at Meadow Dawn. In that moment she felt a deeper connection but quickly brushed it off.

"I get what you mean. It's like, when I get up on a summer's morning and the sun's rising over the hills. The horses wander down from the fields and gather at the gates when I shake the feed bucket. There's no one else around – just me and them."

"How many horses do you have?" he asked, wearing his signature, hard to resist smile.

"None. I just do the leg work." She blew a puff of air out of her nostrils, and her lips tightened to a straight line. "Would you like to meet my first love sometime?" She suggested randomly. A sudden blast of heat flushed her cheeks as she realised how eager it sounded.

His perfect lips separated, and she gulped back her foolishness, waiting for him to make his excuses. She looked away and traced the cool misty glass with her nails, teasing the tiny beads of water.

"If you like horses then you'll love her, she's called Venatrix, but we call her Trixie," she continued in a gust, reinforcing the fact he would visit the horse, not her.

"I'd really like to meet her." His deep voice carried over the bustle of the busy lobby.

She licked her lips. "Whenever you've got time, just text me."

"Tomorrow?" There was no hesitation. He dragged his thumb across his lower lip as his eyes paused at the open buttons leading to her cleavage.

That subtle movement made her pulse thrum, hard and fast. "She's at Meadow Dawn yard." She almost panted as his gaze dallied back up to her face.

"I know the yard," he said huskily. "If she's your first love, then who is your second love?"

Shannon inhaled a shaky breath. "She's my one and only. I don't have time for silly stuff like love. She's my life right now."

"Good to know." He winked in agreement.

The waitress returned with more drinks as if she'd been told to always keep them flowing. The sweet girl vanished, no doubt devastated that he hadn't shown her even the slightest bit of attention.

It wasn't Jamie's fault he was carved to perfection, laced with sex appeal and doused in dangerous intentions. She nibbled the side of her fingernail as he silently spied her over the rim of his glass. Whatever he was thinking right now, was hidden behind his eyes.

"What about you? Did you ever get a horse or riding lessons?" she asked freeing her finger from her teeth.

Just as his jaw dropped to speak, a tall man wandered into view with a beautiful woman draped on his arm as the perfect accessory for the evening. "Hey, Jamie. Why are you down here when all the fun is upstairs?" The man slid Shannon an odd look.

Jamie launched off the seat and threw his arms around the handsome, well-dressed man. "Trent, mate, you came. Marcus said you couldn't make it up from Dublin this weekend." Jamie grinned as the two parted. "I haven't seen you in ages. How's business?"

The attractive woman stood back, lingering on the periphery. Her earlobes were adorned with diamonds and an expensive necklace reflected the light like a rainbow, catching Shannon's eye as it sparkled. Neither of the two men spoke to the woman, nor did they look in her direction. It was obvious that her attention was focused on Jamie by the way she trailed her tongue over her lips and teased the jewels close to her throat when he spoke. The woman was sizing him up, like she wanted to lick him from head to toe, or worse, like she was reminiscing a good time from their past. Jamie ended the conversation with a pat on the man's bicep. Trent strolled away with the beauty traipsing behind him. With one last glance, she flicked her head over her shoulder and winked at Jamie in a playful wicked game.

Shannon gave him a dubious look when he swung back around to face her. A niggling fear rippled in her gut. She could tell Trent was one of those guys who had different arm candy each night. He was an example of the people Jamie associated with. The same people who had zero moral's, zero principles and more money than wit. Suddenly the penny dropped. She wanted the truth to stop spinning like the revolving entrance door, but it was obvious Jamie was just like them.

Coughing into her fist, the words came out with firm tone, "I don't want to keep you back from the party, Jamie. If you want me to leave just say so."

His forehead creased. "I don't. It's filled with a few assholes. It's just better if we stay here a while." He scratched his jaw in an odd moment of awkwardness.

"Assholes? Like that guy? A loaded, pompous prick who thinks he can buy off those who are less fortunate?" she said sternly. "And what's with his pet?"

"Not everyone with money, is like that." He raised his eyebrows.

"Yes, they are. Those type of really rich people think they can do whatever the hell they want, and fuck the consequences, because at the end of the day, money talks."

His arms folded across his broad chest. "Is that an observation or from experience?"

She sighed heavily and set her glass down with a thud. "I'll never be with a guy who has more cash than sense, or more self-importance than honour."

Jamie's eyes flashed. He collected his glass and drained the icy liquid in one gulp. "Shannon…"

Her stomach clenched. "I shouldn't be here. I'll head home now." She lifted out of the chair. "I didn't realise you owned this place, or that the party would be full of those types of people, or more to the point, that you were like them…"

Jamie lunged forward and halted her retreat by grabbing her wrist. "Stop..."

Warning bells rang like the death toll. She had arrived under dressed, understated and under the fucking illusion that a hot guy like him would actually want her company. No doubt he would earn extra points with his rich friends if he fucked a poor country girl.

She had no idea he owned the hotel until this evening. But he seemed so down to earth, and dare she think it, normal, even for a cocky guy. "I shouldn't be here. I just thought you were having a knees-up in the function room and wanted me to come along." She patted down her windswept hair.

Tightening his grip, Jamie pressed against her chest. "That's exactly what it is. Please, I want you to stay."

"I've changed my mind." She looked down to the pretty square mosaic tiles underfoot.

With his forefinger, he tilted her chin upwards. "I asked you to come here, so we could get to know each other."

"Yeah, sex." She swallowed loudly.

He grinned down at her. "I'm not going to lie, Shannon, I'd fuck you right here if you'd let me."

A strangled moan escaped her throat, and she focused on his wicked grin with a narrow stare.

"I'd also be happy to just talk for a while." He shrugged like the idea of sex wasn't on the front of his brain, but the vibrations coming from his body said otherwise.

A lock of hair tumbled over her face as she shook her head. "I'm not dressed properly. I don't fit in with that lot... I don't belong in your world, Jamie."

A low growl reverberated in his throat, initiating a skin tingling shiver down her back. "Shannon, I started with nothing and slogged hard for years to get where I am today. Having cash means nothing if you're a dick with no dignity. This has nothing to do with money and everything to do with enjoying the evening together." Alcohol heated his breath, lingering in the combustible air between them.

His fingertips played with the dishevelled strands that hung over her pink cheeks. "Will you come up with me, for a while, at least?"

She gulped, barely able to acknowledge the sexy little indent that nestled in his cheek. "Fine," she whispered, even though her head was telling her to run like hell.

His hands trailed down her sleeves, meeting her clenched palms. "Like I said, there are a few assholes up there tonight, who'd probably fit your expectations, but I'm not one of them, okay?"

His molten amber eyes held a dark glint as they loitered hungrily on her lips. She waited, without breathing. Her thoughts swirled, craving another taste of Jamie McGrath. That second of insanity was exhilarating, being held captive by him stirred crazy sensations that made her jolt back and tug her hands free.

"Fine."

The awareness of his proximity was making her mind foggy. Tingles shot around her body, reaching places that never knew they needed stimulation. He owned half of a hotel, and she just owned the clothes on her back. Shannon silently cursed herself. Somewhere along the way, in her inexperienced heart, the lines had become blurred.

Jamie swiped her cash from the table, uncurled her fist and placed every penny on her palm. He towered above her, blocking out every sound, scent and sensation other than her galloping heart. His masculine aroma permeated the thick air around them.

"You bought the first round. I got the second. Take the rest of the money and get a taxi home later - if you decide not to come back to my place, that is." His sultry voice drifted through the air like silk, forcing her thighs to clamp shut. "That's highly unlikely though."

A puff of air shot down her nose. "Really?" she smirked. "You seem pretty confident about that, Jamie. The last bus is before midnight, so if I decide to go home alone, I'll use up my return bus ticket. Take the money."

His eyes closed for a second as he inhaled slowly.

"Please, get a taxi. You're not taking a bus home in the middle of the night with drunken assholes."

"I've taken the bus home from Belfast before. It's fine."

His head lowered, but he looked up at her under his thick lashes with a sexy half smile on his handsome face. "I can tell how much you appreciate your independence, or is it stubbornness?" The firmness in his speech gave way to the suggestion that he'd be dominating when it came down it. "Let's put a wager on it. I bet you twenty-four pounds that you come tonight."

"To the party?"

"No, on me."

Shannon gulped, feeling the surge of his wickedness deep in her core. "So, you're a betting man?"

"I don't bet against the odds. And I know you'll be right where you belong, in my apartment, on my face, tonight."

The truth was out there, floating around for them both to see. This wasn't about a date. It was about him. It was about shameless sex and the memory of that game changing kiss in the hotel restaurant.

"Let's see how the party goes. At the moment, the odds are stacked against you, Jamie." She batted her lashes, grinning playfully.

Chapter 12

Jamie inhaled the inevitable, which was meeting his unfinished business upstairs. No doubt blondie's wide green eyes of jealousy would devour Shannon like a python – in one swallow. He'd dealt with shit like that before. Most of the time women joined forces and happily entertained him together. He wasn't sure if Shannon would be part of those antics, and he certainly didn't want to scare her off, until he saw the goods she had to offer. That sweet ass was begging to be devoured, and he was just the guy to do it.

She was like a skittish colt with a hatred for men who had a lack of scruples, which apparently went hand in hand with an abundance of money. Now she knew he had a bit of cash, but he wasn't in a rush to tell her the truth. He didn't make a habit of telling people that he was a billionaire. Anyway, after tonight he'd never see her again.

Jamie watched her palm crumple the paper notes and shove them back into her pocket. The idea of Shannon and blondie sucking him off made his dick pulse, until the fantasy took an unexpected turn, and the extra woman evaporated, leaving Shannon as the leading role, centre stage.

He knew it was a better plan to sit in the bar and sip his family branded whiskey, yet the sinking disappointment that had paled her pretty face when she glimpsed his hesitation, had been a low blow to his balls. A shadow of hurt had crept into her bright baby blues, and her sweet smile had faded to a thin uncertain line - all because she had a crazy fucking idea that she didn't fit in. Yeah, she had a sexy wildness, and her clothes bordered on tom boy rather than pretty doll, but that's what made her different. She was a world apart from the fake money grabbing pleaser's who were zero challenge but tasted good, as any random fuck would. He didn't care if she stripped down to her panties or thermal underwear, as long as he was the one to rip them off with his teeth, tonight. She was complicated and closed off – natural and untamed. Shannon was playing a razor-sharp game with an edge that he would happily cut himself on just to get inside her.

He mostly enjoyed it when blondie sucked him off earlier. As far as blow jobs went, it was fine, but it hadn't revved his engine, not nearly as much as the mega revs he got when Shannon stepped into the picture. She injected him with an unknown feeling, like his destiny was banging at the door, begging to come in. He couldn't put his finger on why she felt so close but so far away. One thing was certain, he wanted to put his fingers on every inch of her skin. Especially now, with her unruly raven hair that framed her glacial eyes with a blue so intense, like icicles that had frozen into disc's, created from the Icelandic blue lagoon.

As they rode the elevator to the top floor, he realised he put way too much thought into the colour of her eyes. Eyes were fucking eyes, and women were fucking women.

The doors pinged open, and he slid his hand to her narrow waist. She peeked up at him under long black lashes as if sensing his unease. His mouth formed a firm line, holding off his apprehension. The vein in his neck pulsated as each reluctant stride brought them closer to the invitation only bash. He waved off the lean security guy, who spoke into a device attached to his ear, announcing their arrival.

Jamie held her to his side, snug to his hip as the door drew back and the music escaped into the corridor. Together they stepped into the lion's den, the seething pit of the rich and unscrupulous.

"You son of a bitch!" Luke Devereux halted their entry. "Where did you find this one?" His corrupt gaze washed over Shannon's curvy form, and his brow cocked with intrigue.

"Luke. Meet, Shannon. My date." Jamie put his cards on the table and straightened his back, nestling a little closer to her petite frame.

Luke's eyes flashed as he chuckled low in his throat. The laugh held a wicked secret that made Shannon shift back. Jamie's palm drifted lower to the dip of her lower back, and he rubbed his thumb along the waistband of her jeans.

"Are we going to play cards later?" Luke's scrutiny ended. His leering gaze leisurely returned to Jamie.

Jamie's ribs squeezed his lungs making him feel like he had to protect her. "Nah, mate, I'll be outta here soon. Business to take care of."

"That's a hell of a lot of business. I'd be happy for a three-way conference call?" Luke smirked as he folded his arms across his chest, and he actually fucking winked at Shannon.

That wink - a simple gesture he'd served up countless times before himself, now pissed him off. His stomach clenched and a jolt of anger rattled his skeleton. He inhaled deeply, settling the odd, unknown sensation and quickly forced a laugh. It was loud enough to rumble over the music but low enough to play it cool. "Not this time, mate."

"Shame."

Jamie nodded. "I'll catch you later. We'll get that card game arranged soon."

"We will, my friend, we will. You know me, always willing to party, and always happy to share. That's the moto, right?" He patted Jamie on the bicep.

Jamie winced inside his steely composure. He was the very asshole who came up with the stupid moto, during a weekend binge in Vegas.

A heavy hand gripped his shoulder from behind. Whipping his head around, he released a gust of relief.

"Jamie, it's about time you showed your ugly face. Lana said you were here somewhere." Marcus handed him a beer.

"He's been otherwise occupied." Luke lit a joint. "Lucky bastard." He drew the smoke into his lungs in a long inhalation, letting it bellow from his nostrils. A devilish glint in his eyes peeked out of the haze. He gave Shannon a lazy grin with the rolled up paper hanging from his lips.

Jamie ignored the bait. He knew Luke was testing him. They always fucked with each other. It wasn't a rare occurrence to fuck the same woman, at the same time.

"Shannon, this is my *old* brother, Marcus." Jamie smirked, emphasising the word old.

Her face brightened. It was obvious she found him attractive, he was a McGrath after all. "Nice to meet you, Marcus." She stuck out her hand. A broad smile radiated under the glow of the twinkling spot lights.

Jamie's gut churned, and he cleared his throat.

"You too, Shannon." Marcus reciprocated her hand shake with a lopsided sexy grin that stretched across his stubbled cheeks.

Jamie tightened his arm, pulling her back with a discreet tug. She turned her head and flashed him a dubious look. Why his brother's innocent grin irked him, was beyond comprehension. Marcus wasn't competition and never had been. Maybe it was her reaction, the way her voice was riddled with nerves, and her heartbeat pounded so hard that he could feel it in his own chest.

Her eyes flared, and it suddenly hit him. Her heartbeat hadn't just sped up. It matched the same galloping tempo from earlier, when he jerked her torso close to his side and held her there.

"What do you do for a living?" Marcus asked.

"I uh, I'm a barista."

"And she rides horses, competitively," Jamie added with a strange sense of pride.

"A horsey girl? Wow, a match made in heaven." Marcus threw Jamie a knowing smile.

Suddenly, Shannon lunged forward, away from Jamie's protection and almost jumped into his brothers startled stance.

"Jeez, I'm so sorry," she panted in a fluster, patting her own shoulder wildly. "My back is soaked!"

Jamie spun around to find the joker who soaked his woman. *His* woman? "This is fucking crazy," he muttered, noting that his elbow was drenched too.

Her black shirt was sopping. Cold liquid seeped into the material from her shoulder all the way down her back, sticking to her skin in an ice-cold layer. Marcus surrounded her, sweeping her dripping hair over her shoulder.

"It's just booze. I'll get a new shirt brought up immediately." He comforted her with a half hug.

Jamie stood silently with his fists balled. He had no clue how she ended up saturated or who did it. Just as well, because a rage was bubbling to the surface, and his usual calm and collected persona was morphing into a demon. His stomach twisted in knots as he watched Shannon lean into his brother's chest and giggle at his stupid ass joke. Since when was he a fucking comedian?

"I'll have to dry off under the hand dryer." She looked up at Marcus.

A surge of jealousy propelled Jamie forward. He gripped her arm and yanked her sideways. "There's a hair dryer in the bathroom," he gritted out. "I'm sorry this happened to you, Shan."

"It was an accident, Jamie. It's not the first time I've been bathed in champagne." She dodged a tall brunette wearing nothing more than a satin teddy.

"This way." Jamie slid his hand down her arm and linked their fingers. Picking up pace, he escorted her towards the master bedroom, failing to smile at the guests who wanted to catch his attention.

It was like déjà vu, and in a turn of events his end goal was ensuring Shannon was dry and comfortable – not wet and begging for it. "I'll dry it for you."

"No, it's okay. I can sort it."

He forced himself to take long slow breathes, holding back the urge to rip the damn shirt off and find out how good she looks beneath. "I'll wait outside the door." He stuffed his hands into his pockets. "There should be a hair dryer in the drawer under the sink. Unless you want me to arrange a new shirt?"

Shannon pushed into the bathroom and looked back over her shoulder with an innocent but sultry expression. Her cheeks were a pretty pink in contrast to her tousled black locks. A deep navy blue darkened her eyes until the light pinged on. "It'll be fine, Jamie, thank you."

"Shannon…" An overwhelming urge to kiss her hard shuddered through him. He hankered after the sensation of her soft lips.

The urgency in his voice was a surprise to both of them. Her chest rose with a sudden intake of air.

"I want to kiss you, Shannon." He inched inside. Excitement shot straight to his groin when he noted her pulse stutter in the dip of her throat.

The closer he advanced, the more his heartbeat drilled against his sternum. Her soft quick breathes landed on his skin with a stimulating invitation. She looked up under thick lashes, darting her tongue over her lips. He could tell she wanted to taste him just as much as he needed to hunt out the sweetness that had sent his libido wild. Threading his fingers through the hair at her nape, he angled her head, tugging her parted mouth closer to his.

"I'm not like those women out there, Jamie," she whispered into his mouth.

"Good," he growled, brushing his lips lightly over hers.

"I'm serious. I'm nothing like them."

He needed to stamp out the whole money diversity issue. Whether she had money or not was irrelevant – especially when he had enough for them both.

"I don't give a fuck about those women out there. It's you who has me ready to blow my load." And he *was* ready, the sensation of her satiny skin was irresistible.

Her head flinched in his tight hold. "I mean it, Jamie. Maybe this is a bad idea."

It was far from a bad idea. His dick was rock hard, and

his intentions had quickly become wild, but the vulnerable flare in her stormy eyes was enough for him to reconsider his rapid pursuit. He wanted to take his slow sweet time with this one. She deserved better than a quick fuck in the bathroom – the same bathroom that he'd been in only hours ago with a hot chick wrapped around him.

"I know you're not like them. Don't worry about it." He knew the slight pressure of his kisses trailing along the curve of her neck, combined with the restrictive grip of her hair would shatter her defences. Each featherlight kiss rained down her soft skin with a bid to tease and seduce. Her fingertips pressed into his shoulders and she whimpered with a light sensual gasp. The rigid walls were disintegrating, her stubbornness melting away with each delicate touch. Shannon responded, nudging her groin into his thigh.

The last soft groan was met with his lips as they covered her mouth. It was one of those ruthless, passionate kisses that was filled with equal parts hunger and need. If he didn't stop, he'd end up fucking her on the floor.

Her breathing hitched when he unexpectedly drew back. Releasing her hair, he growled, "Fuck the taxi, fuck the bus. We both know why I invited you tonight and why you showed up. We don't need to complicate this. I know you want me. So let's just cut to the chase and leave right now. You can give me one night, Shannon. Just one night." Jamie swallowed hard and let go. He stepped backwards, his eyes on her perfect lips. Reaching the door, he winked just before he closed it behind him, leaving her alone.

Chapter 13

Shannon stared at the closed door, panting with frustration. Her shaky palms slid down the fabric of her jeans, tilting her torso until she was stooped over. Closing her eyes, she inhaled deeply through her nose, trying to settle the burning swell between her thighs. Every nerve ending tingled, and her heartbeat bucked in her chest making her dizzy.

Her reaction to him was out of control. The guy effortlessly whipped her up into a frenzy with just a tug and a kiss. The truth was, that kiss, fuck, that kiss made her knees weak and her heart bounce. An explosive swell of heat sparked in her core and spread between her legs. She was hot and bothered and in need of a release - right this second.

Jamie left her in the bathroom to dry off her shirt, but he'd also left her alone with a slickness in her panties. Dragging her fingers through her tousled lengths, she regained composure and stood tall. Carefully popping open each button on her shirt, she thought about the women at the party and the type of playgirl he was used to. She could be like them, of course she could.

The girl looking back at her in the mirror was on a high of sexual adrenaline. Her cheeks were burning, and her eyes were wide. Peeling the shirt from her torso, she traced her short nails across the curve of her cleavage, shivering with delight. The skin prickled, responsive to the light touch that she wished was Jamie's. Sucking in a deep breath, she let the buzz race through her muscles.

With each lonely second that passed, she craved his touch and imagined his dominant body arcing over hers. Tonight she would forget about all the things she thought she knew about him. There was no point playing it cool. He knew the effect he had on her, the cocky asshole had it down to a fine art.

She would give him the one night he wanted because she wanted to experience the sexual power of Jamie McGrath.

Chapter 14

With Shannon barricaded in the bathroom, Jamie dragged his palms over his face, blowing out a puff of hot air. On the other side of the door she was stripped down to ass revealing panties and a lacey bra that showed off her nipples.

Well, that was the image in his head anyway, whether she needed to undress to dry the shirt was irrelevant. Damn, he was getting all sorts of hot and horny as he skulked outside the door like a dickhead with a massive uncomfortable hard-on nudging his zipper. He paced a track in the carpet, letting his mind tear off the delicate panties with hungry hands.

The unfulfilled blond from earlier strutted into view as she entered the bedroom, the same hot ass woman who dished out a mediocre effort in the dick lick department. Her pouty lips held a hint of amusement, and her overly friendly fingers traced the seam of his shirt. Jamie had no clue what her name was, yet she'd had his dick in her mouth without any introductions.

Did he need to know her name? No.

Did he want to know her name? Nope.

"So tense," she cooed. "How about round two?" She pushed her breasts into his chest, failing to stir his sexual appetite.

"Not tonight," he replied flatly, shrugging off her touch. "I'm waiting on someone."

"C'mon, Jamie. I promise it'll be everything you dreamed of." She ran her tongue along her glossy lips and giggled like a little minx.

In any normal situation he'd probably pin her to the

super king bed and do all kinds of filthy things, but for some reason, her attention felt wrong. He side glanced at blondie's partner in crime who sidled into the room with long tanned legs that ended in leopard print stiletto sandals. She looked Dutch, or Scandinavian, whichever of the two countries that spawned stunning, leggy blonde's. Even with her fluttery false lashes and painted nails, she still wasn't in the same league as the wild beauty beyond the bathroom door.

"Are we having our own party in here?" Dutch blond asked with a glint in her eyes.

A flash of possibilities ran through his head. Three girls, one Jamie. Hmm. The night could turn out to be very interesting if he wasn't so damn set on having Shannon all to himself. A niggle of uncertainty twisted in his gut. His self-conscious had finally found a voice and was urging him to get rid of the party girls and take Shannon on the ride of her life instead.

"Ladies, I'm busy tonight." He wrapped his torso with his bulging arms. "Go on."

"We're all friends here, Jamie. Luke told us to make sure you're happy." The unfulfilled blond trailed her pointy pink nail across his chest. "Why don't you ask your pretty little friend if she wants to join in?" She nudged her knee into his groin with light pressure, being so close that he could smell the perfume that clung to her clothes.

That idea had merits, but the one and only reason it would be remotely enjoyable, was Shannon. He shook his head as a low laugh rumbled in his chest. "It's a one woman show tonight, ladies. Sorry to disappoint." He lifted his shoulders to his rugged jaw line and held out his hands.

"Really? You play nice? That's not what we heard? We heard you're an anything goes kinda guy. The fun one, with the big hard dick," purred Dutch blond while walking her fingers up his arm to meet the shaved hair at the side of his head.

"Look, ladies..." He snatched her hand away and let it drop. "Like I said, I'm busy. Now fuck off."

Unfulfilled blondie's gaze drifted over his shoulder and her eyes narrowed. "But, Jamie, you loved coming in my mouth earlier. You promised me we'd fuck later, now's your chance. You owe me, and my friend here will make things a whole lot more interesting. We don't mind sharing." A wicked smirk danced on her lips. "We've heard that your good, really good."

Jamie stood wide and pushed his hands under his armpits. "I'm not in the mood for this shit. Like I said…"

Before he could finish, the Dutch blonde interrupted, "Oh, come on, Jamie, we'll tag team your dick. She can join in, if she's game?" Her head bobbed like she was acknowledging someone - Shannon.

Sweet Jesus.

Shannon stopped at the foot of the bed, keeping her distance, wearing a damp shirt and big wide eyes.

"Fuck off, girls," he growled. Jamie glanced sideward to meet Shannon's unreadable expression before her eyes cut to the elephants in the room.

"No, wait." She stepped to the parameter of the trio, staring up at the beautiful women with her shoulders back and her chin high. "He'll do it."

"Do what?" Jamie scrunched his brow.

"Let them suck you off. That's what you want, right? What you were going to get before I called you? Don't let me stop you." Her mouth quirked. "I'll watch."

A weird silence momentarily passed until light giggles filled his ears. He inhaled sharply feeling his dick rage against his zipper. "I didn't think you were coming tonight, Shannon, but let me tell you this, I most definitely underestimated you."

"You should never underestimate me, Jamie," she said faintly, a smile pulled at the corners of her mouth as her shoulders crept up.

The tiny black circles in her sparkling eyes dilated as she gulped, giving away her nerves.

A slow smile crept over his face. "You really want to watch them blow me?"

The Dutch blonde pushed Jamie backwards, propelling him towards the bathroom. "Let's go," she urged.

"Shannon..." he called, stumbling back. "Come here, now," he ordered, not giving her the chance to back out.

She followed quietly and positioned herself in front of the bevelled mirror above the sink, right next to the exit. Her hip dipped against the sleek marble counter, narrowing her eyes as they adjusted to the lighting. The tiny ceiling lights set the stage and lit up the glamorous women who professionally popped open the buttons on his jeans and released his hardness. Jamie's scorching gaze darted from his reflection and homed in on Shannon's pale face. Her shoulders rounded, and she wrapped her arms around her torso in a self-comforting hug. She looked like a timid kitty waiting to lap up cream.

He was bursting with a mixture of combustible arousal and surprise. Shannon was a dirty girl after all, and this little set up was beyond fucking hot.

There were skilful fingers and lapping tongues all over his erection, with soft moans and slurps. His mouth quirked as Shannon's tongue swiped across her cherry lips. He grabbed a handful of blonde hair and slammed his length into an open mouth, then the other. Under hooded eyes he watched Shannon's chest rise and fall in time with his quickened pulse. Her bright blue eyes flared, darkening like the deepest dangerous ocean.

The kneeling women stuffed their mouths full and hummed out loud. It didn't matter that their swollen lips were warm and wet, not when Shannon was squirming right in front of him. He ate up every sweet gasp, each subtle fumble of her shirt and every nibble of her lower lip.

This was fucking awesome – her reaction was fucking awesome. His wild-eyed voyeur was about to come in her panties, and he was getting off on her unexpected thrill.

The obedient women swapped turns with energetic enthusiasm, kissing each other between sucks. Little did they realise that Jamie wasn't interested in their provocative show. One inhaled his tight balls, while the other engulfed his cock whole. Shannon kept her eyes low, avoiding contact. She reached behind, fumbling for the edge of the counter and gripped it like she was trying her best to stifle a reaction. Jamie's cock stiffened harder than it ever had before when the muscles inside her thighs visibly clenched, and her jaw dropped just a fraction. It was the very thing prepping him to blow his load.

With a deep throaty growl, he fisted the base of his cock, locking eyes with her startled gaze that suddenly cut to his. As he spurted his seed over the faces before him, a soft moan escaped her throat. His eyes shut briefly, calming his racing heart just as the door clicked shut.

Shannon was gone.

Chapter 15

The next morning Trixie pulled out all the stops, popping neatly over the grids, clearing one after the other in close succession. She combined agility with speed, allowing Shannon to predict her every move as the perfect winning team.

The midday sun hung low in the wispy sky as winter prepared to dish out its worst. Shannon, on the other hand, was feeling sticky under her feather filled jacket, exhilarated by her hour-long session.

Harry sat in the sand paddock on his usual wooden bench near the gates with his Irish Wolfhound, Jackson, at his feet. He was a kind man who would rather spend his big bucks on the animals, than himself. A weathered, waxy peaked cap teamed with a matching hunter green jacket was his signature look, both had seen better days, but they added to his simplistic persona. Where Harry went, his buddy Jackson followed. They were best friends and solid companions.

"Okay, darlin', give her a long rein and let her cool off. She went well after yesterday," he hollered, sparking up a cigarette.

Shannon hitched her leg forward, leant down and released the buckle on the girth a notch as Trixie reduced her pace to a slow, steady walk. She patted the strong sinewy russet neck, smoothing her jet-black mane to the right.

"That'll do for today. No lessons tomorrow. Just take her out on the bridal paths tomorrow," Harry called from his seat. "You made me so proud yesterday, Shan. I knew you'd win."

"Trixie did us both proud, Harry." She nodded over at him.

"You both went well." He scratched under his cap. "You've worked hard. It's a dream to work with you."

"Awww, Harry, are you getting sentimental on me?" She tossed him a cheeky smirk.

A mechanical rumble interrupted the peacefulness of the quiet Sunday afternoon, amongst the rolling green hills. Harry jumped up and twisted towards the bumpy driveway that lead to the main house.

Shannon's heart tumbled in her chest when a lightning blue Mustang came into view. It growled along the curved path, reaching a gravel car park at the rear of the yard. The engine cut out and silence wrapped around the atmosphere like a warm blanket.

Its ergonomic design reminded her of a sleek and powerful shark hunting the vast ocean, looking horrendously expensive and way out of her financial stratosphere.

Crunchy footsteps brought the most amazing sight. Jamie strode towards the paddock, each muscly leg hugged by tight denim jeans and a khaki fitted tee poked out from under a jet black leather jacket. Confidence surrounded every stealth step, while his eyes locked in on his prey. His hair was neatly shaved at the sides with styled length at the top, ready for her fingers to sink into.

She watched from the centre of the paddock as Jamie held out his bulky arm and introduced himself to Harry, who matched his hardy handshake.

"Pleasure to meet you, I'm here to see Shannon. I hope I'm not interrupting?" he asked, flicking his eyes up to meet hers.

Shannon felt dizzy the second he nodded towards her. The memory of last night shot straight to her core with a blistering heat.

Harry looked back over his shoulder, waving her over. She kept within earshot but stayed a safe distance away, waiting for her racing thoughts to regain an ounce of rationality.

"Good timing, we've just finished. And you are?" Harry puffed out a whirl of smoke and repositioned his cap.

"I'm Jamie McGrath." His sexy smile made her stomach clench. "My dad, George, knows this yard. I'm guessing you must be Harry? It's a pretty nice set up here." Jamie nodded respectfully.

"Thank you, Jamie. I thought you looked familiar. How is George?"

Jamie's chin dipped. "He's got Dementia." His expression tightened.

Harry rubbed his clef chin with a callused thumb. "I see. Does he still know who you are?"

"Yeah, thankfully." Jamie shoved his hands into his pockets and raised his shoulder a little.

A plume of smoke bellowed from Harry's nostrils. "Well, that's a blessing. You call round here anytime, Jamie. My doors always open for you McGrath lads."

In the distance, Shannon noted Niall's approach before Jamie and Harry had the displeasure of his company. He strode towards them with his back poker straight and his floppy hair smacking his forehead with each step. His mouth was crooked like he had the smell of horse shit stuck up his nose.

"Didn't know you were having company today?" He looked Jamie up and down with an inquisitive half-cocked brow.

"This is my son," Harry announced. "Niall, this is Jamie McGrath. He's here to see Shan."

Niall's head popped back, and he made a snarky grunt. "I know who you are, McGrath. So why on earth are you here to see her, she's no jockey. In fact, she's barely a good rider. I doubt she would be worth anything to you."

Typical Niall. Never a nice word to say about anyone, especially, Shannon. She was well used to his verbal diarrhoea and let it wash over her like rain.

"That's enough, Niall," Harry snapped, shunting his shoulder into Niall's stiffened form. "Shan is the best rider in the yard."

Her cheeks stretched to a wide smile. All the riders at Meadow Dawn knew that Niall was too rigid and cranky in the saddle, and until this moment, Harry had never verbally put her above his son.

Niall scowled, widening his stance defensively like he was ready to brawl. "Bullshit, Dad."

Jamie folded his arms across his chest and stepped closer. "I heard she qualified for the Championships. She must be one hell of a rider to get that far." His tone was clipped.

"Sit on the right horse, and it can take you places. She just has to hold on." Niall retorted. If he sliced open his flesh right that second, green venom would ooze from his bitter and twisted veins.

"Will you be competing in the Championships?" Jamie raised his brow, but the look on his face made her think he knew Niall was an asshole.

Harry interrupted, knowing perfectly well that Niall hadn't qualified and never would. "Niall, let's head up to the house and grab lunch. It was great to meet you, Jamie." He nudged his son in the ribs, beckoning him to follow with a curt nod.

Shannon gathered the reins and squeezed her legs, nudging Trixie closer to the fence. She leant forward and threw her leg over the horse's back in a quick dismount. Her hands trembled as she rolled up the stirrups. How could she be so fearless in the saddle of an unpredictable animal, but with Jamie a few feet away, she could barely breath as nerves buzzed around her body like an electric charge.

Last night had taken a turn for the unexpected. She felt like she was back at school again, yearning to fit in with the pretty girls. It had been a hasty decision to join in with their game, and the reality was like a kick in the windpipe. They tagged teamed his dick like pros. Both of the women knew exactly how to get him off – and it didn't take long. It had been obvious by his dark gaze that he loved every damn minute of it.

Once he released, she knew the events would quickly gather momentum, and the fact she was about to explode, meant it was time to bail. Luckily, there had been a taxi waiting outside the hotel so she could scarper home, with her tail between her legs.

Shannon pulled the reins over Trixie's ears and nuzzled her face into the horse's warm cheek bone. She inhaled an uncertain breath and let it puff out slowly as she drew back and began to walk closer to Jamie.

"Hey. So, this is the love of your life then, huh?" His smile reached out and caressed her insides with a wickedness that tingled *everywhere*.

Her gut churned when they finally came face to face – a stride a part. The corners of her mouth pulled wide with a surprised happiness. "Venatrix Meadow Dawn, meet, Jamie."

Jamie's hand floated towards the silky towering beast. His long fingers met the white star between the set of large brown eyes. He gently swirled his nails over the white patch of hair and Trixie's head lowered.

Shannon peered up at him under the peak of her helmet. "You like this guy, Trix?" She purposely spoke to the horse because she was otherwise dumbstruck by his closeness. "She doesn't usually like deep manly voices."

Jamie chuckled. It was a low rumble that vibrated in her belly. "I'm guessing it's not hard to dislike that prick, Niall?" His sultry voice turned stern. "Isn't that right, girl?"

A soft laugh bubbled in her throat. "And he's not even a man. Although, she sure as hell hates him. There's not much to like about that guy." She rolled her eyes and pursed her lips. "Anyway, I'm going to hose her down. You can wait up there." She pointed a shaky finger to the stable block, praying he didn't notice her nerves. "I won't be long."

Even though the sky was a dull grey and a haze of mist clung to the hills, his presence electrified the air and made everything seem vivid and thrilling. His eyes were the colour of syrupy honey, adding warmth like a blanket on a cold winter's night.

"Can I help you?" he asked, moving closer and sliding his fingers through the reins to bring their hands closer together.

Her stomach flipped when she inhaled the leathery smell of his jacket mixed with his signature cedarwood cologne. "Sure," she whispered.

His fingers gripped tighter, and he carefully removed the reins from her gloved hand, escorting the horse away. For a fleeting moment she stood still, rooted to the earth, gawking at the splendid sight of his perfect tight ass in navy blue denim. She stared at both man and beast walking shoulder to shoulder, towards the hose reel. Both powerful creatures possessed the ability to make her heart pound frantically, and her mouth widen from ear to ear.

"I'll hose her legs down if you want to hold her?" He suggested when Shannon finally joined them.

"Okay, but take it slowly. She's a little skittish when the water hits."

His cheek dimpled when a sexy little grin curved his lips when he chuckled. "Is that where you get it from?" A devilish glint in his eyes forced her to look away. "You left without saying goodbye."

She swallowed hard. "Thought I'd leave you to it."

"You were my date, Shannon. Not them."

"And they could give you what every guy wants. The very thing you hoped for before I interrupted."

He shook his head, sporting a lazy smile. "I didn't want that, until you brought up the whole voyeur thing. That was pretty damn hot, by the way, Shannon. Why did you really leave?"

She fiddled with Trixie's mane, dropping her gaze to her dirty boots. "I'm not that experienced. I guess, I just…"

"I didn't expect you to join in, Shannon." He reached out so his fingers lightly brushed her jacket. "And just for the record, I sent them packing after you left. Nothing else happened. I tried to find you, but you'd already left before I got downstairs."

There was something magnetic about this guy. His smile penetrated her core, turning her bones to mush and her blood to dark rivers of desire. With a subtle wink, he twisted the tap and held the hose away as ice cold water spat out.

"I lost the bet." His palms brushed down Trixie's hefty hind quarters, letting her know he was close by. With caution and care he allowed the water to swell over her powerful legs, one by one until all four had been treated.

"You did. Looks like you've done this before?" Her brows knitted together, observing his diligence.

He remained focused on his task. "I've had plenty of experience getting fine mares wet."

"Seriously, Jamie, not everyone knows how to act around a horse."

His eyes danced. "Like I said. I've had experience. Plenty of it." He paused holding the gushing water away from Trixie, letting it flow to the ground. A dangerous silence passed between them, and she sucked in a deep breath to calm her nerves.

"How do you have experience with horses?" she murmured, filling the silence with words rather than heated looks.

"I own a few," he said vaguely. How many is a few, how did she not know this already?

"Really? How many?" she probed

"About that bet, Shan. I owe you. But you owe me too."

"Really?" She hated that he changed the subject, but despite skirting the issue, she couldn't ignore the possibility that he came to her for sex.

"I said one night. You owe me that. I'm here to both deliver and cash in."

He was taunting her, teasing her all over again. Last night was confusing and thrilling, but it ended with a quick shower and a self-release. It wasn't anywhere near the orgasm she had hoped for, and now he was here, making her spine tingle with his suggestions.

"If you weren't holding Trixie, I'd hose you down too. I'd love to see you soaking wet again," he said with a smirk.

"Again?" she whispered, tugging at the safety strap on her helmet, feeling claustrophobic under his assessment.

He just stood there with his eyes narrowed, lit with an inner glow of mischief and lust. "Last night, you were turned on when you watched them blow me. I know you were. I could tell you were getting off on it. That's what sent me over the edge."

She swallowed loudly as if trying to extinguish the flames of heat that sizzled over her skin. The weight of his gaze settled deeply between her thighs. "I need to get Trixie untacked now. Would you like some lunch?" She changed the subject.

"Is there anywhere good to eat around here?" he asked, bolting the stable door behind her after she led Trixie inside.

Heaving off the saddle, she placed it on the half door and peered out at him, drowning in those amber eyes that watched her every move.

"Yeah, I know this great little place, not too far from here. In fact, it's just up those steps." She pointed behind him, towards a set of stone steps that hugged the gable end of the impressive stable block. "That's my place up there, I live in the loft above the stables. I can make you a bacon sandwich, if you like?" she suggested, tugging off her gloves. "Nothing beats a good old bacon butty."

The sexy dent in his cheek appeared when he threaded his fingers through his thick sandy hair. "Have you got smoked bacon and thick white bread?"

"Yes."

The smile that flashed across his face shocked her. He looked amazed, or delighted. "I can't think of a better thing to eat, or a better person to eat with."

Tugging off her helmet, she yanked out the elastic tie from her hair, ruffling it with her fingers while cloaked in the shadows. There was nothing worse than flat hat hair. She had washed it first thing that morning and hoped it wasn't stuck to her head like a shower cap now. As usual, there was probably an ugly red blotch across her forehead where her helmet had constantly pressed. No amount of rubbing would get rid of it. What a sight to behold, she shuddered at her messy appearance before stepping into view.

Trixie lowered her head gently, letting Shannon slide the bridle free and release the bit from her mouth. Drawing the leather straps over her shoulder, she reached up and scratched the beloved horse behind its ear.

"Good girl."

"She's a beauty." Jamie's voice arced through the air.

"I've put everything I have into training her. There's not a day that goes by when we're not together. She's the one that takes up all of my time." Shannon looked back over her shoulder. "The horses are the pets I told you about."

"You still need some relaxation time, Shannon."

Leaning into Trixie's warmth, she whispered, "Wish me luck, girl. I think I'll need it with this guy."

The water trough was full and the bedding had been skipped out before she rode, leaving her a few hours of freedom. Jamie swung the door open and stepped back. It occurred to her that he looked relaxed, his eyes gleamed, and he wore a bright smile.

"I'll carry the saddle, love." He heaved it over his forearm and followed her into the musty tack room that smelled like polished leather and hoof oil. With ease, he deposited the saddle on the rack above the bronze plaque that read, 'VENATRIX'.

"Thanks." She eyed the material that clung to his ass as he stretched.

Swivelling around his gaze scoured the brick walls that were laden with hooks and draped in horse riding equipment. To his left sat a tall steel bucket crammed full of riding crops and schooling whips. Shannon peeled off her gloves and stuffed them in her coat pocket.

He just stood there for a heartbeat in complete silence with his head angled and his palms balled to fists. "I'm hungry as fuck, Shannon." His tone was low and urgent.

"Me too."

"You use this much?" He snatched the new riding whip that Harry bought at the show the day before. It sat away from the used ones that filled the old milk canister like branches. He shifted, sliding his fingers along the length of the unused leather.

Her lashes fluttered rapidly. "It's new," she mumbled, feeling her insides knot as his nostrils flared.

A low growl rumbled in his throat. "I like this one. Let's go upstairs."

Chapter 16

He ducked down ever so slightly, passing under the door frame. There were a good few inches to play with, but it looked low, given the upstairs space was the top of a barn conversion. Jamie wandered into the cosy sitting room that stretched to a galley kitchen with two doors at the far end. It was small enough to resemble a shoe box but perfectly proportioned for one short person. The walls were painted in pale green, with cream kitchen cupboards and a natural wooden counter. Skylights on the sloping ceiling let in the low afternoon sun, lighting the small space with a hazy glow.

As he moved further into the room, the worn floorboards creaked under his weight. An odd warmth heated his entire soul when he was with Shannon, and being in her personal space felt like he'd been given a winning tip at the bookies.

The seating area was crammed, with a dinky pastel green couch and a tan leather stool wedged in the corner. Both faced a flat screen television that hung on a steel arm above a collage of colourful rosettes and golden trophies.

Shannon slid off her padded jacket and hooked it next to the door. She unzipped her tatty black half chaps and tugged off her jodhpur boots, leaving them in a heap under her coat.

Jamie stared quietly, observing her routine and slapdash movements. He studied her untidy tendrils that tumbled over her narrow shoulders and watched as her tongue poked out of her mouth, held in place by her teeth as she concentrated, trying to balance on one leg while she peeled off knee length chequered socks. Her face was make-up free, with jet black lashes framing those stunning blues eyes. Why her eyes had such an effect on him was a mystery, but they did. Every time she looked right at him, it was like she could see straight into his soul. She was an effortless beauty. A little rough around the edges, in scruffy breeches with speckles of wood shavings stuck to her ass and a wrinkled tee. Nonetheless, in his opinion, she was damn near perfect.

With the whip still locked in his fingers, he growled, "Shannon."

Her eyes flicked up, finding his. "Yes?" The subtle swallow in her throat, combined with parted lips was the tell-tale sign that she was nervous.

"I want more than lunch."

With a quick intake of air, she gulped. Jamie stalked closer with his eyes solely focused on the prize. Sensing the heated vibrations pulsing from her inviting body, he pressed his groin into her belly, trapping her against the wall. Shannon was perfectly petite, not tall and lanky like the Dutch girl. He was getting off on the power he welded, soaking up the thrill of the chase, but weirdly, he was equally overcome by the power she exuded over him.

"Did you really invite me in for food, or do you want more?" His voice was gravelly and hoarse, thickened with lust.

"I want more…"

Chapter 17

Jamie's presence was suffocating – in a blood tingling way. Raising to tiptoes, her tongue swept between her lips, and she paused a breath away from his oh-so-sexy face. Then, she tilted her head, giving the perfect angle to suck his lower lip and tug the satiny flesh into her mouth.

"I want more of this..." she rasped as his lip popped back into place.

His sexy groan reverberated through her core like an electric current, kick-starting the most intense sensation of lust she had ever felt. The heavy whisper of his fiery breath ignited thrilling sparks that rocketed down her spine. Slotting the whip under his arm, his fingers threaded her unkempt tousles, and he pushed his mouth onto hers. Their hot lips smashed together, their tongues swirled. His hand locked her head in place, and his entire masculine body imprisoned her against the wall.

Their lips clung together with slow seductive sweeps until he drew back, and the warm sensation turned cool and lonely. She panted softly when a hungry hand roamed her breasts, drifting to the waistband of her tight breeches. His skilful fingers unclasped the top hook and pulled down the zipper.

"Hold this, love." A swirl of thick lust made his eyes almost black as the night. "In your mouth. Open wide." He freed the whip, lifting it to her face.

Her jaw dropped, more out of shock. It was sexy and dirty, way beyond her experiences and everything she wanted him to teach her.

Flipping the thin black whip horizontally, he rested it on her bottom teeth and nudged her jaw shut. Pressing lightly, he pushed it further inside, so it bit into the corners of her mouth with a pleasurable pressure. His gaze lingered on her face, making her chest heave into his.

"Good girl."

With leisurely restraint, Jamie dragged the breeches down to her ankles, bending at the knees until he was crouched. She heard the subtle hitch in his breath.

"I thought my thing was slinky lingerie," he growled. "These are unexpected."

She squeezed her eyes shut and clenched her teeth down hard on the leather, barely peeking through narrowed slits under her lashes. There was a perfectly acceptable excuse on the tip of her tongue, well actually, there was something else on her tongue right that very second, but she mulled softly knowing she couldn't explain.

"Practical panties." He squeezed her buttocks through the thick white cotton. "Soft and baggy, easy access for this…" His nails traced the seam, and her insides quivered. "I like them. They're my new thing, Shannon. You… and these. The perfect fucking combination."

A throaty hum followed searching fingers that brushed over the cotton in a teasing game. "You're even more fuckable with these." On his knees before her, his nose nuzzled the front panel. The elastic smacked against her skin as he pinged it with his long finger. "But they have to come off."

With both hands, he slid the fabric down her freshly shaved thighs. His large palms stroked the insides of her legs, pushing them apart with a quick shunt. She happily obliged, opening as wide as possible with the breeches at her ankles like shackles.

"You liked watching them suck my dick, didn't you?" he growled.

"Uh-huh." She groaned as he found her wet folds and pulled them apart with his devilish fingers. With a long-drawn lick, he ran his tongue over her swollen clitoris.

"You liked it when they licked my balls?" His eyes cut to hers.

She barely nodded, stupefied by the heady sensation of his sinful tongue. He looked so damn sexy, kneeling before her like he was a slave to her pleasure. Their eyes locked, her composure melted between the slats in the oak floor boards.

"Did you want to play too?" he said with a huskiness to his voice.

Sucking in a ragged breath, she expelled it as a hum.

He chuckled low in his chest. "I knew you wanted to take your turn." His tormenting tongue swiped her heat again with a teasing pace.

She whimpered, every nerve ending exploded in a flurry over her skin.

"Did you enjoy watching me come?" he rasped, his breath caressing her swollen, wet flesh.

She swallowed back her lust, wanting to scream at him to fuck her raw and hard. Her fingers reached for his thick hair, threading through the choppy length at the top and she nodded wildly.

"I'm going to watch you explode, just like you watched me." Jamie held her gaze before his mouth returned to her heat and his bristles scratched with a thrilling pleasure. "You like it when I do this?" His tongue dragged upwards, and his eyes glistened wickedly.

Her fingers curled in his hair and a groan slipped from her mouth when she nodded.

"How about when I rub it, Shan?" The pad of his thumb circled.

Her head flew back, spinning giddily, and her teeth almost bit through the whip still clamped between her teeth. Bucking her hips, she began to lose control as he circled the sensitive flesh, then he gently blew a puff of air directly onto her heat.

"Look at me, Shannon."

Latching on to her swollen bundle of nerves, he sucked and flicked his tongue at the same time as two fingers pushed deep inside. A guttural moan echoed in her ears as she became victim to a quick and dirty orgasm.

Jamie rose to a stand, holding her quaking body prisoner, slowly teasing the whip from her jaws. "That was so fucking hot, Shan." He pressed his lips to the tip of her nose, making her drift forward into his chest.

With a low rumble deep in his chest, he laughed. "We're not done yet, love. Turn around and put your hands on the wall. Spread your legs," he ordered.

She quickly toed out of the fabric at her ankles, turned away from him and widened her legs like she was waiting to be searched by the drug squad.

Excitement bubbled through her veins like champagne, the anticipation like a flurry of fizz waiting for the cork to pop. Jamie skimmed the wound leather along her quaking thighs, barely giving her time to recover

"Do you know how much my cock needs you, Shannon?" His voice strained. "My cock wants to fuck you, but I want to play with you first."

She gasped, feeling the narrow rod meet her warm, wet flesh. He skimmed the tip along her folds, back and forth. The foreign object nudged her entrance, then swiftly entered. She inhaled a gust of his woody hot scent. Her jaw went slack, embracing the deep intrusion – a delicious, enticing secret that would stay in her memory for eternity.

He knelt, her peachy ass now at eye level. Opening his mouth, he sucked in fleshy bites of her like he wanted to leave delicate pink bruises. He continued to tease, dipping the whip in and out.

"Turn back around," he barked.

Leaving the whip buried inside her tight walls, he grabbed her hips and spun her around to face him. "Look at me."

Her gaze dropped, locking with his eager wicked eyes. A slow curve of his lips made his alluring dimple join the show just as he extracted the whip from her heat. With a flick of his wrist, he twirled it around, so the leather loop was at her folds. With a light pressure, he tapped her pulsating nub, then gave it a subtle smack that sent volts of ecstasy through her begging body.

She was enthralled by his torture, inspired by his actions and consumed by his sheer presence.

"Lean your back against the wall," he ordered, rising from his knees, peeling off his shirt and unbuttoning his jeans.

She obeyed because right that very moment, caught up in his potent indecent behaviour, there was nothing else in the world that she wanted more. Her legs shook as his hands roamed. His chest was ripped and curved with every pronounced muscle, leading down to a heavenly v shape that pointed straight to his magnificent length. Never had she ever seen a body like his, nor did she ever in her wildest, wettest dreams imagine she would be able to touch a man of this calibre. Just above his naval were a mash of letters and on his right shoulder a detailed tattoo of three wolves sprawled down his bulging bicep.

He was utterly dirty and divine, and Shannon would willingly succumb to whatever titillating acts that he wanted to indulge in. She was captivated by every inch of him.

Dropping to his knees again, Jamie tugged one of her legs upward and rested it on his shoulder. "You smell like sex and leather," he said huskily, grappling with the whip by his knees. "Two of my favourite things."

Gently running the whip from her ankle, up and over her tingling skin, he created a path of desire that lead right to her bare slick folds. She'd held a whip around for countless courses, but never once imagined using one for pleasure.

"Widen your legs further," he ordered.

With light taps, the pressure increased until the rigid leather loop smacked her sensitive nub. Flashes of excitement capitulated through every muscle. Spreading her flesh open with his forefinger and thumb, he tapped, a little harder this time, then again – an erotic excitement pounded in her heart making her light headed. Groans spilled past her lips, her eyes searched for his, only to find his lustful, dark gaze fixated on the task at hand like he was enthralled by the action.

The thin leather handle entered her again, sliding in and out in time with her thrusting hips. She gripped his hair, writhing with the intense feeling that detonated in her core.

"Fuck me, Jamie. Please, fuck me!" she screamed.

His heavenly torment stopped, but he kept the whip inside her and drew back.

"Hold it inside your pretty pussy," he commanded.

Shannon clenched her pelvic floor muscles and sucked in the whip, letting it hang between her legs while Jamie palmed his hard shaft and rolled on a condom.

"You're so sexy. I've never fucked a girl with a whip before. I'm so hard and ready; I might tear you apart."

"I don't care, just fuck me, Jamie," she begged.

The corners of his mouth rose into a seductive, mesmerising smile. He tilted into her trembling pelvis and slowly pulled the whip out of her wet centre. He stood, towering over her, caging her like a savage beast ready to devour his innocent prey. The pad of his thumb brushed her chin, nudging her head upward. His molten gaze drank in every detail of her face, then he shunted his cock forward, pressing it into her stomach.

She wrapped her arms around his neck and let him hoist her up, so her legs wrapped his hips, keeping her back pressed against the wall. Shannon inhaled sharply, wanting and needing him. Jamie pushed in half way, waiting for her to adjust to the width.

"More?" he asked in a low growl.

She nodded, incapable of words. He pushed in hard and fast, impaling her on his rigid length. She was stretched wide, a feeling of completeness and fullness brought her head to his neck, biting his shoulder to stave a scream.

Chapter 18

Jamie was losing his shit – Shannon was a wild ride that was about to make him explode within seconds of thrusting into her tight entrance.

Her insides wrapped his cock like a warm glove, massaging his length with an erotic sensation like none other. Tight muscles squeezed his dick so tightly that he swore she was the best fuck he'd ever had. His heart thundered in his chest as the smell of her skin, laced with arousal, wafted in his nostrils. Her greedy pussy sucked him back in every damn time. She fitted his size to perfection, and the constant biting of his shoulder turned him on even more.

Shannon was close to detonation, he could sense her need build. "Not yet, don't come until I tell you," he snarled, trying his best to keep himself from blowing his load. He'd always had a thing for leather and red lace lingerie, but that fantasy had become predictable. Who would've guessed Jamie McGrath would be turned on by a pair of cotton briefs? Was it the briefs, or the fact that Shannon's pretty ass was inside them?

Her erratic panting became deep and steady when he slowed the pace. The biting sensation of her nails digging into his flesh made his skin tingle. Lifting her head from his neck, she found his mouth and tugged his bottom lip, looking up at him under thick ebony lashes. Her swirling pools of ocean blue begged him to take her to the highest wave and let her fall into the deep. She was calling to his soul, pleading for a release, imploring him to fuck her hard, fast and dirty.

She crushed her cherry red lips to his, violently and

passionately. Barbs of electricity sprinted down his spine.

"Now," he muttered breathlessly.

She let herself soar, shattering the silence with guttural moans. Jamie grunted as he pumped his seed into the unwanted condom, throwing his head back. "Fuck!"

With her legs still wrapped around his hips, Shannon brought her gaze back to his. "Would you like that bacon sandwich now?" Her sexy voice was raspy making her sound well and ridden.

"I'll need extra bacon after that." He squeezed her ass with his large hands.

His lips lingered, uncertain if they should move away altogether. Then he nudged forward and let them rest on her mouth. He let them stay there, savouring her intoxicating taste with a gentleness that was both caring and enigmatic.

One more kiss.

A mind-blowing kiss.

A game-changing kiss.

Chapter 19

The sex was unbelievable, and the hot sensuous kiss after was filled with alternatives.

The kiss was incredible.

The sex was incredible.

Jamie was incredible.

Shannon had stumbled upon something her soul wanted to keep – but it wasn't possible to hold onto a man like Jamie. Her life didn't have any room for options, and he would drift on to the next wanton female by tomorrow.

He broke their confusing kiss, hesitating at her mouth with a ghost of a smirk on his wet lips. "I don't need to ask if you enjoyed that," he announced with amusement in his tone.

The removal of his lips and the loss of his fullness left her feeling lost and empty. How could this guy breath so much exhilaration into her lungs with such an intensity, leaving her craving more? He wasn't boyfriend material, and she had her sights set on a career, with zero room for distractions.

"Don't get all cocky, Jamie. Next you'll be asking if it was the best sex of my life."

She eyed his retreat. Watching as he pulled up a pair of bright red boxer briefs that hugged and moulded the curve of his ass and the bulge of his manhood. The fabric wrapped his muscular thighs, rising mid-way to his hip bones with a thick waistband. His jeans were the next item to cover up his perfect physique, and she found herself wishing he would stay undressed, just so she could fully enjoy the sight of a real man before he walked away for good.

Leaving his shirt open, he strolled to the kitchen to dispose of the condom with a confident masculine gait, that had her secretly swooning.

"I think we both know it was the best sex of your life, love."

She grabbed her strewn clothes and scuttled past him towards her bedroom door. "I'll be out in a sec," she muttered, closing the door behind her and putting much needed space between them.

Of course it was the best damn sex she'd ever had. How could she even compare Niall to a man like Jamie. But he didn't need to know that, it was irrelevant in the grand scheme of casual no strings sex.

Rummaging through her drawers, she selected a pair of running shorts and quickly slipped them on without her big old cotton knickers. The idea of him rushing out the door while she was getting changed pinched her heart. She tried to pretend it wouldn't matter if he was gone by the time she went back into the kitchen, but a flare of hope was begging him to still be there. Why did she care? The odd yearning gave her cause for concern. She was getting into unfamiliar foolish territory because she'd already told herself that it was just sex. So why did she want his company too?

Changing into a clean white tank top, she trailed a brush through her hair and held a deep breath, then slowly opened the door with a sudden bashfulness. There he was, leaning against the counter with his muscle toned chest on show, mussed up hair and a glint in his eyes.

"For a moment there, I thought you wanted me to find you on the bed wearing nothing but high heels," he said.

She took a steadying breath.

He stayed. He actually stayed.

The tanned fantasy, loitering in her kitchen was filling her with a powerful lust. The urge to lick the dimple right off his striking face was hard to ignore. "I never renege on an offer of lunch," she said with a shy smile, feeling his gaze settle on her tight tank top, assessing her bra-less situation.

"I'm looking forward to food," he said casually, taking a sip of water from a coffee mug. "I haven't had a proper bacon sandwich since I was a kid. I hope it's worth it."

"Believe me, it will blow your mind." Her fingers crossed behind her back. "I might not be able to cook up a five course meal, but I sure as hell can make a killer bacon sandwich."

"You've already blown my mind, Shan. The bar has been set pretty high." He set the mug on the counter and sauntered towards her, the light dancing in his roguish eyes. "I like the shorts." His eyebrows rose, brushing long fingers across her thighs. Shannon twitched under his electrifying touch, loving how he gently pressed into her flesh.

She was melting all over again, but her mind was trying to run away from the hold he was silently wrapping around her body.

"We'll never eat at this rate." Holding her palms to his chest, she put a little distance between them, even though she desperately wanted him again.

He exhaled silently, teasing her cheek with his breath. "You shouldn't wear shorts like that when you're in the kitchen." Suddenly, he nipped her ear lobe between his teeth and tugged gently. "What can I do to help?" he murmured, giving her a swift slap on the ass.

Her head shook, declining the offer. "I've got it covered."

While the smoky bacon sizzled under the grill, Shannon buttered a few slices of crusty bread having just cut her way through a large loaf.

After her jaunt around the cross-country course the day before, she had to wait for the final times to determine the winner. While Harry talked business, Shannon scooted around the market stalls in the large marquees. With only a ten pound note stuffed into her breeches, she spent the last of her weekly food budget, and now she was happily sharing her rations with Jamie.

"Are you a brown sauce or red sauce kinda guy?" she

asked, looking over her shoulder.

"Red."

"Lucky, because that's all I have." She whipped her eyes away before she liquefied internally.

"My dad used to make these for my brother and I. I'd forgot how good they smell." His chest rose as his lungs sucked in a deep breath.

"They're my all-time faves." She threw him a sweet smile over her shoulder. In reality it was a low cost meal that didn't require too much prep or time. Well, it was either that or a bag of salty potato chips washed down with a slug of green tea.

"Mine too, reminds me of happier times."

"Oh yeah?"

"Yeah, my dad used to cook breakfast when my mum worked the late shift at the bar... and then when she was killed, Marcus made them for me. Every Sunday." His chirpy tone took a dip.

Shannon stopped turning a slice of half cooked bacon and faced him. "Your mum was killed?"

His chin dipped. "Drunk driver. I was just a kid. My big brother, the guy you met at the party, pretty much raised me."

"I'm sorry to hear about your mum, Jamie. It must've been tough being raised by your brother."

"Marcus isn't that bad." He chuckled. "I know he's a cocky shite at times, but he's got a kind heart."

"I'm sure you were a handful." She giggled softly, turning back to focus on the bacon. "How is your dad?"

"He's with Rebecca. She's been warned to keep him close, so he doesn't wander off again."

A strange and powerful connection was pulling them together. He was opening up about his life, talking freely about his family and involving her in the matters of his mind.

Usually, in this type of scenario, guys like him would have made an excuse to leave after already tasting the goods, but Jamie was still there, sitting in her kitchen, talking about his past.

The heat from the grill radiated through the small kitchen. He whistled loudly when the hem of her jersey shorts hitched up her ass cheeks as she bent down to get the sauce from the refrigerator. Each natural and innocent movement seemed to stir a reaction.

"What's your set up, Shannon? How did you arrive at Meadow Dawn?"

Tossing the tongs on the counter, she said, "When I was sixteen, I begged my parents to buy me a horse. They contacted Harry and arranged for me to work here instead. I think it was supposed to be some sort of life lesson. You can show a girl hard work, and she'll run away screaming. That kind of thing." Her eyes rolled ever so slightly. "Harry agreed to let me work for the summer, mostly skipping dung out of the stables and grooming. When the summer was over, he said I was more dedicated than any of his other stable hands, so he kept me on and taught me how to ride in his spare time. Eight years later and I'm competing on one of his top horses."

Folding his arms across his chest, he nodded. "Impressive. So why do you work at Coffee Kicks, if Harry pays you?"

"I'm saving to buy Trixie. She's technically Harry's horse, even though he lets me train her. One day I'll own her. Sooner rather than later, I hope."

"I'll lend you the cash, then you can buy her tomorrow." He shrugged like it was nothing to hand a stranger a wad of cash. And they were right back at the beginning.

"No!" she snapped. "I'll never take your cash - or anyone else's. I'll earn the money myself and pay for her myself." The words spilled out in a fluster.

His eyebrows shot up. "Understood. I'm sorry. It would be a loan, that's all."

"No thanks. Like I said, I'm saving."

"Your pretty fucking hot when your devoted to your cause." He grinned, making light of her sudden hot headed outburst.

Fiddling with the metal tongs hooked on her thumb and forefinger, she turned away. "I don't know you, Jamie. Anyway, I'd prefer to take care of it myself."

"I get it, love. I respect the hard work. I've been without money, so I know what it's like. I haven't always been the good-looking rich guy before you." The bar stool creaked as he shifted his weight.

She scooped up the sauce bottle and napkins, setting them before him on the breakfast bar. Slice by slice, she built the perfect bacon sandwich, making sure she gave him four bits of bacon, leaving herself only two.

"Tuck in." She fluttered her eyelashes.

"Thanks, love." He winked, grabbing the chunky cut bread in his long fingers and sinking his sparkly white teeth straight in. He hummed in his throat while he chewed.

Jamie was a sight to behold, perched on a wooden bar stool, half dressed, his shirt skimming his smooth pectorals. The muscles in his jaw worked hard while he chewed the bread.

"It must be frustrating – not owning her?" he asked, before taking another bite.

"Kind of, but then that's what us poor people have to do when we want something. We work hard for it." She giggled, throwing a scrunched-up napkin at him.

Jamie dodged the tissue, pretending it was a missile. "Watch it, love, or I'll have to throw you over my knee." His eyes flashed.

Shannon bit into her sandwich, grunting with appreciation. His eyes flicked up to her face. Wiping the corners of his mouth with her used napkin, he paused. "That sound drives me fucking crazy. We need to have more meals together. Next time I'm gonna record those sweet sexy sounds so I can play it back when you're not around." He smirked. "Like audio porn."

The slight slip of her tongue meeting a smudge of sauce at the corner of her lips made his chest visibly rise.

"I'm just enjoying my lunch."

"There's something else you can enjoy when you've finished." His suggestive gaze lingered on her mouth.

"Oh yeah? You got something else to add to the menu?" Her mouth crept up at the corner, and she took another big bite.

"I've got something else you can put in that pretty little mouth."

Her insides lurched. Her heart bounced like a lucky leprechaun who just found gold at the bottom of the rainbow. Jamie McGrath wanted her again. He wasn't bolting out the door like a man slut on a mission to forget.

"I'll have to see if I have room after this," she teased, sucking sauce off her finger with a pop.

"Finish your lunch." His tone held a rasp of sexual eagerness. The last bite of his sandwich was devoured, he stood and sauntered towards the couch.

As he sank down, his head drop backwards, and his hands rested on his sinewy thighs. She noted the quick rise and fall of his broad chest making her insides quiver. The thought of taking him in her mouth outweighed the need to eat and overruled the need to finish her food. With only a few bites left, she padded across the room, standing before him with the remaining sandwich in her hand.

Rooting herself between the television and the couch, she continued to chew. Her tongue traced the edge of the bread, while she dished out her best come-hither look. The quick lick of gloopy red sauce from the edge of the bread evoked a low rumble from deep inside his chest.

"What are you doing to me, Shannon?" he growled, pushing himself forward.

"Ah, ah, mister, I have to finish my lunch before I get dessert." She waved a teasing finger back and forth like the devil in disguise. She was loving the game and trying her best to be like the women who pleased him.

Nibbling a little more of the bread, she dragged out her seduction with a wicked grin on her flushed face. She inhaled in a sharp gust when he lunged from the couch and grabbed her biceps in a firm grip.

"These lips need to be on my dick, now," he ordered dragging the tip of his tongue along the seam of her mouth.

The guy was actually turned on by her little display. The flutter in her belly made her continue, just to see how far she could push him. Gazing into his golden eyes, she shoved the last bite of bread into her mouth, so her left cheek bulged.

A slow rise of his lips dimpled his cheek as she taunted him with a smirk. "I should take you over my knee and use that whip properly."

Keeping her gaze focused solely on his sexy face, she lowered to her knees and located his zipper. Featherlight fingertips walked the happy trail that lead to the waistband of his boxer briefs, tugging them down at the same time as his jeans. The tight grip fisting her hair locked her head in place. She couldn't lift her chin to see the look on his handsome face.

Flicking her tongue, she teased the tiny slit at the crown of his cock. He suddenly yanked her head back so that her throat was vulnerable. His fingers tightened with a silent bid for her to sink his length deep in her throat. Coaxed on by his enjoyment, Shannon pulled against his hold, tracing a wet trail down his shaft. Taking his magnificent manhood in her hands, she engulfed most of his length, dragging her lips up and down in long sweeping pulls.

Devouring him was like the best meal she'd ever had. The salty release of pre-cum was exquisite, and she wondered why it had never been this exhilarating in the past.

"I'm gonna blow," he snarled, jerking back her ponytail with one hand so her wet lips slid off the tip. His other hand took over, sliding up and down his shaft readying a release.

"Did you want me to join in with those other girls last night?" She remembered the look in his eyes when he released and wondered what he was actually thinking about when he exploded.

His breathing hitched, and his hand strokes quickened.

"I wanted your mouth on my dick. I just wanted you, Shannon."

Chapter 20

The captivating pull of her blue eyes held him in a steamy daze. Shannon was a sexy little siren who made him think of multiple ways to get inside her, with just one flash of her sultry smile. His release was coming but not before he found his way back into her tight walls. Rising to the darkness in his soul, Jamie pounced on her with the same hungry need that she returned.

Together they tore off each other's remaining garments in a frenzied blur. His fingers dug into her thighs, dragging over the curve of her ass as she tore the tank top up and over her head. Burying his face in the hollow of her neck, he inhaled the sexy scent of her hair and threaded his fingers through the black waves.

Inviting moans electrified the hairs on his scalp, bringing him closer to the end goal. He plunged into his jeans pocket, discarded on the floor and collected a golden foil packet. Hurriedly sheathing his new hardness, he willed himself to hold on. Cupping her fleshy buttocks, Jamie hoisted her into the air and swung around. They crashed onto the couch, her back slamming against upholstery. Securing her body beneath him, he noted the wildness in her eyes and let his mouth cover hers with a deep passionate kiss, fuelled by hunger. With clashing teeth and roaming hands, Jamie impaled her, pushing deep inside. He clawed at her silky flesh, biting her plump lips and savouring her erotic whimpers.

Her climax came quickly after, both of them lost in each other's taste and overwhelming arousal.

"Holy fuck, love, you'll be the death of me." He held her small frame in his powerful arms, holding her close to his rapidly beating heart.

His father had a medical appointment that afternoon, which meant he had to leave in the next few minutes. The sex had been good...actually it had been a complete mind fuck. He couldn't describe the emotions that were knocking on his brain with question marks. The smell of her hair, the dip of her back, the sensation of her soft shallow puffs on his skin – they all joined forces, into one big motherfucker of lust. He was in lust with Shannon Colter, and he wanted to repeat the whole lunch time session all over again. She had surpassed his expectations and surrendered herself to him.

It wouldn't be hard to charm her into submission again. There was no doubt she'd want to have dinner with him at the end of the week. No fucking doubt in the world.

Chapter 21

Filling her lungs deeply, Shannon accepted Jamie as the best thing ever.

The best of the best.

An A plus in all things hot and filthy and satisfying. Not only did he inhale her like she was his only source of life, but he gave her a taste of what life would be like with him, and it scared the living daylights out of her. The warmth of his chest felt like home, and the gentle strokes along the curve of her back were heavenly.

The only sound was the rapid beating of her heart and the chatter of crows gathering on the roof. Then a lorry engine rumbled, followed by dancing hooves in the cobbled yard. It was a sign. A reminder of her life outside of this random sex session. Jamie was here to get what he was owed from last night, and now she'd paid her debt. Stables needed skipped out, horses needed exercised – her life would carry on without him.

An invisible line was etched. Whatever *this* was, would never happen again. She had plenty of time for a relationship with men in the future, when she owned a yard of her own.

Jamie would be long gone by then, more to the point, Jamie would be charming his next victim the minute his sexy ass walked out the door. With a soft sigh, she sat upright, accepting the casual encounter for what it was.

With her leg pressed against his, she was reluctant to break the close contact. "I've got stuff to do now." Her silly heart pinched at the surrender of their intimacy when she stood. "You'll have to leave now."

"Yeah, I've got to go anyway." His voice was distant.

There's a difference between lust and love. Lust is an aphrodisiac that sucks you under a temporary infatuated haze. This is where Shannon sat, on the fence of lust. Nowhere near the path of love. That meant walking away from him would be easy.

Peeking from the corner of her eye, she watched him peel off the used condom. His expression was soft, his hair tousled and his lips all pouty and sexy with a deep red 'just been kissed' shade. The battle between her foolish heart and stubborn mind began, with revolvers at the ready.

Jamie hauled himself off the couch, all naked, sexy and buff. Had he caught her gaze, he would've seen the ruthless conflict unfolding behind her eyes.

"I'm going away on business for a few days. Maybe we could go out for dinner on Friday night, when I get back?" he announced suddenly.

"Like a date?" Her heart bucked wildly.

His brow creased. "Uh, yeah. Like a date," he said slowly, obviously thinking about the correct terminology to use for a repeat sex invitation. "We can get to know each other a bit more. Eat more food." He scooped up her shorts and tank top and held them towards her.

A light puff of air burst from her mouth. "Do you remember what I said when we first met? I don't have time for anything right now, especially dinner dates."

His eyes narrowed as she snatched the garments out of his hand. "Then it's not a date. Just two people eating food and talking shit," he persisted. "We can talk shit together, right?".

Shaking her head, Shannon kept her gaze low, knowing in her heart that if she looked him right in the eye, she'd do anything he asked. "Best not. I'm really busy. Working here and at Coffee Kicks takes up all of my time."

Her mind loaded the gun and took aim at her pounding heart, ready to pull the trigger.

Jamie sauntered towards her with a confident grin pulling at his lips. Those damn amazing lips that had magical powers, especially when they touched her skin.

"Shan, it's only food."

The sensible bullet shot straight through her foolish heart, sparking a glut of disappointment in every cell of her being. She wanted to say yes, but her head said no. If she continued to see him, then all her plans would be pushed aside, and her focus compromised. Jamie was a distraction that she couldn't afford to indulge in. Her rules were in place for a purpose. Hard work and dedication would pay off in the end, earning her enough cash to pay the bills and buy Trixie outright. Nothing else was permitted in between.

"Like I said…"

"You need to eat, don't you?" he interrupted. "Or do you live off fresh air and horse hair?" His eyebrows rose, and a hint of amusement flashed over his handsome face.

She clucked her tongue and smirked. "Don't be an asshole."

"Would you have dinner with me if I wasn't an asshole?" He stepped into his boxer briefs. A glimmer of disappointment made her sigh lightly. His magnificent manhood was covered away, and she would never see it again.

"Jamie." Her hands moved to her hips.

"I'll pick you up at 7:30 p.m." He took a step closer and tipped her chin upwards with two fingers, locking his dark suggestive stare with hers.

She put her palms to his bare chest, drawn to his heat yet giving her an inch of space to think. Tilting her head back, she nudged out of his hold. How could she resist him? He was absolutely gorgeous. She nibbled her lower lip as her bleeding heart stuttered, rose from the ashes and took aim at her cautious mind. It will all end in tears – her tears.

"Let's see how I get on."

"So that's a yes?"

"It's a maybe."

He chuckled. "It's a fucking yes, Shannon." Angling his head, he pressed his lips to her temple.

This time her heart squeezed the trigger, blowing her

sensible mind to smithereens. What she needed right now, was to walk the hell away from him, but his lopsided smile was tugging at her heart strings and stirring a mounting pressure between her thighs, all over again.

"I need to get dressed now." She shunted past him, toed into her shorts and pulled them over her shaky knees. "How about you text me on Friday to confirm. I'll let you know if I can make it at that point."

"Uh-huh." Jamie grabbed his shirt from the floor and covered his chest. "I'll be in touch. But, not to confirm. The date is going ahead as planned."

The tingles on her skin were a pleasurable reminder of his touch that still burned with satisfaction. She smiled inwardly, secretly enjoying the warmth left from his rampant thrusts as she swiped his jeans and tossed them his way. "I like those boxer briefs," she said eyeing the strained bold fabric.

"You wanna wear them today?" He smirked. "They'd be a good fit to ride in."

Her skin flushed to a deep crimson. "No."

"Go on, Shan. Wear them today," he cajoled.

"No way, Jamie." There was something hot and sexy about the idea of having his boxer briefs close to her private parts, and the idea was making her squirm.

Dragging them down his thighs, he stepped out of the designer briefs and held them out. "Wear them," he ordered. "I want to know you're riding in my boxers."

"You're a kinky fucker, aren't you?" This was not how she planned her escape from Jamie McGrath. He was supposed to leave. To saunter away with confident swagger and on to the next female, but now he was watching her kick off her shorts and slide on his underwear. He was standing in front of her with his legs wide, his splendid cock on show and a filthy look in his eyes.

"Fuck!" he sighed, crossing his arms over his chest and nodding. "Now that's hot."

"It's time for you to leave, Jamie." A smile tugged her lips. "I'm going to grab my breeches from the bedroom.

You know where the door is."

"I'll be here at 7:30 p.m. on the dot, Shannon. If you don't want to go out, then I'll bring take out. Either way, we will be having dinner together."

Stepping into his jeans, sans boxers, he covered up. She shook her head lightly, acknowledging her stupid infatuation. He slipped on his boots and ran his fingers through his hair, fixing the agitated strands back into place.

Only seconds ago he was dishevelled, naked and banging into her like a wild animal. It was a distant dream that could be questioned of its integrity had he not been standing in front of her like a kissable fantasy, in the flesh. Placing his palms on her cheeks, he tipped closer and kissed her lips with a leisurely tenderness.

The silly crush had escalated, she was besotted. The cocky asshole had won. Pulling away from her lips, she took a second before opening her eyes, catching her breathe.

"Gotta go. I need to take my dad to a check-up at the hospital." His voice was almost strained, and he scratched his head. It was like he was struggling to gather his own thoughts.

Chapter 22

Jamie had left the loft hours ago, yet Shannon was still floating on the apex of satisfaction. Her heightened senses were all consumed with the lingering aroma of his woodsy scent. The loss of his clawing fingers on her skin made her heart pause, and the memory of his taunting sexy dimple made her thighs clench.

This was not the damn plan. Everything had turned into a complicated mess.

Jamie was under her skin, in her mind, in her body and now his name was on her phone as it lit up on her bedside table.

Jamie:

That was the best bacon sandwich ever.

A rising flush warmed her neck all the way up to her scalp, making her toes curl. She recalled the temptress who took over her body and teased Jamie into oblivion with the remnants of her lunch. He had a way of luring out the sordid sexual side of her, that both shocked and elated her beyond recognition. Maybe he was a good thing, a guy to push her past the dull boundaries and take her life to another level. Perhaps she could channel this new-found energy into her riding and still see him when it suited.

Shannon:

That was the best dessert ever.

Jamie:

Send me a dirty pic, cherry lips.

She giggled to herself, feeling a slow heat creep between her legs. There was no way she was going to send him a filthy picture of herself. It could serve as leverage for bribery if they ever broke up. Wait, they weren't even in a relationship, and her mind was running away with silly ideas of commitment – because that's never going to happen. Needless to say, she didn't want to spoil the moment, so she padded out of the bedroom and found the whip propped up under the coats by the front door. She quickly snapped a picture.

Shannon:

This is dirty. Shall I clean it...or would you like to keep it.

He instantly replied.

Jamie:

I'm hard again.

Shannon:

I would help you out, but I'm too far away.

Her phone buzzed, only this time Jamie was calling her.

"Hey," she answered immediately.

"Are you still wearing my boxers?" His voice was low and husky.

Running her fingers beneath the elastic covering her hips bones, she grinned. "Maybe…"

"Hmm. I can come over, if you promise to misbehave?"

"As good as that sounds, I have a 5 a.m. start tomorrow. Not this time, Jamie."

"But you'd be happy for me to come over another time?" His voice was husky with a sexy rasp.

"We agreed on Friday, when you get back from your business trip."

"So, it's definite then? I'll have my phone set up to Dictaphone so I can record your sexy groans as you eat."

"I like pizza, by the way." She didn't want him to hang up. Shannon was being sucked into his tornado like Toto, into a new world where happiness included a man. Unfortunately, she knew only too well that her reality would be to wake up in a different world, one filled with heartbreak and no Jamie.

"I like your pussy, by the way."

"Jeez, Jamie, say it out loud why don't you." She slapped her hand over her eyes feeling the rush of blood to her cheeks. "Such a romantic."

"Is that what you like – all the romance. Flowers and shit like that?"

She swallowed hard. "Nah, romance is over rated."

"I agree. What's the point in all that mushy stuff when the end goal is sex?"

"Yeah, I guess the sex was good." She sucked in her lips staving a grin.

A low chuckle rumbled down the line. "I'd say the sex was fucking awesome, Shannon. That's why you like me, isn't it? Admit it."

"I haven't decided if I like you yet."

"Sure you do, love. I can feel it." Her heart lurched. "Good night, Shannon."

"Good night, Jamie," she whispered.

***

A strong wind battered the hay barn, making it creak like it was about to fall down. Every night she checked on Trixie, even though Bucky was responsible for ensuring all the horses were safe and sound. She liked to do it herself, for peace of mind.

Trixie was safe and sound, standing in a sleepy daze with her long neck lowered. "Hey, girl."

She hitched the stable door open, clanking the stiff metal bolt loudly. Trixie's triangle ears shot back.

"It's okay, girl. Only me," she whispered in a soft calm tone. She moved further into the stable with slow steps. Reaching her favourite horse, she nuzzled her face into its warm neck. "I love you, girl. Have you got enough water?"

A loud bang startled them both and Trixie scooted to the side. The noise was quickly followed by hushed voices. It sounded like there were people a few stables down. Shannon peered into the water trough and noted it was full. Patting Trixie with her palm, she kissed her soft muzzle before leaving. "See you tomorrow."

A lull of music filtered through the strong wind,

dancing with the notes and blending them with nature. Shannon pottered down the yard, peering in each stable to check on the other horses. Nearing the feed room, she held back in the shadows. The door was ajar and dark silhouettes moved like ghosts in the dim light projected from the energy saving light bulb overhead. Giggles were followed by groans.

Edging closer, she glanced through the slit to find one of the female stable hands flat on her back. Not only was she naked with her legs wide open, but she had a long trail of white powder from her navel to her black curls.

"Don't fucking move, Gracie, or my coke will go everywhere," the male with his back to the door growled.

She recognised the voice instantly. It was Niall. His shoulders dipped, and the sound of air being sucked through a small tube was followed by an almighty sniff. Turning to the side, Shannon watched in shock as he covered each nostril in turn and snorted up lingering powder.

"Your turn, Gracie. Then it's shots."

Gracie sat up and hummed low in her throat as he smashed his lips to hers. Chocolate curls tumbled down her bare back, and she wrapped her thighs around his hips. Shannon held her breath. Niall's taking drugs. Gracie too. No wonder he's turned into a self-absorbed prick. Inching away, hidden by the night, she bumped into a rock hard figure.

Spinning round she gazed up at the shadowy figure. "Bucky, you scared the shit out of me," she half laughed palming her breast bone.

"So, you've seen the party?" His eyes glowed in the moonlight.

"Yeah. Guess it explains a lot."

"The guy is an asshole, with or without cocaine," Bucky snapped gruffly. "You'd best head inside before he sees you."

Shannon agreed and patted Bucky on the arm. "Good night."

She hastily jogged to the stone steps that took her back to the loft, locking the door behind her. Thankfully, Niall was oblivious, with no idea that she was privy to his little late night party with one of the young stable hand girls

Chapter 23

After his father's appointment in the city, Jamie returned to his apartment with an antsy tightness knitting his ribs together. He wanted something to do - someone to do.

Grabbing the whiskey from the shelf, his fingers drummed the tall bottle. A certain female had his dick growling – Shannon Colter. Her fuckable lips and dazzling blue eyes were blazoned into his mind, manifesting a deep sensation that snarled in his gut like a hungry animal. There were plenty of candidates, all ready and willing for a good time, but he wasn't interested in any of them now.

He poured a dram of whiskey and sat back in the recliner, flicking the TV channels on the flat screen. Scanning the listings, he hoped to stumble across a new series on Netflix, something to stop him from obsessing over the black haired vixen.

How could she fuck his brains out and make him feel a sense of belonging all at the same time? What part of 'just one night', turned into wanting 'just another night'? There was no harm in going back for seconds. Neither had time for a relationship, so maybe they could consider a new arrangement. One where he fucked her, and she fucked him. When it suited, of course. It wouldn't be a relationship, more of an understanding. That way, when temptation creeps in, which it always did, he wouldn't feel bad when he moved on.

Grabbing his mobile phone, he sent a quick message to thank her for lunch… and the hot sex session. The frustrating thing was, his text message was just an excuse to reach out to her again.

As soon as her reply lit up the screen, his pulse had

raced like a high-speed train teetering close to the edge of the tracks. A wide grin stretched across his peppered jaw. After a few sex texts, he resorted to a phone call, craving to hear her damn voice. Now he wasn't just turned on, he was bordering on crazy. In fact, he had bought himself a condo in crazy town, right on the corner of crazy street with a perfect view of crazy city.

The infatuation wasn't normal.

Rolling his head back, he cursed his loss of levelheadedness and internally advised himself to get a goddamn grip.

Spending time in Las Vegas with Marcus over the next few days would help add perspective to his absurd runaway emotions. Business was the priority, and the little dick cherry could take a back seat until he returned. He wouldn't tolerate a mediocre approach from anyone, least alone himself. It was essential that he snapped out of his weird funk and rectified his distorted focus.

Shannon was like an atomic bomb, annihilating every other woman in her wake. This girl felt like the real deal, and the realisation of her sudden importance in his life scared the crap out of him. A few nights away from Northern Ireland would clear his mind.

***

The following morning, Jamie rolled out of bed with a dull ache of dehydration pulsating in his skull. He'd taken to his bedroom with a half bottle of whiskey and an iPad, browsing the X-rated videos. It was a waste of time, the filthy clips failed epically. Shannon was still there, on the tip of his dick, pinned to his memory like a postcard from heaven.

There was unfinished business between them. A situation that needed taken care of before he could fly thousands of miles away. The flight from Dublin was in the late afternoon which left him time to run a few errands.

The wooden sign for Meadow Dawn swung in the blustery wind and droplets of rain splattered the windscreen as Jamie sped towards the stable block. An electric buzz powered through his muscles when he thought about seeing Shannon again.

Exiting the car brought a gust of ice-cold wind that tried to cut him in two, but the throbbing between his legs spurred him on. Finding the paddock empty, he jogged to Trixie's stable in the hope of finding Shannon. Her husky voice sang in a low murmur, her words left unanswered. Looking inside the dark stall, a wide grin spread across his face when he caught sight of her glossy hair pulled back in a shaggy ponytail, relaxed in her surroundings.

"That's all your hooves picked out, Trix. You're such a good girl, aren't you?"

"One day she'll answer you back." He chuckled, resting an arm over the stable door.

Her head flicked up to the sound of his voice, her mouth forming an o shape. "Jamie, I thought you were away on business."

The veins in his dick pumped at the curve of her mouth. She was pleased to see him. This was going to be epic.

"I leave this afternoon. I'm only here to give you these." He raised a white carrier bag and waggled it over the door.

"You bought me something?" Her brow scrunched, and she stepped closer. "We said one night. I hope you're not getting all romantic and mushy?" She smiled shyly.

Jamie shrugged, hiding the fact he was secretly pleased with his intentional purchases. "Neither of us are into all that romance shit. And just one night can be just a bit more sex, right?"

"You're here for more?"

"Look, we're adults. We can have a little fun between the sheets. No commitment. You've got your life, and I've got mine."

An odd look flashed behind her eyes, and her palm slid to her belly. "Sounds fair."

"Great!" Fucking awesome. "Here…" He hung the bag in the air.

Shannon accepted the offering and peeked inside. "A lead rope? Knee length socks? What's in the other bag?" She nodded at the brown paper package snuggled in the soft leather of his biker jacket.

"The lead rope is for your horse and the socks are for you," he lied. "This stuff..." He patted the crumpled bag. "I'll let you see later."

Her fingers choked the plastic like she was holding a bag of stolen money. "You didn't need to buy me anything."

"I know."

"Or bribe me to have sex with you."

"We both know I don't need to bribe you."

Shannon folded her arms and dipped her hip. "You think I'm easy, Jamie, don't you? Like I'll do whatever you want, whenever you want? Do you think you can show up here with an offer of just sex, no strings, and that I'll happily fall at your feet?"

His eyes loitered on her sensual lips. "You won't fall at my feet, love. You'll sit at them. Now, can we go up to the loft?"

He loved how her eyes flared when she was angry and how her gaze fell to the floor like she couldn't look at him without coming in his briefs.

"Like right now?" Her hands drifted to her hips.

"Right. Now."

Jamie slid the bolt free and held a clear exit for Shannon to amble out. With her thumbs in the belt loops at either side of her hips, she put on her best casual strut. Each swagger was teamed with a teasing backward glance. He purposely lagged behind, letting her climb the steps before him so he could watch her wiggle in tight breeches.

The loft was snug and warm with the familiar smell of Shannon. She tugged off her boots and slipped off her coat, setting the plastic bag on the ground.

"Do you want a cup of tea?" She padded to the kitchen and grabbed the kettle. "That's weird," she said. "The water is already boiled? I've been out since 5 a.m."

Jamie kicked off his shoes and lifted the white bag. "It must be faulty." He couldn't care less if the water was warm, and he certainly didn't want a cup of fucking tea.

"Hmmm," she hummed before turning around to meet his body.

The black circles in her eyes widened, almost sucking up the piercing blue. He set the bag on the counter and folded his arms across his chest. "I may have told you a tiny white lie."

Shannon's sweet smile dropped, and a crease on her forehead deepened. "Oh?"

This was going to be fucking amazing and his cock knew it. "Yeah, the lead rope. It's not for Trixie. It's for you."

"Well, I kinda knew that. I'm the one who'll use it to lead her to the stable." A puff of 'is that all' air blew past her lips.

"It's not for the horse, Shannon." His voice was low and raspy. "Do you trust me?"

That delectable wet tongue he dreamed about darted from her mouth and swept over her pretty lips sending him into the realms of darkness.

"I… think so."

"I'm not going to hurt you." He placed a light kiss to her temple. "You tell me to stop, and I'll stop. Okay?"

"Okay."

"Do you trust me?"

"Yes."

That magical three letter word. So small yet so powerful. It gave him the green light to rip her clothes off. It let him know she wanted him as much as he wanted her. It indicated her trust, in him. Lunging forward he grabbed her jumper at the hem and roughly heaved it over her head, ensuring both of her arms were freed. Underneath, a lavender camisole was in his way, so he tore it from her chest, ripping the stitching apart at the seams with both hands.

Her gasps only fed his desire and fuelled his hunger.

Dropping his head down, their lips mashed in a furious kiss. He tasted every inch of her mouth like it was the only remedy to his new obsession. Sliding his hands to her breeches, he flicked the button free and let down the zip. Her hips jutted forward, and he stepped back. Jamie had played out a scenario in his head before he had fallen asleep, and he knew exactly how he wanted it to go down.

"Strip," he ordered with a husky growl.

Each quick breath made her chest rise and fall as her fingers fumbled and tugged. The breeches came down, along with her dusky pink cotton briefs that had replaced his. Peering up at him under her thick ebony lashes, she toed out of the fabric at her feet. Shannon quivered, standing before him with an uncertain look in her wide eyes.

Selecting the navy long socks, he yanked off the plastic tag and held them out. "Put them on, right up to your knees, Shannon."

"You have a sock fetish?" She giggled nervously.

"No, I have a Shannon fetish. Now do as you're told," he growled feeling an unbearable arousal charge through him.

Hunching over, Shannon rolled a sock up to her left knee and then repeated her slow torture on the right leg. A mass of inky black hair tumbled over her slender shoulders. It was messy and ruffled from the wind outside, with an 'I want to get fucked look'. Standing tall, her mouth rose with an impish grin hitched up at the corner like she knew he was getting off on the show.

"Like what you see, Jamie?" Her voice was low and sultry.

"Yes, Shannon. I like what I see."

Without taking his eyes off her, he reached for the rope. It felt warm and inviting in his palm. Soft and smooth, with a hard metal clasp at one end. Threading it around the back of her neck, he looped it, so the fibres nestled snuggly on her skin. "Walk to the bedroom. Slowly."

With the rope around her neck like a collar, Shannon

stepped forward. "Slowly, Shannon. I want to watch your ass."

Shannon raised onto her tip toes, placing one foot in front of the other with a sexy swagger that tested his restraint. He gave the rope a subtle tug and growled, "You like being mine, don't you?"

"Yes," she said with a throaty rasp.

Is that what this was? Did he want Shannon to be his for the long term?

Reaching out, he snatched the brown package and followed behind, entranced by her beautiful lean figure. When her shins hit the mattress, Jamie released the rope and let it fall away from her neck. Drawing up behind her, his palms drifted over her soft round hips, and his needy lips grazed the shell of her ear. "Bring your hands behind your back."

"Jamie, I.." she stuttered.

"Trust me. I won't hurt you, Shannon." He lightly brushed his lips over her temple. "I'm asking you to trust me, love."

Slowly, her elbows drew back, and her hands pressed together above her buttocks. Winding the rope in a figure of eight, Jamie wrapped her wrists but left the remaining rope hanging. "On the bed."

Placing his hands on her hips he guided her forward, so she rested on her knees. Drifting a hand along the curve of her back, he prompted her to tip her torso down onto the mattress, so her ass was in the air and her head to the side. The sight of Shannon tied and waiting for him initiated a fucking hot fever. Every cell in his body was burning to taste her, to own her, to take her.

He took his time to drink in the sight before him. Shrugging off his jacket, he tossed it to the floor and tugged his tee over his head. He'd been with countless women before and got off on the sex high every damn time, but something about this was more than a turn on. It felt right and wrong, hot and heavy, needy and greedy. The pounding in chest felt like his heartbeat was banging the jungle drums, and the pulsating in his dick was so intense that it almost hurt.

The silky soft skin on her pale ass cheeks deserved the rosy glow that came from a swift spank. The fact her toes curled made it even more of a thrill, and the sweet sound of her moan carried his face to her folds. Her legs quaked, and her body almost convulsed, but his fantasy didn't end there.

He loved how she lost herself in his torture, never mind the musky taste that he wanted to bottle for the days she wasn't with him.

With a suck and a bite of her delicious flesh, her legs shook. A powerful orgasm rocketed through her core. Her breathless pants were muffled by the duvet, her hands pulled behind her back, she was completely at his mercy. It was erotic and sexy and everything he thought it would be.

While she swirled down from her lust cloud, he dragged off the socks and freed her muscular calves. Grabbing the rope twisted around her hands, Jamie yanked her backwards, lifting her torso off the bed. He sucked in deeply when her fingers nudged his groin. She was warm and soft, sexy and vulnerable. Nuzzling her black locks, he inhaled the sweet scent of Shannon Colter and noted how her milky flesh prickled with each light kiss. Turning her hips, he brought them face to face.

"I haven't finished with you yet." He winked.

Her whimpers were sexy, her smile was dreamy and her responses were a power house of emotions and sensations. "What do you have in mind?" she barely asked as her voice was thick with lust.

"As much as I adore those big blue eyes..." Cupping her face, he pressed his lips to each eyelid, until she closed her eyes. Her ribs expanded quickly as he replaced his mouth with the nylon material. "Jamie," she gasped.

Shannon's vision was blanketed with a long sock tied tightly behind her head. "Jamie?" Her voice trembled. "I don't know about this."

Without her sight, the other senses would kick in. He knew she'd love it. "Trust me, Shannon."

The heat from her ragged gasps sizzled on his skin, and the beating of her heart thrummed in the hallow of her vulnerable neck, begging him to feast on her innocence. Dragging his fingers over her lips, he distorted their position with gentle movements. There was a chemical reaction taking over his mind. He could sense her pleasure was mixed with hesitation, arousal sought in the unknown and the anticipation of his touch.

"You want to know what's in the other bag, Shannon?" She was isolated in darkness, his body removed from hers. Their heat no longer combined.

"Yes," she whispered.

A small silky solid globe touched her moist lips. "Take a bite," he said huskily.

Sinking her teeth down cautiously, she licked her lips and sucked the rich sugary substance.

"What do you taste, Shannon?"

"Hmmm, chocolate and... cherries," she purred.

"Now you know how good you taste. You're addictive." His tongue swept across her parted lips. "You're sweet." The chocolaty orb traced the seam of her mouth and dipped inside. "You're intense." Rough prickles scratched her face as he pressed his mouth on her cheeks with feather light kisses. "When I left here yesterday, I had this fucking need to come straight back. It's like you have me on a string, tugging me back."

Pressing his fingertips to her hips he turned her back to face the bed and growled, "Fall again."

She prepared to crash face first into the duvet, but as she tipped, he snatched the rope at her wrists and lowered her down with one arm. Scooping his hands under her pelvis, he angled her hips upwards a fraction and parted her legs. It was like heaven. Soft curls and glistening red folds, so wet, just for him. Soft seductive moans whispered from her throat as he grazed her buttocks with his teeth.

Crawling up her body like a panther on the prowl, he rolled her to the side and rubbed melting chocolate over her pouty lips until a succulent red cherry was exposed. With slight pressure he slid the glossy fruit into her mouth with a push of his tongue. Her lips were streaked and muddy, ready to be devoured.

"Eat up, Shannon," he ordered, watching as she relished the luxurious taste with licks and chews.

Her tongue darted free, swiping across the velvety dark trail and her teeth dented the fleshy pillow of her bottom lip. Shannon was lapping up her treat like the dirty girl he knew she would be. Innocent on the outside and filthy on the inside. A soft mull echoed in his ears, and she sighed. "That was so good."

The reality had become even better than the fantasy. He wanted those soft lips all over his dick - all chocolaty and perfect, mixed with cherry. Nothing could've prepared him for the mega hard-on that drained all the blood from his appendages, flowing straight to his dick and making him light headed. He pulled at the loose knot behind her head, whipped the sock away and revealed her enchanting ocean blue eyes that punched the breath from his lungs.

Keeping his focus solely on her chocolate covered mouth, he edged off the bed. His zipper slid down, breaking the electric silence. "You know what I want right now?" His jeans hit the floor. Shannon nodded. "But first." He slotted his hand in the paper bag and selected another chocolate covered cherry. This part was a new addition to his midnight fantasy. "Open your legs."

She obeyed. Sliding his hand between her thighs, Jamie trailed the chocolate over her wet heat, melting it over her skin. "I'll lick this up later."

Her gasp was like a surge of excitement bubbling alongside apprehension. "You're so fucking edible, with or without chocolate cherries. I want you on your knees. I want that dirty mouth all over my dick, Shannon."

Her eyes turned navy blue like the deep unknown ocean and each little gasp pushed her breasts higher. She was so eager to please, so willing to satisfy him. He hoisted her off the bed, helping her to the floor, resting on her calves. Sitting tall, she arched forward and took his hard shaft deep into her throat.

"Good girl." The sensation of her warm mouth tightened his balls. Bringing his fingers to her tousled hair, he maneuverer her head so he could see those big baby blues gazing up at him.

"Slowly, take it slowly," he growled. The sensation was tight and warm.

Shannon dragged her sinful tongue up his shaft like she was licking a lolly, getting him so wound up he nearly burst. Fisting her messy strands, he yanked her head back. "Fuck that. "

Slotting both hands under her arm pits, he lifted her off the wooden floor in a flash. He had hoped to savour the torture of her wicked mouth, but the truth was, it was too damn intense, so fucking good. In one gentle movement, he pushed her face first onto the bed. She willingly shifted her hips up and spread her knees wide, moaning loudly when his tongue found her entrance. With repeated long sweeps, he lapped up the melted chocolate combined with her musky taste. It was the best fucking confectionery experience he'd ever had. But his dick wanted in too. Rising up, he thrust inside her with one deep push. Her walls clamped, and in that moment of insanity he was forced to withdraw. "Are you on the pill?" He prayed she would give him the green light to go ahead without protection.

"No," she panted.

Now that he'd felt the real deal, he wanted more. He was determined to experience the intensity of Shannon Colter at some point, but right now he rolled on a condom and chased his orgasm.

He crashed to the mattress beside her. The crook of his arm slid over his eyes as he waited for his breathing to steady and his head to stop spinning. Feeling the bed dip, he dropped his elbow and turned his head to find Shannon wrestling against the rope.

"Fuck, sorry, love. Here, let me." The thick rope fell away. "I've made a mess of you." Leaning into her face, he ran the tip of his tongue over her chocolate streaked mouth and hummed low in his throat. "I'll get a towel."

He jumped off the bed and strolled to the bathroom like he lived there. It was small and compact, probably the same size as his pantry in Fermanagh. Snatching a purple towel, he strode back into the room to find Shannon in the very same spot he'd left her. She looked so beautiful and fragile. Inky black locks framed rosy cheeks and the tip of her tongue traced her messy lips. With gentle swipes, he erased the chocolate chaos and moved down to her thighs.

"What are you doing?" her voice was high pitched.

"I'm just cleaning you up, love. Open your legs."

A deep line settled on her forehead. "That's just weird. I can do it myself."

Jamie chuckled. This girl wanted to do everything herself. "Open your legs, Shannon, or I'll force them open."

"Are you threatening me?"

"Yes. Do you want to test me?"

"Maybe…"

"Fine." Jamie crawled up the bed on his hands and knees. His eyes locked with hers and his mouth tipped forward. Their lips clung together with slow, warm kisses. Her arms automatically reached around his neck. Drifting a hand to her waist, he tugged her close to his thundering heart, pouring his soul into the passionate, heady kiss.

He didn't want to let go.

He didn't want to leave.

If he was honest with himself, her kisses were equally as astounding as the sex.

Their lips parted, and he breathed deeply, absorbing the sensation of her weary body next to his. Jamie had finally found a connection, and it was incredible.

"Won't you miss your flight?" she mumbled.

"I know, I know. I have to leave, or Marcus will kick my ass." He half joked, trailing his nails over the dip of her waist.

Her head lifted, and she stared at him momentarily.

"You bought me chocolates. Some would say that was romantic."

A low rumble echoed in his chest. "And melting them all over you - is that romantic?" He met her curious gaze.

"Not romantic, as such."

"But you enjoyed it?"

A wash of pretty pink warmed her cheeks. "I'll never be able to look at a cherry again without being turned on." She giggled softly. The delicate tone of her happiness settled in his heart with a weird flutter.

"Well then, Shannon. Mission accomplished."

"Jamie, I don't need presents or affection, right now. You don't need to buy my stuff." Her eyes were dark, and he knew her tongue was covered in lies.

Rising to his elbow, he tucked a wavy tendril behind her ear so he could see her entire face. Shannon actually thought a rope and socks were presents, if only she knew what he'd really wanted to buy her. If she wasn't so damn edgy about money, he would've acquired a cherry orchard in Turkey, or even California, just for her. "They weren't really presents, but you have to admit it..." His brow quirked.

"Admit what?" she said with quiet contemplation.

"They were a good choice. They got your engine fired up." He knew he had the ability to spark up a woman with just a quirk of his mouth, and up until this point, he never felt the need to ask if their response was real or not, but something inside him prompted reassurance.

She nodded, agitating her unkempt hair. "They did..." Her voice hinted a tremble. "It was different." She looked away from him like she hated admitting to anything, let alone the fact he rocked her world.

His head dropped, hovering over her face as the last word left her mouth. "I'll think about cherry's and chocolate... and you, until I see you again this Friday, love."

Jamie kissed the tip of her nose and clambered off the bed. Catching a glimpse of the time on his gold watch, he cursed. The minutes had rolled into hours without even realising.

"Sorry, Shan. Gotta fuck and run. Don't be mad at me?" he half asked half stated as he stepped into his jeans and slid on his tee. Sliding his arms into his favourite leather jacket, he quickly ran his hands through his messy hair. "We're all good here?" He jogged to the doorway and looked back over his shoulder. "Shannon? All good?"

"All good." She smiled, hugging her pillow to her chest. "We're good, Jamie. See you on Friday."

Chapter 24

Las Vegas was a den of powerful men and even more powerful women who could charm a few thousand bucks out of any man's hand with a shake of their best assets.

Having left on Monday afternoon, he travelled through time zones, almost like time travel, and landed in Sin City on Monday evening. Jamie arrived with one thing on his mind - business. Well, that, and one other thing. Hopping off the private jet to meet the bright lights of the Vegas Strip, he sent Shannon a quick text message to ask if she was still naked or wearing his boxer briefs that she still had.

This wasn't the first time that a woman had played on his mind. He'd been spoiled for choice over the years. There was the odd one who teased and tempted, but none of them had the connection he longed for. Shannon was like an atomic bomb, annihilating every other woman in her wake. This girl felt like the real deal, and the realisation of her sudden importance in his life scared the crap out of him. A few nights away from Northern Ireland would clear his mind. It was just sex.

He walked into the hotel near the empty ground where he and Marcus were planning to erect their own mega casino. Hitting the lift call button, he messaged his brother to let him know he was on his way up. Riding the lift all the way to the top, he let himself into their suite.

"Holy fuck, mate. That's the last thing I need to see this evening." He covered his eyes for the sake of Lana, who was folded around his brother like wrapping paper.

"Jesus Christ, Jamie. You haven't changed. I told you to give me a head's up when Lana is with me." Marcus sounded like he was angry, but Jamie knew otherwise.

Clearly, he'd been preoccupied and hadn't noticed the incoming text, with said warning. The guy was like a happy prairie dog who popped in and out of Lana every time he saw her.

"Sorry, Lana." He peeked through his fingers. "Okay, guys, I'm right here, in the room. Stop with the touching… and biting… and put on some clothes on."

A cute giggle arced through the large room. "It's great to see you again, Jamie. I'll get dressed, then I'm going to Facetime Freddy, so you can have this one all to yourself." Dropping his hands away from his eyes, he watched a half dressed Lana crawl off Marcus like a panther. Marcus swatted her ass with a loud slap.

"Fuck. That shouldn't turn me on. But it did." Jamie laughed, knowing Marcus would rise to the bait, even though it didn't. Not even a little bit.

"You owe me, dickhead," Marcus growled. "Big fucking time."

"When's the meeting?"

"Tomorrow. You ready to take the lead on this?" Marcus stepped into his jeans and tugged a tee over his head.

"Sure thing." Of course he was ready to take the lead. He'd secured the contract with Emilio Falcone, even though Marcus tried to fuck it up by swiping Lana out from under Emilio's nose pre deal, and then nearly died just to top it off. He shivered. The memory of his brother laying in blood like a carcass.

Fuck, at the time he tried to let on that it didn't bother him, but it did. The whole thing bothered him. Marcus was his life, and he nearly slipped through his fingers. Between Marcus's near death drama and his father's mental deterioration (and yeah, sometimes the guy was pure mental), Jamie just wanted to live his life with the pedal to the metal. Only now, that thrill was coming from a woman, Shannon Colter, his tasty little dick cherry.

And on that note, he shifted his arousal behind the zipper on his jeans and strode across the room to join

Marcus on the couch.

"You do know I was talking to you?" Marcus dipped down to catch his eye.

Throwing him a look of disbelief, Jamie added, "You must've been talking shit. I zoned you out. Turned down the volume on your Lana chat."

"I wasn't talking about her, but maybe you were thinking about a certain ball crusher?"

"So, what if I was? I'm man enough to admit it when I like a girl."

"You like her... like, like her enough to invite her round for Christmas turkey, or just to hook up with a few times?"

"Christmas fucking turkey, Marcus? Do I even know who you are anymore? What man talks about bringing a woman home for turkey. I could understand if you were talking about a cut of rump steak... but turkey?" Jamie shook his head while he dished out a fake look of disgust.

Marcus laughed and winced, clutching his bullet wound. Jamie's eyes homed in on his brother's movements. "Awww, Jamie, you cut me deep. It's all her fault." He nodded to the bedroom where Lana was dressing. "She's been talking about a family Christmas. Don't worry, I'll spank the idea out of her."

"Please, Marcus. She's like my sister now. I feel all protective over her. You can't say shit like that to me. It's just icky," Jamie said playfully, sitting back in the sofa and stretching his arms up. "How did you know Lana was it?" There, he asked the question. The very question he'd asked himself on the long flight to the US.

Marcus's brow scrunched, and he gazed into the open space with a stupid look on his handsome face. "The second my lips touched hers. It was like... home."

"Right. Home. I get it. Shannon made me a bacon sandwich. It reminded me of those morning's when Dad made us breakfast."

"You do like her."

"I do."

Chapter 25

It was Tuesday morning and Shannon checked her phone to find out what time it would be in Las Vegas. Jamie told her the flight was around twelve hours, and by her reckoning, it was only Monday evening on the other side of the world.

She switched on the radio, dancing around the small kitchen in a particularly jolly, 'just had fucktastic sex recently' mood. Glancing down, her mobile phone screen glowed with yet another message.

Jamie:

You awake? Just landed. Hope your wearing my boxers or better still, are you naked?

A broad grin ached her flushed cheeks. His sex texts added to his charm, they thrilled her to bits, well that, and his tight muscular body. Before the plane took off, he sent a message saying 'back soon' with a tongue emoji and a winky face. From there, filthy text messages bounced back and forth until she texted goodnight and fell asleep.

Knowing he was collecting her on Friday, scattered a burst of bumps over her scalp, tingling down her spine in a flurry of excited anticipation.

Shannon knew his visit would lead to more mind-blowing sex, and her body was on high alert, waiting and wanting it sooner. She also knew it was equally a bad idea to let him waltz into her bedroom with the doors wide open, but Jamie was a delightful itch that she so very much wanted to keep scratching. He was her crack, and she had fallen into the realms of addiction.

Shaking her head to free her mind from his sexy behaviour, Shannon reminded herself of the busy schedule she had planned out over the course of the next year. There was no room for hot, horny, hedonistic distractions. A few more steamy sex sessions would bring the whole thing to a satisfactory ending. She told herself this, as a way to prepare herself for the let down when he finally decided to move on.

What would she wear on Friday night? It's not as if she's the sexy kitten with lacey undies and titty tassels, but anything was better than those hideous, bigger than a parachute knickers that he seemed to get a kick out of.

If all went to plan and he arrived as promised, they probably wouldn't make it out the door. A mischievous grin tugged at the corners of mouth, and her teeth pressed down gently on the soft plump flesh of her lower lip in hopefulness. Maybe she shouldn't wear anything at all, other than the tan cowgirl hat she bought last year at the country festival.

Shannon:

I've got my outfit sorted for Friday. Just a Stetson.

Setting the phone on the counter, she savoured the torturous swell between her thighs. The exhilaration of his hands tightening around her wrists, combined with the feel of his seductive kisses that held her lips, was burned into her memory.

The front door flung open. She spun around to watch Niall march inside with the usual sanctimonious look on his face. His pale denim jeans were pristinely clean for a guy who was meant to help out with the horses, and the gingham shirt under an olive fine knit jumper was styled more like a grandfather than a primped gentleman.

"What's got you smiling like a bitch in heat?" he snapped, dragging the back of his hand across his nostrils.

Shannon puffed out her cheeks, letting the air blow out in a steady stream. Talk about a mood killer. He was a big wet drip of swamp water dangling above, ready to drop on her forehead at any moment, saturating her with his ugly disposition.

"Let yourself in, why don't you. Perhaps you should learn how to knock, or is it too late to teach an old dog manners?" she said firmly. Thankfully the kitchen counter separated them, allowing her to keep a safe distance.

"Why would I need to knock, Shannon? Are you afraid I'll find out your dirty little secrets?" he retorted, exhaling loudly from his nostrils.

She rolled her eyes to the sky light. "It's called privacy, and another little word you know nothing of – respect."

Niall inched closer, his thin lips crept up into a smarmy smile. "It's not like I haven't seen you naked before. Maybe I'd like to walk in on you sometime. I bet you think about me when your touching yourself, don't you?"

This guy was unbelievable, not only had he just wandered into her home, but now he was implying she fantasied about him. As if. Slamming her fingers in the door would be more pleasurable than visualising Niall's naked body. Unbeknown to him, he'd taught her a valuable lesson about men - the more money they had, the more they expected, and if they didn't get what they wanted, they went ahead and took it anyway.

The year before, Harry had held his usual Christmas party in the main house. Shannon and Niall were in a relationship at that point. In typical fashion, Niall proceeded to get drunk and flirt with anything in a tight dress. Shannon had been informed that he screwed some eighteen-year-old in the tack room after giving her a grand tour of the newly extended stable block.

Shannon had become immune to his insecurities and compulsive attributes. She planned to dump his sorry ass after Harry's big party. However, while Niall was entertaining his mistress, Shannon struck up a conversation with Mitchell Ashfield, one of the top international riders in Europe. He was funny and sweet, and not at all daunted by her many fan girl questions. They quickly developed a rapport, connecting over their passion of all things horse related. There was zero sexual spark, but his witty humour made her laugh. Once Niall had emptied his lustful load, he returned to the party in a drunken state with his shirt tails flapping.

It wasn't the first encounter of Niall's fiery temper that simmered to the surface of his cold steely eyes. She knew he was selfish and conceited, but that night he revealed his true ogre of an ugly soul.

Snatching her away from Mitchell in a jealous rage, he trailed her to the boot room at the back of the property – away from the watchful eyes of the guests. Niall had the nerve to suggest she was flaunting herself like a shameless whore and caged her against the wall. Forcing his slobbery mouth onto hers only added to her rage. She slapped and punched, until he snatched her wrists and pinned them to the wall. With a swoop of her knee she banged into his groin, sending a gust of air into her mouth as he convulsed in pain. The fact he was so drunk and disorientated, made his fists easy to deflect.

When his punches failed to make contact, Niall grabbed the lengths of her hair, swinging on the strands as he lost balance. She toppled to the ground meeting his boot on the way down. Straddling her pelvis, he messily grappled with her dress, dragging it to her waist and thrusting his hardness into her groin. She couldn't quite recall all the repugnant nonsense he spat out, all she could remember was throwing her forehead into his face and hearing the satisfactory crack as his nose poured with blood.

Harry bounced into the room like a lion. His yell drowned out Niall's growl and he was dragged off her writhing body by a few of the other guests.

The next day Niall conveniently disappeared, only to return a few weeks later with a scripted apology minus the sincerity. He threw a wad of cash at her as a payoff for his alleged grotesque behaviour – yeah, because part of his apology included a statement saying he was intoxicated, not in his right mind, and couldn't remember the minor *scuffle*. She was furious, not only by his blatant refusal to accept his full actions but at the gesture of a payoff. A financial sweetener to make the whole ordeal vanish into thin toxic air. Needless to say, she felt obliged to accept, to keep the peace for Harry's sake, after all, Niall was his only son.

Shannon took the money begrudgingly, relinquishing any future relationship, friendship or otherwise. Niall wasn't pleased that she was the one who dumped him. In retaliation, he spread rumours that he was the one that kicked *her* to the kerb. From then on, he made it his mission to hunt her down every day, just to piss her off. If she didn't hate him so much, she might just feel sorry for him. The only reason she stuck around, was Trixie – and the fact Harry was like her second father. He made Shannon a sworn promise that his son would never be abusive towards her again, ever.

She believed him.

Her mobile buzzed once, signalling a new message.

Jamie:

My dick is ready for the ride, Cowgirl.

Niall's eyes flicked down to the illuminated screen. His hand shot forward, snatching the phone before she could get to it. Reading the message aloud, his usual stuck up enunciation became more pronounced, with mocking cadence. "I always knew you were a slut. Unbelievable. You and McGrath, are at it? Is that why he was sniffing round here?" he gritted out with a threatening look.

"The only one sniffing around here, is you, Niall."

"Excuse me?"

"Have you got so much cocaine up your nose that it's blocking your ears?"

"Quite the little goody goody, aren't you? Suppose you're going to trot off to my dad and spill?"

"You need help, Niall. I always knew you had anger issues, but drugs?"

"It's recreational, you dumb fuck. I party hard because I can. Something you wouldn't have any idea about because all you do is ride horses. I'm sure McGrath has had a few laughs at your expense. The dull country girl with no sex drive. Guy's like him win big bets for being able to pull weirdo's like you. We all know Jamie is a betting shark."

She shook away the thoughts of Jamie luring her in to win a bet and told herself that Niall was just being twisted. But his words cut through her flesh, right to the bone and into to the marrow.

Shannon leaned forward, seizing the phone from his curled fingers. "Get lost, Niall, and shut the door on your way out," she snarled, slamming the device on the counter.

His face contorted with an ugliness that matched his soul. "You're such a fool. A pathetic nobody, who really believes a McGrath would actually be interested in you. Do you like rich cock? Is that it, Shannon?" he cackled.

This conversation was going nowhere, fast. Striding to the door, she yanked it open letting a frosty swirl breach the warmth. "Get the hell out, and don't let yourself in here again."

A slippery shadow of anger slid behind his grey eyes. They thinned to slits like a venomous snake. His breathing was fast and shallow, his hands fisted at his thighs. Stomping forward, he shoved her back. Her fingers fell away from the handle. Niall thrust the door shut with so much force that she swore everyone outside would've heard the bang. But loud noises weren't unusual on the yard, it was a normal occurrence to hear hefty gates slam or horse hooves banging the stable doors. Shannon knew no one would bat an eyelash.

"You and I need to have a chat, Shannon. *You* need to learn some fucking respect." His jaw clenched with an angry visible tick.

Her hands shot to her hips. This time she was ready for him with harnessed anger as her friend. She could take him on, no problem, after all, she knew exactly what he could deliver.

"You're nothing but a coke head. A waste of space. Your dad will see that soon enough. One day you'll trip up, Niall, and I'll be watching. I'll be clapping and cheering the day he cuts off your funds. Now get the hell out!" she yelled, feeling the bit of rage shake her bones.

His head tipped back and a low grunt slid from his

throat. "You think he'll be influenced by you? Haven't I told you already, Shannon, you're a nobody. You don't own anything, not even this loft. What have you got going for you?"

Her hands cinched her waist. "I only regret two things in my life, Niall – the first is having sex with you, and the second was putting up with your lame sex efforts because you couldn't even satisfy a fucking week old corpse."

Darkness swallowed the room, and a bolt of panic struck her ribcage when his fury erupted like a volcano. In slow motion she watched helplessly as he lunged forward and grabbed the abandoned whip propped against the wall - the very whip that had treated her to so much pleasure only days before. Niall clutched it so tightly that his knuckles whitened. Raising it high above his head, he launched into a full attack, flogging her with force.

The first crack that lashed her skin, sent searing pain through her flimsy top. The second wallop stung like a volt from the electric chair. Shannon yelped with a strangled sound, leaping forward into his chest with her palms scrunched to fists. Wrestling with his firm grasp, she attempted to free the whip from his grip. With her attention focused on winning it back, Niall lifted his other hand and seized her hair, yanking her head down with a jerk. Her body twisted, her gaze fell to his powerful knee that smashed into her ribs in one brutal blow.

Her legs crumpled, crashing her body to the floor, crouching in a defensive ball like a hedgehog minus the protective prickles. The breath left her lungs as the pain screamed through her muscles. Sheer disbelief and burning pain swallowed up any intention of fighting back. Her winded lungs left her defenceless.

Even through her clothes, the slaps of the whip felt like he was branding her flesh with fiery metal. Each slap exploded into flames as he unleashed his violent tirade on her unprotected curled form.

The last crack of the whip felt like the hundredth. Niall held it high above his head. Shallow breaths and a low growl were the only sound he made. The whip remained in limbo, the warning of more pain lingered like the threat of thunder after lightening.

"You tell anyone about this little misunderstanding, and I'll ruin your life, and your precious fucking horse. I'll pay her a visit in the dead of night and do her so much harm that she'll only be fit for dog food. If you think I'm joking, then take a look at yourself right now." The final lash spliced through the air, connecting with her lower back leaving a deafening imprint. Her core shuddered with pain. "And one other thing, you keep that asshole, Jamie, away from this place. Stay the fuck away from him."

The sound of the whip hitting the floor was a distant thud, and the whoosh of cold air engulfing her misery was a welcomed reprieve. Gently clicking the door shut behind him like he'd exerted enough energy for one day, Niall left her in a crumpled heap. None of the staff working in the stable yard below would know he'd brutally flogged her into submission.

A quiet melody emanated from the digital radio like eerie interval music at a horror show. An interlude between the atrocious sensation of leather lashing her flesh and the whimpers that waited on the periphery of her shock.

Shannon stayed on the floor, hugging her fiery limbs, perfectly still and ever so quiet.

There it was, inches from her face.

The whip.

Her awakening and her ruin.

Chapter 26

Marcus lifted his finger, signalling to the waitress for more drinks. The bar was pretentious and stylish with peacock blues and low-level tables so the top floor's 360 degree views were unobstructed. A pianist, wearing a satin tuxedo, played smooth jazzy rhythms, and a wall of suited men with ear pieces blocked mingling guests from joining their exclusive party. The powerful men around the table oozed wealth and entitlement, their eyes trailed over the beautiful women circling like vultures, all of them except Jamie. His eyes were drawn to the screen on his mobile phone.

"Gentlemen, thanks for coming out to Vegas." Benji Finka, the club owner, clinked his glass with the man to his left. "Let's do business before we invite the entertainment to join us," he said casually, because this was how they rolled. His wavy salt and pepper hair teased the creases around his eyes when he raised his glass to the closest little hottie wearing a slinky dress with puffy white hair like Marilyn Monroe.

Jamie's phone slid along the glossy black surface. A solitary ice cube rattled in his glass when it tipped to meet his lips. The cool liquid drained in one long gulp. His knee bounced, and he flipped a spare coaster into the air, snapping it tight between his fingers. Every voice, sound and glance had him on edge.

Marcus slid him a knowing look. "Problem?"

"Nothing I can't deal with." His elbow nudged into his brother's arm and winked like the world was perfect.

A barely dressed waitress carried over a tray of drinks, skilfully balancing them on one hand high in the air. Sure, she had curves in all the places and thick fluttery lashes framing feline eyes, but her act was too fucking predictable. There was no challenge, no hunt, no thrill. He didn't flinch when her hips brushed his arm, or when her ass lingered before him in full view as she oh-so-slowly set down the six glasses in turn.

The other men in his company were only too happy to lap up her flirtatious performance. Each inviting stroke and seductive trace of her dewy cleavage received their full attention.

It was just too easy.

"Will you excuse me, gentlemen. I need to make a call." Jamie's seat flew back and he stood.

Marcus grabbed Jamie by the wrist just as he turned away. "Later," he ordered. "Sit down."

All he needed to do was call her, just one more time. "I said excuse me."

Marcus's eyes flared, and he rose up tall to meet his brother's scowl. "Business first," he replied with a new found calmness since Lana had softened him up.

Business, fucking business. If he had to hear that term one more time, he'd smash his fist into the mirror behind them. How could he concentrate on business when Shannon was ghosting him?

"I'll be right back. It won't take more than five minutes tops." He nodded curtly, skirted the group and jogged across the room. Pushing through pin tuck velvet doors, he sighed heavily, thankful for space to think. Shannon had stopped replying to his messages. He didn't have time for games. His concentration had gone to shit, his focus had singled her out, and his goal was solely aimed at making contact with her.

Their frequent sexy texts had been fun, flirty and bordering on god damn kinky. He'd even disappeared into the washrooms for a quick self-satisfaction release when she announced her lack of outfit for their date on Friday. Shannon had him riled up like a bronc waiting to buck in the stalls. But now, fuck if he knew why she'd gone cold.

The ring tone ended. Her voicemail automatically

began, for the tenth time this evening. He strode back into the bar, feeling uneasy and tight. His jaw almost locked from clamping his teeth together.

"Sorted?" Marcus asked, narrowing his green eyes.

Jamie dropped his phone on the table and began to roll up his shirt sleeves. "Not yet. I'll handle it."

"You sure about that?"

Throwing his brother an 'Are you for real' glance, he nodded. The frustration in his eyes signalled a silent plea to shut the fuck up and keep business, business.

"So, what have you got for us, Finka? You know we submitted the planning permit like a fucking century ago?"

Marcus cleared his throat as one of the men sat tall and pressed his lips together in a firm line. "Jamie, I heard you were an asshole, but if we're gonna help each other, we need a little respect."

Jamie's eyes cut to the mobile phone. He pressed the home button just in case his battery had died, even though he'd charged it to one hundred percent before they left the suite.

"Are you even listening to me, you cocky fuck?" Finka growled.

Jamie steepled his fingers. "Yeah, I heard your little bitchy yap from all the way over here."

Marcus jumped up, knocking his seat back roughly. "If you'll excuse me, gentlemen. My brother and I need to have a quick word."

He was tugged off his chair and frog marched to the bar. "What the fuck is wrong with you?"

"Nothing." Jamie looked down feeling like a kid who'd cheeked up the teacher.

"Seriously, Jamie. Why are you pissing all over this? We need these guys to get this off the ground. It's huge for us. This Vegas hotel will be the biggest one we've ever owned… never mind built, and you're acting like a brat. Either you tell me what's going on here, or I'll take over the deal and cut you out."

Jamie dragged his hand down the scruff on his jaw and

sighed. "I'm not in the mood for tits and ass, Marcus."

"Is that it? Fuck sake, Jamie, leave with me. They know I'm not playing anymore."

Peering at his mobile phone for the umpteenth time, his irritation simmered. It had been way too long since their last text, and he was acting like a pubescent teen.

"Shannon. That's the problem. She's not answering my texts, or my calls. I feel like a fucking stalker now."

His brother's large palm rested on his shoulder, the welcome touch left a warmth that he craved to feel from Shannon. "Women are curious creatures." His mouth curved in a lopsided smirk. "Did you piss her off? You have a talent for rubbing people the wrong way. Like, Finka."

"No. Things have been really good between us. Better than good, until she just cut me off." Jamie shook his head and slotted his hands under his arm pits, taking a wide stance.

"Go home, Jamie. Sort your shit out. You obviously really like her, so go and do whatever you have to do. I'll cover your ass here."

"Thanks, Marcus."

"I mean it, Jamie. Pull yourself together. Not every woman on the planet will fall for you. If she's not interested, move the fuck on."

Jamie shook out his arms and pulled the phone from his pocket, glancing at the blank screen. "Of course she's interested." He was in too deep to consider the idea that she wasn't. There was a connection between them, and he knew it, she knew it. Hell, the universe even knew it. His crazy thoughts were racing down a one-way track with Shannon as the only destination.

Marcus puffed out a long steady breath. "Then go get her."

Chapter 27

Multiple unopened messages waited on her mobile phone. It was game over between her and Jamie, whatever had dared to spark was ruined here forth.

Now she was more driven than ever to stick with the original plan and focus on her career, without getting preoccupied by sex. The harsh decision to ignore Jamie wasn't solely due to Niall's request to keep him away from the yard. The reality was his just sex suggestion. That's all he offered, and that's all it would ever be. She hadn't expected him to come back for more, and she certainly never imagined agreeing to a casual sex arrangement, nor that she would actually have feelings for him. Yes, she had feelings for the guy. Where they came from or why she let them escalate was beyond her. Perhaps it was the tenderness in his touch, the meaning in his sensual kisses, or was all that just the Jamie McGrath charm package.

The whole idea had been doomed from the start. This was the perfect time to pull the plug. With a heavy heart, she pushed him to the farthest gloomiest corner of her mind, then caged her heart in barbed wire and drained it of all emotion. If she could hook on a lock and throw away the key, she would do that too.

Rule number one was reinstated - no men. She would never allow herself to be vulnerable at the hands of a man again. Jamie manipulated her heart and body, whereas Niall chose brute force to evoke fear and evil.

Shannon abandoned her emotions, accepting a bleak numbness into her heart. Everything had changed and she desperately wanted to shut her feelings down.

No more fear.

No more lust.

No more men.

Hiding in the loft that evening with a duvet and the last of her red wine, Shannon cloaked herself in a shroud of shame. For the first time in over a year she hadn't ridden, and she was riddled with guilt and disappointment. The ache in her belly became more unbearable when she let herself think about Jamie.

Draped in misery, she sipped the syrupy wine and stared at the blank walls, mulling over her options. The door handle rattled and her hearing pricked on high alert. A loud series of thumps followed.

"Shan, open the bloody door!" Harry hollered from the other side of the front door

Wrapping the duvet over her shoulders, she made sure her body was covered, then she scuttled through the kitchen like a giant marshmallow with legs.

Pulling open the door, she came face to face with Harry. "Jeez, Shan, you look like shit!" he gasped, tactless as ever but filled with concern.

Shannon spent hours with Harry on a daily basis. She even spent more time with him than she ever did with her own father. It wasn't that she didn't adore her parents – they just didn't have the same passion, nor did they try to understand hers. They left her to her own devices, which suited her fine.

Shannon was the daughter Harry never had, and his equine prodigy. Every rosette won was met with a huge knowing grin and a congratulatory hug, even the silly plastic awards from the country fares made him proud. From the very first day she sat in the saddle, Harry told her she had a natural riding flare that couldn't be taught, but merely refined. Day after day, he coached and mentored. She willingly took on board his critique because Harry had been one of the best riders in his time, retiring from competing to produce winning horses instead. He understood her drive, her passion and her effort. Their bond was a far contrast between the relationship he had with his son.

She hugged the hefty duvet close to her chest, brutality hidden beneath. "Flu," she muttered, failing to meet his furrowed gaze.

"Need the doctor? Or your mum?" he asked, scratching the grey prickles on his jaw.

"I'll be riding tomorrow, Harry," she mumbled, swallowing back the lump in her throat.

"All right. Niall's gone off again. I've put Trixie in the walker. If you're not up to riding tomorrow, then I'll get someone else to take her out for you. Okay?" He cocked his head like an attentive dog. "Shan?"

Her eyes misted. "How long is he away for?"

Harry shrugged lightly. "A few weeks, maybe. Who knows what he's up to this time? He said he was looking for another mare, but at this point, I've no fucking clue what he's up to."

Shannon was gripped with both relief of Niall's absence and dread for his return. At least it gave her time to recover and decide how best to approach the asshole (with a shotgun).

"Look, Shan, I'm worried about you. Did Jamie do something to upset you?"

"No, Harry." Her voice cracked. She couldn't tell him the truth, it would break his already lonely heart. For all of Niall's faults, he was still Harry's son – they were blood, and blood ran deep. If it came to the crunch, Shannon would be turfed out on her penniless ass and Niall would succeed in ruining Trixie's beautiful spirit.

"Really, Harry, it's nothing. I'm under the weather, but I'll be back at it again tomorrow." She glanced heavenward, staving tears.

With a deep sigh, he nodded in acceptance. Before turning away, he patted her shoulder. "I'll bring you some stew down later."

Sweet Jesus, no!

The thought of Harry becoming Meals on Wheels sent her stomach into a rinse cycle. All she needed was solitude.

"It's okay, I've got something defrosting. But thanks," she lied, mustering a smile that barely moved her cheeks.

"Come on, we both know that's not true." The creases around his eyes softened. "Get in the Jeep. The fire's lit and there's a pot of stew simmering."

Jackson nudged through the gap and rested his nose on her belly. Big eyes as black as the night pleaded with her to follow them to the main house.

She sighed deeply. "Emotional blackmail, Harry? I'm sick, you know? I should be in bed."

"Jackson here wants the company." Harry nodded to his dog who was playing the game along with his master.

"He's got you to keep him company."

"He has me every night. Anyway, he wants to make sure you're okay." Harry tipped the peak of his cap, knowing perfectly well he was using Jackson to get what he wanted.

"I'm fine."

"You're not. I know when my girl's upset. Let's go."

She relented with a puff of her cheeks, wishing she could hide away in isolation under the covers with the last packet of potato chips and a two-day old end of a baguette. "I'll get my coat."

"There it is." Harry crouched down. "I'll put this in the horse lorry for the next comp." He lifted the whip.

The whip she wanted to keep because it reminded her of Jamie.

The whip she needed to burn because it reminded her of Niall.

The fucking whip.

Her stomach roiled. Harry tucked it under his arm and turned away from her. "Come on, Shan. Grab a coat."

It was gone. Drifting her hand to her mouth, she sucked in a deep shaky breath. The duvet fell from her shoulders, trailing behind her staggered steps. Letting it fall, she tossed it on the couch. Choosing the biggest, longest waterproof coat she could find. Working outside meant she was prepared for everything mother nature could chuck at her, aside from Niall fucking Ross.

Cloaked in an aubergine rain coat that ended midway to her calves, she pulled the door shut behind her and trudged down the stone steps.

The rain pelted down on her hood and bounced like stones on the cobbles. "Are you sure Niall is away?" She eyed Harry as she gingerly slid into the passenger side, her words muffled under the spluttering engine.

"Come on, old girl." Harry tilted forward like he could will the Jeep to roll forward. "He's long gone. It's just me, you and Jackson."

As soon as his name was mentioned, Jackson peered through the gap between the front seats, panting happily.

The wheels spat up stones under the chassis as it raked along the track to the main house. Harry always did have a thing for speed, but he was as careful behind the wheel as he was in the saddle.

The house lights twinkled amidst the stark black countryside. Her heels barely touched the ground when she dropped out of the Jeep, jogging to the back door with her arms hugging achy ribs with each juddered step.

Warmth radiated from the large stove that was housed under a brick arch in the cosy kitchen. Shannon had spent many a night sat by the giant oak table, drinking beer and chatting with Harry... and Niall. Even though she hated Niall with every cell in her body, the main house still represented home. Harry was family, even if his son was a douche bag.

"Hang that coat up in the boot room and go on through. I'll bring you a bowl of stew once I've dished it out," Harry instructed.

Teetering on tip toes, she hung up the coat and made her way through the cluttered kitchen to the lounge. The fire glowed with a bright red flame, coaxing her closer with a promise of comfort. On the dark red walls were portraits of Harry's ancestors, with horses and landscapes scattered with whimsical flare. Dark mahogany furniture was littered with golden cups, trophies, plaques and the odd random sheet of paper that he stuffed to the side. Drawing closer to the fire, she chose the hunter green leather wing back chair to her left, because the one on the right was, and always would be, Harry's. No one sat on his chair, or they'd face the consequences with a trip to the dung heap.

"Here we go. There's a glass of wine for you." Harry set a large glass of red wine on the circular side table and handed her a hearty bowl of stew. Leaving her alone for a few minutes, he returned with his own portion and a healthy measure of brandy. Harry and brandy went hand in hand, as did Harry, brandy and cigarettes. And, Jackson should be added on there too.

As she popped a carrot into her mouth, she did a quick check of her limbs, to ensure there was no flesh on show. "Thanks, Harry," she said between chews, feeling a warm sensation of homeliness wrap her wounded body.

"Anytime." Harry dunked a chunk of bread into the gravy. "Didn't like the thought of you being all alone when you're like this." He nodded to her drawn in knees and hunched over position. "You look lost."

"I'm right here, Harry. Where I belong." With a broken heart and a beaten body.

Harry picked out a large piece of meat and held it out for Jackson, who waited patiently at his feet. The fire crackled and spat, filling the comfortable silence. They didn't need to talk to be in each other's company. She picked at her food with a fork and watched Harry feed most of his dinner to the dog. The large ornate clock on the mantle ticked rhythmically with a soft beat that captured her attention.

She didn't realise that her eyes were rolling or that her head was lolling as sleep secretly welcomed her. So when she opened her eyes and the bowl was nowhere to be seen and her torso was swaddled in a patchwork quilt, she blinked with surprise. Harry was slouched in his chair with fingers wrapping a glass of brandy that rested on his thigh. He could be drunk as skunk, or fast asleep, and the man would never spill a drop of alcohol. It was like an unconscious gift of saving precious brandy. Jackson was curled up on the rug in front of the dying embers. His head lifted when she shuffled off the chair and stretched.

"It's okay, boy," she whispered.

Glancing at the clock she noted it was just after midnight. Spending time away from the loft had been a welcomed break, even if it was in the home of the asshole who abused her. She gathered herself up, tiptoed through the quiet kitchen, tugged her coat from the hook and crept out the back door. A shiver skittered across her skin when the cold breeze howled, prompting brisk quick strides back to the yard. The rain had stopped but the night sky threatened more with an oppressive darkness suffocating the stars. Nearing the stables, she caught sight of Bucky weaving his way through the yard.

Waving over, she called out, "Hey Bucky!" Feigning a smile, she kept her pace brisk.

"Feeling better, Shan?" His voice drifted out of the shadows.

"I'm getting there, thanks. See you in the morning."

Bucky continued to check the stables as she bounded up the steps. The door was ajar. She could've sworn she had slammed it shut. Peering through the gap, she waited for movement. Nothing. Holding her breath, she stood perfectly still. A flurry of fear made her pulse slam.

"Hello?" she called, then cursed herself for being so stupid. If anyone was lingering, ready and waiting to murder her, they surely wouldn't call back with a friendly 'hello, can you come inside so I can kill you'.

The small lamp in the seating area cast shadowy caricatures of her furniture on the walls but the room was otherwise empty. Releasing her breath slowly, she teetered on the balls of her feet, creeping inside, making her way towards her bedroom. The thundering beat of her heart rose up into her mouth when she saw the duvet, folded neatly and set back on her bed. Hadn't she left it on the couch? A flurry of panic tore through her body. Dropping to the floor she checked under the bed, nothing. The bathroom door was open. It was clear to see that no one was hiding in there either. Flinging open the wardrobe, she gasped with relief when she found her clothes minus a freaky masked man with a knife.

Running back to the door, Shannon secured the lock and pressed her back to the slats giving the room another visual once over. Maybe she left it on the bed herself and her mind was messing with her after the trauma? After all, Niall was long gone and Jamie was in America.

Once Shannon was confident the loft was safe, she curled up under the covers. Before falling asleep, she considered switching her phone back on to see if Jamie had stopped his hunt. After thirteen unanswered text messages and the nine missed calls, she had turned it off, resorting to the cowardly act of ignoring, hoping he'd get the hint.

She was broken and Jamie would only mess up the pieces with his just sex offer. There was no way she'd let him near her now, not with bruises and threats hanging over her head.

Shannon refused to let the world see what was hiding under her baggy clothes. The last thing she wanted to endure was pitiful glances and assumptions. Her cruel secret had to be buried in the past for the sake of her love for a horse that wasn't even her own. It would be a small sacrifice to deny herself the unforgettable thrill that came with Jamie McGrath. All she needed was her career and the commitment she made to herself from the beginning. It was irrelevant that Jamie had kick started her heart, igniting a fire in a world that had been so cold. He plagued her subconscious and made her crave his wicked hot lips on every inch of her flesh.

Was she losing her mind? Surely horse riding would be enough for her now?

Chapter 28

Shannon slept like her mattress was stuffed with nails. The morning routine didn't bring any relief either, nor the pathetic shower that dribbled like a leaky watering can. Warm water flowed over her bruises, nurturing and kind, not like burning wallops that still stung. There was no point staring at her pitiful reflection, looking down was hard enough, let alone seeing them all in their glory.

Carefully dressing in a long sleeve top and breeches, she covered herself from neck to toe. Partly due to the howling wind that stabbed like an icy fingered demon outside, but mainly, she wanted to hide away under the loose fabric. One day the hideous marks would fade but the mental scars would remain, deep rooted in her memory until her dying breath. Her belly rumbled, but the cupboards were empty. Breakfast was the last packet of potato chips and a mug of green tea. The thought of going to get groceries made her groan.

She pushed the small button at the top of her phone, turning on the device. A flurry of beeps tallied over twenty-five. Every missed call and unanswered message was from Jamie, with the final one a solitary question mark. None of his messages received a response. Her heart sank, hating herself for leaving him high and dry, without even a goodbye. He deserved a reply, but she couldn't face it. She couldn't build up the courage to actually let him go.

Her head shook. He was a grown man who'd have no issue rolling on to the next woman. He'd get over it, sooner rather than later. Jamie didn't do emotions, he did sex. Just sex.

Routine would keep her busy. The busy schedule

would fill the void.

Harry was lunging Trixie in the sand paddock, preparing for Shannon's first lesson since the attack. She wasn't ready to get back in the saddle, but it was important to stay on track with her training. Every slight movement felt like her ribs were going to snap and her skin burned at the closeness of her clothes.

"You should've stayed the night, Shannon. You know there's always a bed made up for you. Are you sure it was the flu?" Harry asked, raising a bushy eyebrow.

She kept her gaze to the sand and nodded. "I just wasn't feeling well. Women stuff. Your stew made me feel better. It always does, Harry, you've always looked out for me." She tipped into his chest and rested her cheek on his shoulder, inhaling the smell of his waxy jacket. His arms closed around her. Even though his tight hold ached her wounds, she let him hold her close. She wanted him to. She needed his comfort. Blinking back tears, she swallowed the lump forming in her throat. "Let's get started."

Harry squeezed her wrist, when she pulled back. "We'll not spend too long outdoors. There's a storm brewing." He nodded towards the dark clouds in the distance. "After this you can come up to the house for lunch."

Climbing the mounting block, she ran her hands over Trixie's withers. As much as she despised Niall for stealing her self-respect and allowing him to hurt and degrade her, a swell of relief overpowered the hate. Trixie was safe.

He may have won this time but that would be the last time - the very last time. A constant surge of hatred powered through every cell, every nucleus, every minuscule component of her flesh, begging revenge. Fucking bastard.

Lying to her boss at Coffee Kicks had only added to her humiliation. She despised lies and deceit, but there was no way she could face a week of shifts, or people for that matter.

Flipping her leg over the tan leather, she sat deep in the saddle. There was no place on earth she would rather be.

Trixie was her salvation. Jamie was just a fantasy, a man beyond reach.

Harry fiddled with the bridle while she strapped on her coffee coloured gloves and clipped the safety clasp of her helmet. Gathering up the reins she squeezed gently. Trixie walked forward with a sultry pace. It had been two days since she was beaten into a hunched mess, two days since she last rode, and two days of sheer hell. But now, she was fighting for her sanity the only way she knew how.

The training session began with a warm up leading to a course of jumps. Shannon rode fearlessly, with a demanding persistence. Trixie was pleased to have her rider on board, instinctively clearing every fence. Shannon focused on the strides and bounces as they followed the course to perfection. She embraced the thrill, a welcomed sensation that masked the hellish emotions suffocating her existence.

A low mechanical growl crept down the laneway towards the main house.

"Jamie's here!" Harry shouted as she cleared the last oxer.

The sound of his name ripped through her skull. Whipping her head around, she saw Jamie McGrath exit the glossy blue Mustang. His signature leather jacket clung to his bulky torso, and his choppy hair looked messy, yet sexy. Confident strides matched his hunting gaze, quickly finding her, yet too far away to see the pain in her eyes.

Panic seized her windpipe, choking her breath. It squeezed her chest and chilled the thrumming blood gushing through her veins. Without conscious thought, she urged Trixie to a bouncy canter, directing her to the rear of the paddock. Leaning over her right thigh, she unhooked the back gate leading to the bridal paths.

"Shannon! What are you doing? The lesson isn't over," Harry yelled.

His warbled words were drowned out under the blood pulsating in her skull. The squalling crows circled overhead like vultures watching her emotional carnage.

Keeping her neck stiff, she refused to look back.
Do not look at him, Shannon.
No. No. No!

Her heart crashed into her ribs, and her breathing became fast sharp bursts. She wasn't ready to face him. To look him in the eye and be strong. Why they hell did he turn up unexpectedly, unannounced. It was only Thursday, and he wasn't due back until Friday evening.

Fighting against her will, she flipped her head around to find him marching towards the paddock, with fierce determination.
I don't need him.
I don't need anyone.
I just want to be alone.
I'm lying to myself.

With a squeeze, Trixie responded instantly. Exuding excited horse power, she kicked out her hind legs with a playful buck and lunged forward into a gallop.

Jabs of icy rain hammered her jacket. Trixie carried her under the inky black clouds, filled with the first winter storm. Tumbling chants crowded her mind. None of it mattered anymore, she needed to forget, to run, to hide and to never look back at the man who could be her redemption.

A forceful wind battered her cheeks, stinging her eyes. Adrenaline pumped in her narrow veins, scorching and burning with impulse. Trixie's pounding hooves hammered the compact soil thrumming through her core, surging power to her chest.

She was free. Safe. Out of reach.

This is where she was meant to be, galloping for freedom, hunting her resurrection. Green fields sprawled for miles, framed by skeletal trees that creaked and twisted in the storm. Shannon found her solace and located a place to hide from her emotions.

She inhaled the damp air, filling her lungs with recklessness – with cowardice. It was wrong to disappear, but that was of no consequence now. Jamie would leave, and she'd quickly become a distant memory.

In reality, there wasn't an inch of room in her life for him, even friendships had taken a back seat over the years. She constantly sacrificed nights out with the girls until they stopped asking, eventually Jamie would do the same.

The wind picked up to a gale and the harsh rain drenched her breeches right through to her underwear. Trotting Trixie back through the paddock, she looked for his sporty Mustang, it was gone. Her heart dropped.

The clip clop of hooves in the yard, alerted Bucky of their return. He rushed out of the tack room, sheltering his eyes in the crook of his arm as the rain lashed down.

"What the hell are you playing at, Shannon? It's been over an hour."

"I needed to clear my head." *I was running away. I was being weak.*

His assessment irked her, like he was trying to figure her out. She just wished... wished she could let Jamie back in her life.

"Clear your head or catch pneumonia," he said sharply. "I was going to hunt you down myself." Bucky collected the reins as she dismounted. "Give her here. I'll get her sorted. Go and dry off. You can't be pulling stupid shit like that with the comps coming up. You've put in too much effort to let it all fall apart now."

A raindrop trickled down her nose, rolling off the tip when she nodded. "I know, Bucky. Sorry."

"Has this got anything to do with, Niall?" *What did he know, what did he see?*

Her eyes widened, wondering if Bucky was trying to piece everything together. "No... I... It's complicated." She raised her hand with a subtle flippant wave.

Bucky scowled behind the rain pouring off his peaked cap. "Everything is fucking complicated with that bastard." He turned away from her.

Shannon ran to the tack room, peeled off her jacket, helmet and gloves and hung them to drip dry. She unzipped her half chaps, kicked off her boots, then tip toed up the stone steps in her wet socks.

The door was unlocked. Thankfully Niall was away, probably visiting whore houses with his father's cash and snorting bags of cocaine like it was icing sugar. How would she cope meeting him face to face again? She had no idea, other than shoving a whip up his nose until it punctured his brains.

Traipsing inside, a deep hearted sigh puffed her ruddy cheeks. She tugged the long sleeve top over her head and tossed it on the floor in a soggy heap.

"What the fuck?" A voice cut through the silence.

She froze. Jamie bounced off the sofa, his brow creased, and his eyes blazed with a ferocious glare. He could see them. Every single one. Unsightly bruises were splashed across her trembling body, visible to his searching eyes.

"They weren't there when I last saw you. What the fuck is going on, Shannon. Who did that to you?" he gritted out. "Fuckin' hell." Those strong hands of his dragged through the textured lengths of his hair.

Drawing her arms close to her chest in a self-hug, she huddled herself into a ball like form, trying desperately to hide her tortured skin. He took one step closer. She flinched. "Stay back," she whispered.

"Shannon?" Her stomach knotted when he looked at her, with pity.

Pushing past him, she fled, darting through the kitchen like a startled deer. She ran into the bedroom, tears glittering her eyes. In a heartbeat Jamie filled the doorway. He just stood there, arms folded, mouth tight, and his eyes - they flashed with an emotion she couldn't read.

"Leave," she blurted out, turning her back to him. In a wild panic she tossed clothes from her drawers until she found a clean hoody. With shaky hands she slid her arms in the sleeves.

"No," he commanded hoarsely.

In two quick strides he towered over her trembling body, his sexy dimple nowhere to be seen. Her dripping wet hair clung to the tears streaking her cheeks, and her nostrils flared as she bit back sobs.

"What happened, Shannon?" His voice was thick and his features softened.

Her head shook slowly. No one could know. "You need to leave, Jamie. I don't want you here." She swallowed. The words lingered in her throat, drifting past the swollen lump in her throat.

His jaw clenched. "I'm not going anywhere, Shannon. You need to tell me what the fuck is going on." He crossed his arms and widened his stance. "Tell me."

She sucked in a ragged breath. "Please, Jamie. This has nothing to do with you. Just go." Her gaze fell on the ruffled bed sheets, the same sheets that she fixed neatly that morning. "Did you do that?"

The crease on his forehead deepened. "What?"

A shaky finger pointed to the rumpled bed sheets. "I made my bed this morning." Or did she? Thinking on it, she could barely remember brushing her teeth. "Forget about it. Doesn't matter."

Stretching out his hand, the pad of his thumb swept a tear from her jaw. The jerk of her head made his jaw tighten. "Sorry," she whispered.

Jamie McGrath was here, in the loft, with her. All she wanted was to feel the softness of his touch, the tenderness of his kisses, but her mind was too far away for him to reach.

Rule number one. No men.

Focus.

Trixie.

She looked up at him, fighting the need to bury her face into his chest.

"Let me in, Shannon." The tips of his track shoes nudged her toes. Her heart stuttered. "Is this why you stopped texting back?" Soft strokes swept wet strands from her cheek. She absorbed the electric sensation of his skin next to hers, initiating a flutter in her chest. "I'm not leaving until you tell me who did this to you - what did this to you? I'll fucking kill them." His voice rattled with anger, and the balled fist at his hip contracted.

"Please, go," she mumbled faintly with zero energy to project her voice.

Calmly angling forward, he scooped her up in his arms, effortlessly carrying her to the bathroom. She stiffened in his arms but didn't struggle. Setting her down on the fluffy mat at the entrance of the shower, she noted his Adam's apple bob as he gulped. He flicked on the shower and held his hand under the water waiting for it to heat up. Their eyes met. A flash of something unknown hid behind his eyes. Her head chanted warnings, but her heart begged to let him stay.

With a steady, calm touch, Jamie unzipped her breeches and dragged them passed her hips, crouching to his knees as they slouched at her ankles.

"You're wearing them."

His red boxer briefs were saturated. The only thing she had left of him, a comfort blanket. A way to keep him close. She'd lied to herself about their importance when she slipped them on earlier.

"They're comfy. That's all."

He nodded, smiling up at her with a shy smile. Her fingers landed on his broad shoulders absorbing a featherlight touch that traced the bruises on her thighs. A shuddered breath left his throat, but she kept her gaze focused on the door.

Don't look at him. Don't look down.

"Shannon," he growled. "Who hurt you?"

His gentle touch was a welcomed source of shelter to hide in. As much as she wanted him to leave, she needed him to stay. "Don't look at them," she croaked, expelling a strangled gasp. "And don't fucking pity me. I'm fine."

She let him peel off his boxer briefs and tug off her soaking wet socks, one by one. She remembered how it felt to let him take control, how Jamie asked for her trust and she willingly gave it to him, right from the start. Shannon had feelings for him. It never really was 'just sex'.

"This isn't who I am, Jamie. I'm stronger than this."
Jamie needed to know that she had strength - the girl who
fell off Trixie mid competition, broke two fingers, got
straight back in the saddle and powered on to the finishing
fence. Shannon had more guts than most men, but this
whole ordeal had broken down her defences and knocked
her self-esteem sideward like an out of control truck.

He rose to a stand, slowly putting his arms around her
torso and unhooked her bra, sharing his heat. "I know.
Being vulnerable doesn't make you weak. Surviving this,
whatever this is, makes you the strongest women I've ever
met." His lips pressed to her shoulder, and the warmth
stayed there, even after they moved away.

Shannon's body drifted closer to his chest. The
closeness felt like home, and she cursed herself for wanting
to stay there. Her saturated garment fell away, and her full
breasts bounced out. His breathing hitched, sending sparks
to her core.

Nodding towards the steamy water, Jamie held out his
hand, helping her balance as she stepped into the cubicle. A
shudder wracked her bones as the drizzling water met her
ice-cold flesh.

Jamie held back, with his bare arms wrapped across his
chest like her bodyguard, his hip resting on the counter.
"Who did that to you, Shannon?"

The corners of her mouth slid down, and her head
shook lightly. "Leave it, Jamie."

He gave her time to absorb the comforting temperature
before crouching down and selecting a bottle of body wash
from the shower tray. The cheap lavender gel that was
almost all used up, bubbled out onto his palm. It spread
between his hands when he rubbed it slowly in a circular
motion. Her eyes widened when he stood, and her chest
tightened, anticipating touch. Could she keep her
composure? Would she abandon rule number one? She was
naked, exposed and completely at his mercy.

Knowing Niall was off the scene for a few days made it
easier to let his hands roam freely over her shame and

allow him back into her life, if only for a few more hours. She craved him more than the water that warmed her bones. Niall would never know that Jamie had been back in the loft, it was their little secret.

The sensation of his palms sliding over her curves was like wild fire spreading a heat between her thighs. His eyes blazed, like he was fighting with himself to keep his hands steady. They smoothed over her skin but never reached her breasts or drifted down to her soft curls. Hesitation was followed by ragged breaths. She wasn't afraid of Jamie's touch, but she feared the feelings that were bursting inside her heart like a rainbow.

Jamie McGrath had the ability to crush her delicate heart without a second thought. She wanted to let him play in her bed, but the monster that lurked beneath was too dangerous.

The silky feel of the soap lathering over her shoulders was like heaven. Pleasurable chills flurried over her skin. Sparks blasted to every cell in her body. This was a dangerous game. She had too much to lose.

"This isn't a good idea, Jamie." She swallowed hard, backing away with no room to retreat. "You shouldn't be here."

The muscles in his jaw ticked. "I'm not going to do anything, Shannon." He continued to caress her wounds. "Relax, love."

Relenting to his magical touch, Shannon placed both hands on the tiles to steady herself. Her eyes followed the gentle movements of his hands as they floated down her thighs. This was an act of kindness, not a sexual request or a chance to seek arousal. Jamie was taking care of her the only way he knew how. For a cocky asshole who only wanted sex, this was caring, needed, right... wrong.

Chapter 29

The porcelain glow of her skin was stained by multiple purple hued wounds smudged across her back, shoulders, ribcage and down her shapely thighs. It was a painting of fucking torture. Each blemish made his stomach twist and his anger spark.

She was stunning, even with marks of violence blazoned across her body. Exquisite but fragile – like a hairline fracture on a sheet of thin ice, ready to shatter into millions of dazzlingly shards.

Even though she trusted him to wash and sooth, he knew there was a line he couldn't cross. She trusted him. The strong, stubborn woman kept giving him her trust. It didn't matter that his dick had hardened with an insatiable need to have her raw and exposed, he would never break that trust. It's the very thing that bonded them together, that's part of their connection. The missing piece to the female equation.

This shit was real. He needed answers. Like who the hell hurt her, but he also had to find out why he had to be with her from sunrise to sunset each day. A part of him needed to let her love him, but he didn't know if he could truly love her back. He doubted his ability to commit. So why did he feel this way. Torn up. Lost. Angry. Hurt. He'd gotten used to being the person she laughed with, touched, kissed and then she backed off. The flirty text messages stopped abruptly, like she ripped the band aid off a wound and left it open and stingy as hell. The fact he had been miles away from home, a day away from Shannon, made the whole situation even worse.

He endured a soul destroying flight back to Northern

Ireland. Staring at the bland cabin walls was akin to being stuck in a fucking asylum. He urged the time to go faster, but instead, each painful second passed like repeated drops of water torture.

Back on home turf, his staff had the Mustang waiting for him at the airport, ready to drive straight to Meadow Dawn. The plan was to play it cool. To arrive unannounced and charm his way back in. If he had to fight that lame ass guy, Niall, he would happily do so, and win hands down. The guy was a self-obsessed prick with a massive chip on his shoulder.

When he finally locked eyes with her, Shannon had bolted. Spurring on her horse and galloping straight into a howling storm like a woman possessed.

What he hadn't anticipated was the fire blazing in Harry's eyes when she took off. The guy actually thought Jamie was the reason she fled - or maybe it was Jamie? Did she finally find out he was a billionaire? Was his face plastered over the media with a few lucky ladies from last month? There hadn't been any reports of media attention, and Marcus had assured him he was on top of it.

Now, she was before him, vulnerable and broken, far removed from the temptress who entertained him earlier in the week. A life-changing switch had flicked, and everything had gone to shit. A secret darkened her mesmerising blue eyes, turning them the deepest shade of pain.

Secrets had a way of ripping people apart, and he would do everything in his power to tease the truth from her lips.

When she closed her eyes, his heart burst with all sorts of unknown and fucked up emotions. It was an unfamiliar feeling that scared the hell out of him. The peppermint shampoo wafted around the small bathroom. He gently rubbed her scalp with the pads of his fingers, mulling over the next move.

Once all the shampoo had swirled down the plug hole, he lifted her towelling robe from the hanger and spread it open. She tentatively stepped out, sinking her arms into the baggy sleeves. Wrapping himself around her waist from behind, he pulled the cord and tucked the robe neatly around her body, tying it loosely at the front.

"I'll put the kettle on." He backed away, drying his arms with a towel.

Shannon looked over her shoulder, gratitude swirling in her eyes. "Thank you," she muttered.

Jamie peeled off his damp tee and hung it over the hot radiator in the sitting room. She lingered in the bedroom, blow drying her hair and keeping a noticeable distance. He flicked on the kettle, leaning into the counter as the room spun with his deep set fury.

A while back he had helped his brother Marcus, rescue Lana from a sleazy murderous asshole, throwing in a few jabs and kicks when they finally caught him. Jamie easily detached himself from the whole ordeal until his brother was shot. The thought of losing Marcus still played on his mind. It still haunted him. And somehow the thought of losing Shannon was just as painful.

He was overcome by a wrath so dark and deep that it slashed open his flesh and stabbed his heart. Her pain was his pain, her vengeance was his vengeance.

The water bubbled to a boil, snapping him out of his chaotic whirlwind. The last thing he wanted was a mug of tea, fuck that, he needed something to burn down his throat and make him feel alive. The first cupboard he opened, housed a solitary bottle of unopened vodka, nothing else. Breaking the seal, he poured a large measure into the mug set out for tea. With a jerk of his chin he downed it straight without flinching.

Light footsteps carried Shannon into the galley kitchen. Having rough dried her hair, she tied it back in a messy bun at the nape. An oversized fleece drowned her torso and black sport leggings covered her bottom half. She was mummified in clothes and misery and reluctant to say why.

Turning his head, he inhaled her sweet scent and then sighed at the sorry sight. "Tea or coffee?" he asked with a quirk of his eyebrow.

Keeping her gaze glued to the kettle, she fumbled with the cuff of her sleeve. "I can manage myself, thanks. You should go now."

The girl had encountered hell, and he wasn't about to leave her alone now. "I'm sure you can, but I'm offering to make you a cup. So, what will it be, love?" His eyes burned into her false composure.

"Fine, chuck a green tea bag in then." She barely shrugged.

He poured the hot water and dunked an organic teabag into a mug, then he stepped closer with his smooth chest on show. Shannon hesitated, her eyes lingering on his muscles.

"Thanks," she mumbled, scooting past him towards the couch.

He loitered in the kitchen, this was new territory for him. She was like a caged broken bird with hidden secrets. The urge to protect her made his heart hammer, and the need to seduce her stirred in his groin.

"So, Shannon." He paused to swallow. "Did someone call in to see you?"

Silence. Her hands cupped the mug, her shoulders sagged.

"Maybe we should go away together for a few days? Give you a chance to get your head around whatever happened?" He sauntered to the side of the couch.

Her head spun around, and her brows snapped together. "No!" she spat.

He felt the vodka heat his belly, but he could feel the fury from her hot glare even more.

"Why not? You need to talk to someone, Shannon, and I'm that person. We can go away right now if you want, I'll get a chopper to collect us. Just say the word, love. I'll take care of it."

A veil of irritation shrouded her eyes like a swarm of wasps. "Who the hell do you think you are, coming in here and telling me what I need. You don't even know me, so don't pretend to care. We both know I'm just another girl to fuck."

"Shannon, wise up. You're not just some random woman."

"Well, what else am I, because I seem to remember telling you that I had no time for guys in my life, and I fucking meant it – didn't you get the memo, Jamie?" she hissed through her lying lips. "We said just sex, and I can't even give that to you now. I have nothing else to offer."

Jamie hesitated a moment, unsure if he should speak. "Come on, Shannon," he finally replied with a slight smile. "It could be more than just sex."

"Get out of here, please," she pleaded. "And out of my life. I'm sick of men like you, throwing money around like it'll solve everything. Men who think they can have all the control." She slammed her mug down on the corner table, splashing hot water over the surface. Standing tall, her petite body vibrated with fury. All her pent-up anger was projected towards Jamie, rightly or wrongly, he was in the line of fire, receiving the brunt of her break down.

He inched closer, unwilling to share with her that he didn't just have a few thousand pounds in the bank, he had one point seven billion. Now wasn't the time to share.

"Get back. I'm warning you, Jamie," she spat, balling her fists ready to fight. "I can't just go on a whim. I have responsibilities here. I've worked so hard to get where I am today, and no man is going to take that away from me, EVER! Now go!" she yelled.

The situation had quickly plummeted to the depths of despair. Jamie didn't want to leave her, especially in her current state, but she was adamant. His heart danced wildly, and adrenaline shot around his body in jolts. He scraped his nails over the scruff dusting his jaw. "Shannon, I only want to help you. I wasn't trying to take control. It was only an idea. Forget it, we can sit here together and just drink tea for the next few hours."

"Sweet Jesus, you don't get it!"

"I'm trying to help!" he demanded.

"I don't need your help, or your charity," she seethed.

Jamie rounded his shoulders and tucked his hands under his armpits. "Charity? Are you fucking serious?"

Her eyes narrowed, glaring up at him, filled with desolation. "I have a life here that you don't fit into. Stop making me like you. Stop making me want you. Just leave me alone."

Jamie's chest tightened, and he cleared his throat. "Fine." He strode to the radiator, ripped his tee off the heat and quickly dressed. Words rambled in his head, too many thoughts to say out loud.

"Jamie...." she whispered, blinking back tears. "I'm sorry. It has to be this way. I told you from the start."

"Yeah, you did, love. If I ever find out who did this to you, I'll kill the bastard myself." He stormed out to the sound of her ragged sobs.

Chapter 30

A week came and went in a haze of coffee orders, lonely bus rides and horse riding. Winter had taken hold, and the mornings were dark and wet, matching the later afternoons with no reprieve. The days were long, bleak and unappealing. Jamie McGrath was nothing but a painful memory.

"Why the heck are you so down in the dumps, Shannon?" Jess finally asked when their shift finished.

Shannon shrugged with little effort. "I'm just really tired. There's been a lot going on at the yard. I've been riding more of the horses because my boss's asshole son ran out on him. I'm tired all the time."

"Seems like more than that. Man trouble?" Jess's eyebrow quirked.

Shannon sucked in air. "You know me, I don't have time for guys, Jess."

"Girlfriend, you need to get your rocks off. You're so uptight."

Jess had a valid point. She *was* boring and drearily slipping into a dull life coma. Without Jamie, there wasn't much to look forward to, other than the riding competitions. When he left, her life reverted back to the mundane existence of all work and no play.

"Sex isn't be all and end all, you know?" Shannon protested. *Unless it's with Jamie, and then it's everything.*

"Ugh! What are you – a nun?"

"No. I just have priorities."

"You're gonna be one of those old spinster weirdos, living in a barn with chickens."

"I'm going now, little miss perfect," Shannon replied,

rolling her eyes.

Not surprisingly, Jamie hadn't been in touch. She hated herself for throwing him out when he was only trying to help. Even when he washed her in the shower, he didn't make a move. He said it could be more than just sex – what did he mean by that? It was irrelevant now anyway, being nice to her would turn the whole situation into even more of a nightmare. She was already attracted to him. A collection of emotions had already gathered in her heart; desire, need and something so strong that it nearly tore her apart when he left. Niall's threat was so very real. It was imminent. It was cruel.

The fact remained, she wanted Jamie – more than she wanted to ride.

The daily grind was pitiful, and the long bus journey home gave her too much time to wallow. At least when she got home, Trixie was there to comfort and entertain her until it was time to hide away in her small, lonely loft. She couldn't face her usual glass of wine because exhaustion was weighing her down like the entire world sat on her shoulders. Clambering under the sheets, she groaned at her own miserable mood.

The front door rattled and shook. Her spine stiffened and her hearing pricked. A thump from outside made her jolt upright. Cracking open her bedroom door, she waited, holding a breath. Her heart pumped so fast that tiny blobs danced across her vision.

"Shannon!" the male voice bellowed, alongside a further bang. "It's me, Jamie."

She tiptoed to the door, pressing her palm on the wooden slats.

"Why are you here?" she called out.

"I wanted to hangout, and this door is making it fucking hard to do that. Can you open up and let me in? It's baltic out here."

"Jamie, that's not a good idea."

"Yes, it is. Look, I'm gonna get hypothermia out here. I sent my taxi away."

Slowly stepping back, she unlocked her sanctuary and peered through the slither of space that blew a gale of chilly wind through. There he was, shivering in a pale blue tee and fitted denim jeans, worn at the knees. Those amber eyes of his swirled in the moonlight, and his killer dimple dented his cheek when he smiled shyly. Alcohol and cedarwood wafted in the breeze.

"Thanks." He pushed his way inside without waiting for an invitation. As he bounded into the heat, the whole space lit up with his presence. Or was that just her silly heart. Everything seemed brighter, and the jitters of being alone drifted to the back of her mind. She inhaled his cologne with every quick breath.

"Where's your coat?" she asked, feeling dizzy from the chaotic beats in her chest.

"Jeez, Shannon, if I thought you were going to make me stand out there all night, I would've worn a bear skin. I sent the taxi away." He rubbed his arms and blew into his cupped hands.

"Seriously, Jamie, why are you here?" she asked, grappling with her slouched tee, making sure her bruises were hidden.

Flopping down on the couch, he looked up at her with wide eyes and a half smile. "Had a few drinks after a meeting. Went home and had a few more. Got lonely and decided I had to see you." He shrugged like it was nothing to turn up unannounced to her home at midnight, reeking of booze. "Got anything to drink?" he added.

"Ugh! I was in bed." She groaned in protest. "Fine. I've got vodka or green tea."

"Baby, I ain't drinking that green shit." His lopsided grin made her involuntarily smirk.

"Just one drink, then I'll order you a taxi."

She turned away, cursing the irritating waves of excitement that rolled in her core. Pouring a slosh of vodka, she slowly walked back to him. Jamie had already made himself comfortable, by kicking off his shoes. He gifted her with a quick wink, invoking a sudden delicious shiver.

"Cheers!" He held the glass up and nodded towards her before sinking the whole lot.

"Were you celebrating?" she asked, perching on the arm of the couch.

He held her gaze for a second, with a glimmer of something she couldn't decipher swirling in his honeyed eyes. Patting the empty space between him, he flipped his left ankle up to rest on his right knee. "I wanted to see you. Let's watch television, got any good movies?"

"I have to get up early."

"Me too. Sit with me, Shannon, please." His captivating sultry tone seemed huskier after a round or two of drinks.

"Fine."

Shannon sank into the couch, her thigh nudging his. She didn't want to enjoy the delightful pressure of the contact or give in to the thrum of excitement powering through her. Nor did she want to look left, to fall into the irresistible charm that sucked her in every damn time. "I've got Netflix."

"I'm starving. How about one of those amazing bacon sandwiches? I'll make it?" he suggested with an ever so slight slur.

Her insides cringed, she was unprepared and the worst hostess. "I haven't been to the shop. What about a packet of potato chips?"

"Nah, it's okay. I'll order a pizza." He pulled out his phone and rang through an order for the biggest pizza in the world. "Hope they can get that thing through the door!" His laugh rumbled in the air and settled on her skin with a pleasurable sizzle.

"Why are you really here?" She glanced at him out of the corner of her eye, keeping her back stiff.

His legs stretched out, and he dragged his fingers through the textured cut of his hair. "Truthfully..." He sighed. "I couldn't get you out of my head." His lips curved at one corner. "I think about you all the time, Shannon."

A flurry of prickles skittered down her spine. "I'm sure

you have plenty of women to think about. You're only here tonight because I'm something you can't have. That makes you want it even more. That's all, Jamie."

He shrugged. "That's not true," he answered quickly and directly. "I've already had you. Remember?"

She remembered alright and thinking about it now was too dangerous. She wouldn't let her mind go there. He was setting a trap. "I threw you out. You shouldn't be here."

Shannon studied his perfect side profile, with plush lips that glistened, and a strong curved jaw scattered with fawn bristles. The television clicked on, bringing a wave of sound into the quiet room. With his gaze focused on the list of movies, she dared herself to reach out and touch him. To run her fingers through his thick hair while straddling his taut powerful thighs, right here, right now. No, that's his plan. He's only here for sex.

"Yeah. You did throw me out, but I know you didn't really mean it." He turned around and winked with cocky confidence, then drew his gaze back to the television.

"I did mean it," she countered, feeling a swell mount between her legs.

His molten eyes cut back to hers. "Shan, you and I both know there's something going on here."

"Jamie." Her heart paused. Was it true, was there something happening? Did he really feel it too? Or was this just the game, the charm offensive - the end goal. "I've already told you. I've nothing to offer you anymore."

Ignoring her plea, he grabbed the remote control. "I like gangster, vampire and action, or porn. Let's see what's on."

"I like action," she added, leaning back, absorbing the feeling of safety that he brought with him. He was here now, and the pizza would arrive in a few minutes. After that, she'll ask him to leave.

Jamie scrolled through the list. "This one is cool. It's scary but you can cuddle into me if you need to." He smirked without looking for a reaction. "I'll always protect you."

Did he mean that?

"I doubt it's that scary," she muttered, slipping her hands into the pocket of her hoody to stop herself from touching him. Even when he smirked, she wanted to lick the sexy dimple off his chiselled cheek.

By the time the movie started, his mobile phone buzzed. "The pizza guy is outside. He can't find us. Wait here." He sauntered to the front door and disappeared, returning moments later with a huge flat box. "Smells good, huh?" He set the pizza box on the wooden floor, grabbing a slice and held it up. "Here ya go, Shan. Ladies first." Their fingers brushed, his jaw clenched, and his hand retreated without uttering a word.

Her tummy gurgled. When was her last meal? "Thanks." She swallowed down the flutters, ordering them to back the fuck off so she could keep her guard up.

Slumping into the couch with his own slice of pizza, he sank his teeth straight in. This time he stared at the TV screen without surveying her every mouthful. An odd feeling settled in her gut. Did she want to tease him with soft happy groans? Or was she just crushed that he decided to ignore them.

They sat together in silence. Shannon noted how his body tensed when she shifted position and how his breathing hitched when her shoulder pressed into his arm. She couldn't recall a time when she had done something as simple as watch a movie with a guy. Niall wasn't that type of boyfriend. He preferred eating at fancy restaurants and tossing his cash around for show. Tiredness swept over her body making her eyes involuntarily roll. Her arms became heavy, and her cheek crept down to his chest. A powerful arm snaked her shoulder and fingers lightly stroked the lengths of her hair. The sound of his quickened heartbeat lulled her to sleep.

***

Sunlight burst through the tiny skylight in the kitchen, stirring her from peaceful dreams. Blinking rapidly, she realised the firm chest her face nuzzled into was Jamie McGrath's.

Nudging free from his hold, she took a minute to gaze at his beautiful features. The curve of his lips, the tawny prickles shadowing his jaw and dark lashes resting on his cheeks.

Her heart bucked almost cracking a rib. Warning drums battered and banged to the same erratic rhythm. What if Niall came back and saw Jamie leave? Lifting off the sofa, his hand suddenly grabbed her wrist. "Please, tell me you have coffee?" he mumbled.

Tingles scattered down her spine when his eyes slowly opened and his sleepy gaze found her flushed face.

"I've got green shit." She smirked, pulling away.

Jamie sat up and rested his arms on his knees. His hair was messy and his expression coy, almost reticent. "I didn't mean to fall asleep here, Shan. I'm sorry. You looked so peaceful, so beautiful. I didn't want to wake you up. I just sorta fell asleep too."

"It's okay. There's coffee out in the staff room. I'll go get it." She wanted to scout the yard for any sign of Niall and check on Trixie, just in case.

"Don't worry about."

"It's no trouble. I'll be right back."

Chapter 31

Shannon bolted out the door still wearing her track pants and baggy tee. All of sudden he felt aware of his intrusion. The drinks coaxed him to call her, but he knew she wouldn't pick up. So he took the drunken bull by the horns and jumped in a taxi.

The plan seemed plausible, at the time. Just swing by and say hi, but when he finally got there, he didn't want to leave. His boozy plan to seduce her, quickly evaporated the second he saw her sallow face and the dark crescents under her eyes. Then she actually fell asleep on his chest. All soft and warm and contented. The combination of her shallow breathing mixed with the sensation of her warm body so close to his... There was nowhere else on earth where he'd rather be. Not in Vegas, not in his hotels, not with his friends, no, he wanted to be right there, with Shannon Colter sleeping on his chest.

He lifted from the couch and ruffled his hair. Opening every kitchen cupboard door, on the hunt for food, which revealed bare shelves. She didn't just need to nip to the shops for a few groceries, she needed to fill every cupboard. There was nothing to eat, apart from cereal crumbs and one bag of potato chips. He quickly dialled the local café and negotiated an urgent order for delivery, paying a hundred pounds extra to ensure breakfast arrived warm and within the next half hour.

The door clicked shut, and she ambled in sheepishly. "Got it!" Her smile lit up his hangover.

"Hope you don't mind, but I ordered breakfast." He put the kettle under the running tap water.

"Really? I didn't know anywhere in the village

197

delivered?" Her arms folded over her chest as she lifted her brows to match her surprise.

"Eh, yeah." He kept his eyes low, not willing to spill the beans on their overpriced order.

"I need to freshen up. I usually jump in the shower after I've cleaned out the stables. You can take one before you leave, if you like." She leaned against the counter with silky soft hair flowing over her shoulders and blushed cheeks from the cold air.

If at all possible, her eyes were even more piercing than before, and a natural sweet smile blessed her sexy as sin, cherry red lips.

"Thanks, Shan. How are you? It's been a long week."

Her eyes dropped. "I'm fine. Really busy with riding and working at Coffee Kicks."

"You've got fuck all in your cupboards. You should look after yourself better."

"I haven't had the time, that's all. I'll go later."

"I'll go for you. Write me a list of things you need."

Her eyes popped. "No, it's okay. I'll go tomorrow."

"Come on, Shan, let me help you."

"Like I said, Jamie, I don't need your money."

"You can give me the money."

"Don't worry about it. I'll probably go up to Harry's for dinner tonight." Her lips pursed and the tone of her voice dropped. He knew she was lying, and he also suspected that she didn't have either the money or the inclination to go food shopping.

"I'm going to get ready now. I've got chores to do." She kept her gaze low as she walked past him.

"No worries."

Shannon left him alone in the kitchen, waiting for the food order. He knew she was naked behind the closed door, and it was busting his balls to not kick the damn thing open. Pacing the floor, he gathered himself together. Paying her a midnight visit was the last thing he should've done.

It didn't take long for the order to arrive. The entire

breakfast bar was filled with food. Shannon pottered back into view with her hair scraped back in a low ponytail, skin tight navy breeches clinging to her curves and an old hoody shamefully covering her perfect hourglass figure. His heartbeat skipped when her eyes flicked from the breakfast spread to meet his.

"I made you breakfast, Shan." He winked.

Her lips pulled in, holding back a smirk. "That's some feast. I'm sorry, I can't eat too much before I ride, or I'll be sick."

She swiped a rasher of bacon from a towering heap and took a bite. "Tastes good."

He stood, blocking her exit. "Can we do this again?"

She gulped down the last mouthful of bacon. "Don't, Jamie."

"We'll take it slow." He stroked her arm, squeezing her hand as his fingers grasped, but she pulled away before their fingers could join.

"I need to focus on myself. I've been honest with you from the start."

"I know you feel something for me."

"It doesn't matter."

A simmering anger flickered in his chest. "Fuckin' hell, it does." His knuckles skimmed her pale cheek, and his lips hovered, debating a tender kiss. Hoping she would lean in, praying he could taste her one more time.

Her gaze lingered on his lips, lasting for a moment until she freed her breath and stepped back. Nibbling the inside of her cheek was a clear indication that her resistance was wavering.

With a quick swipe of her tongue she moistened those taunting lips of hers, just as her pupils flared. She had a look in her eyes that begged him to taste her, yet her back remained rigid and folded arms protected her heart.

In a flash, he reached out, grabbed her wrists and jerked her into his chest. She sucked in air like he'd winded her, but they both knew it was the thick cloud of lust filling her lungs. The intense thrum of her pulse vibrated in the dip of her throat, matching the rapid heartbeat that hammered against his ribs. Sliding his hands to her soft cheeks, Jamie secured her head in place. He gazed down at her, holding his breath momentarily as he felt himself sink under the surface of her stormy eyes. Light puffs left her nostrils, caressing his skin like a lover's sigh. Shannon was relenting, her breasts pressing against him with silent permission. Her fingers followed the hem of his tee, until they rested on his hips and tightened.

This was it, the lonely days dreaming about her lips ended here. With a long sweep, he licked her top lip, lifting it from her teeth. His stomach flipped. A low whimper whooshed from her mouth teasing his limited restraint. Then he covered her soft lips with his mouth and savoured the silky warmth that felt like heaven amidst the tormented hell she had captured him in.

Their lips grazed and brushed with a delicate pressure, not too hard and not too rough. Just enough to make his head dizzy with need and his dick nudge into her hip. Seductive sucks and bites drove him wild until he drew back. Staring down at the dark lashes fanning her cheeks, he silently studied her plush top lip, with its perfect cupid bow that made her lips look pouty even when she was mad at him. They were naturally blushed and juicy, so much so, that he craved to feel them on his dick all over again.

Her eyes pinged open, revealing dazzling blue gems that glistened with wide eyed wonder. His mouth crashed down again, deepening to a hungry frenzied kiss that opened the door to her body and promised more to follow. Their lips clung together, tasting and devouring, while his tongue teased with a playful wickedness. Shannon tasted even better than he remembered, even more sweet and satisfying.

"I have to go," she mumbled into his teeth, breaking the seductive torture. "Don't make this any harder than it already is." She lifted her hands to his, tugging at his palms for freedom.

"I want more," he said huskily. "You have to admit it,

Shan, you want it too."

"No, no, I don't." She shuffled back putting space between them.

His brow creased with a pained expression because his dick was begging to get out of his trousers, and she was ordering it to stay put. She was shutting him out again. Pushing him away.

Sliding him an apologetic look, her gaze drifted from his crotch to her toes.

"Shannon, don't do this," he barked, almost losing touch with himself as anger shook his hands.

The slight curve of her mouth was meant as a smile, but she just looked dejected instead. "It's for the best."

Jamie dragged his hands down his prickled cheeks and growled with frustration. "Tell me what the fuck has got you so messed up?" The loud tone of his voice boomed.

She yanked the cuffs of her hoody over her hands. "Don't push this, Jamie. Just take the fucking hint and move on. Find some other girl to fool around with. Like I said, it's for the best."

"The best for who?" he demanded, reaching for her wrists.

Stepping out of reach, she tucked a strand of hair behind her ear and said softly, "It's best for the both of us."

"Bullshit!" Jamie's turbulent gaze burned into her pale face. "That kiss was so much more, Shannon, and you damn well know it."

Her startled eyes grew wide and dark. "Don't, Jamie. Just don't. You shouldn't have come here. What we had was just sex. You offered it. I agreed. I don't want it anymore. The fun's over now. Please, just go." She put her hands up towards his chest to stop him from getting any closer.

Jamie took a second to process the words she blurted out. "I don't believe you." He scowled. "You mean to tell me that you'll be happy this will be over the minute I walk out of here?" His voice was tight and strained.

Her blue eyes were filled with swirling emotion and

pain. "Yes," she said with an unconvincing murmur.

He almost dared her to say it again. To make her deny their connection wasn't real. She turned her head away. "I've got to go now."

Adrenaline buzzed through him. He wanted to push her up against the wall and force her into submission, but he just stood there, stunned, hurt and angry.

With lowered eyes and a cool, sedate tone, her voice broke through his internal debate. "Thanks for ordering breakfast. Take the leftovers with you."

He glanced at the mountain of fresh food, feeling his hunger slip to the soles of his feet. "You can keep it. I've lost my appetite." Slotting his hands into his pockets, his shoulders drew back. "See ya, Shannon," he said huskily before side stepping her completely.

As he marched to the door, her eyes searched frantically, and her chest rose in quick bursts, but he just left, like she told him to.

Chapter 32

A blustery storm howled through the yard, rattling buckets and creaking old beams. Shannon checked her phone on route to the coat hooks in the loft. The subtle drop of her heart was of no surprise. Could she really blame the guy for his five day silence? Especially after she dished out the means and told him to leave, again. In fact, she more or less hitched him up by the boxer briefs and froze off his nuts with her ice-cold expression.

She longed to catch the scent of his manly cologne and watch his cheek dent with the sexy dimple that made her swoon. They'd only known each other for a short time, but he was right, there had always been something more to their passionate kisses. They burned through her core, searing her veins with an intense need that she nearly melted all over his flexed body.

One thing she knew for sure, Niall was going to pay dearly for messing with her. A glimmer of hatred rattled her bones when she thought about his unwanted return. If only she could fix that problem, then maybe Jamie would take her back. Keeping Trixie safe was the issue.

Swaddling up in a padded jacket and beanie, she braced herself when the wind blew through the open front door. There on the doorstep sat a hefty cardboard box. It had a courier label slapped on the front with an arrow and the words, 'this way up only'. Her name was emblazoned in black marker. Shunting it inside, she debated opening it. What if it was from Niall? What of it was a nasty warning, or a bribe? Then she caught herself, Niall wasn't that smart.

The box was heavy but easily skimmed along the wooden floor. Slicing along the tape, she lifted the flaps and pulled out the wad of filling stuffed in at the top. Beneath the protective layer was a sturdy hamper. She heaved it out, staggering back with the weight and slammed it down. Unbuckling the leather straps, she peered in, gasping at the luxury goods packed tightly in cellophane. It was crammed full of essentials from fancy cheeses, to croissants, and even a bottle of rich tomato sauce. There was a decanter of freshly squeezed orange juice, pressed in Italy, apparently one day ago, and to the side was a small jar of gourmet maraschino cherries. The crazy flutter in her chest made her giddy. Jamie. He hadn't given up on her.

She flipped the lid closed and ran her fingertips along the bumps of woven willow, noting the initials JMcG etched on a gold rectangle. Her heart cracked open and tears pooled her eyes.

The thoughtful gift was just what she needed. It was like he instinctively knew she still hadn't bought any groceries. And even though she fooled herself into believing they were over, they were still connected.

Leaving the hamper, she braved the night chill, trotting down the stone steps and into the yard. When she reached Trixie's stable, the first thing she noticed was the empty hook where her head collar should hang. It was second nature for Shannon to hang the head collar up after use. So why wasn't it there? Maybe Bucky was cleaning them all.

"Hey, girl," she said softly, peering in at the sleepy horse. Trixie was safe and content.

A chill flurried down her spine, and she spun around to find an empty yard. The steady beat of her pulse began to strum faster, and she felt uneasy, like eyes were all over. Shadows danced as the wind shifted. The weather vane spun and squeaked like a rusty wheel. A thunderous thud made her heart jump and she pressed her back to the wall. Suddenly Jackson bolted out of the night's shadows, all legs and vigour with a small plastic tub in his jaws. His nails tapped the moonlit cobbles until he stopped in his tracks and stared right at her. After a beat and a whirl of the wind, he darted away with his prize for Harry. Her boots splashed in puddled rainwater when she ran across the yard and bounded up the steps back to the loft.

The warmth and soft lighting in the loft was a welcomed reprieve from the silvery glow and gales outside. Locking the door, she eyed the luxury hamper. Shannon had always been capable of taking care of herself, but his gift was more thoughtful and considerate than charity.

She wanted to tell him everything.

***

The following morning Shannon found another present waiting on her doorstep with a signed card from Jamie McGrath. The second box was packed with jars of bright red candied lips that tasted sweet like cherries. Her doorstep surprises were respite from a relentless storm. Shannon was the anchor at the bottom of a cold murky ocean and each present was a link in the chain leading to Jamie's warmth and safety. His persistence shone a ray of light into her darkness.

Could he help her? Would it make everything worse if he knew? She debated the most important question of all, could she allow herself to be indebted to him? They weren't together. He wasn't the settling down type, but he had enough money to buy Trixie and remove her from Meadow Dawn – and Niall.

The internal struggle continued throughout her evening shift at Coffee Kicks. While Shannon poured coffee, she weighed up the pros and cons. Jamie had offered her the money to buy Trixie. It was a daunting idea to loan that amount of cash from him, to owe him, but every time she considered her next move, she agreed with herself that he was her only hope. She was ready to risk it all and tell him everything.

After working for four hours solid, with only a quick break, Shannon began to count the change in the cash register so she could close up a few minutes early. Jess had spent the last hour of her shift applying layers of makeup and strip lashes for student night at the local club. She bounced off a few minutes early when her boyfriend showed up. Shannon had urged them to leave when she was forced to witness the guy ramming his tongue down the poor girl's throat. It was like watching a Python swallowing a kitten.

She flicked off the music and grabbed her coat. Nearing the door, she hit the lights. Darkness fell on the over turned chairs that rested on the tables. The orange street lights shone brightly, casting pretty streaks across the tiled floor. The door opened behind her.

"We're closed." Her head flicked back over her shoulder, and her deep breath held in her lungs.

"Well, aren't you the busy little bitch."

The breath gusted from her lips. "Niall. What the hell are doing here?"

Darkness covered his face with only the whites of his eyes glowing with a menacing glint. "I'm staying clear of the yard for a while. I've got a crash pad here in the city where I can do whomever I want."

"Yeah, snort as much coke as you want too," she sneered. Her bold reaction shocked her after feeling on edge from constantly looking over her shoulder. She wasn't scared this time, she was pissed off at his arrival back into her life.

"Are you judging me? Shannon Colter the gold digger."

"I don't give a fuck what you think of me, Niall."

He moved closer. "Well you should. I told you to stay away from that bastard, McGrath. Do you think I'm stupid? Did you think I wouldn't know that he was in the loft again, or that he was sending food parcels. I mean, how pathetic are you when the rich guy has to send you food. Aren't you embarrassed? I always thought you had more pride than that."

Rage mounted in her belly, and her palm shot out, striking him across the cheek. The sound cracked through air like a gun shot. His head flinched to the side, but the low threatening laugh that followed chilled her bones.

Suddenly a cold sharp edge was at her throat. The

glistening point bit into her skin when he moved around behind her, holding the blade closer to the curve of her neck. "Phone him. Now."

"Why?" Her breath juddered.

"It would be such a shame if that silly old daddy of his actually went missing. The old man is a dumbass, right? He could just disappear one day. Poof." He emphasised the word, blowing hot air into her face. "Phone the rich bastard and tell him to stop sending you stupid gifts. And Shannon…" Her chest rose and fell with fury. "If he comes back to my yard once more time, I'll shoot the fucking horse."

"You can't threaten me, Niall. I'm sick of your shit."

The knife dug in harder. "I can. And, I think you'll just find that I did. Phone him so I can hear you cut the feet from under him."

"No, Niall. No." She sobbed. "Why do you hate him so much?"

"I don't hate him, Shan. I fucking hate you," he said through a chuckle. "You think you're better than me. You always have. Even my dad thinks of you as family. Shannon did this. Shannon did that. Shannon did a shit and it fucking sparkled." He mocked. "It makes my skin break out in hives." His hand wrapped her waist jerking her back into his chest. "Get your phone out and ring him, or George will go missing and darling Trixie will get her legs done in."

"I hate you, Niall. I hate you." Sliding the phone from her pocket, she lifted it high so she could find Jamie's name, all the while still being held too close to Niall.

It rang twice. "Shannon. How are you?" Jamie's voice was husky and inviting like he was surprised and glad to hear her voice.

I'm not okay. Jamie, I don't' want to do this. "Please don't send anymore presents." Her words were shaky.

After a beat he replied, "Shannon, what's wrong? Where are you?"

The knife tightened against her throat. She knew what

Niall was capable of, hidden scars were his specialty. "Did you think sending me food would make you my hero?" She bit back a sob. "That it would make me fall for you?" Silent tears rolled down her face. "You can't buy me, Jamie." When she said his name, her voice wavered. Niall yanked her head back further until her neck was completely vulnerable.

"Finish it once and for all," he whispered in her ear.

The heat of his close contact made her stomach heave. Slowly he released her head so she could talk.

"Shannon…"

"Look. Get the fucking hint, Jamie. You don't know me. I don't know you. It was just random sex. Now back the fuck off." She ended the call before he heard the breath shudder from her lungs and the sobs bubble from her throat.

"Good girl." Niall lowered the blade. "Just remember. I'm right here. Watching and waiting." He slotted the knife into his pocket and turned away. The doorbell chimed as it swung closed behind him.

Shannon sank to the floor. Her heart broken. Her body shaking. Her mind dizzy with hatred.

It was over.

Chapter 33

It had been a week of hell. The gifts stopped arriving. Her phone never beeped. Shifts at Coffee Kicks dragged, and even riding had lost its thrill. Shannon was going through the motions. Trudging through life feeling empty and numb.

The bus hurtled away from Belfast. Shannon huddled in the back seat with her hood up, mulling over her options. What were her options? Tell Harry that his son had beaten her, threatened her at knife point that he'd kill Trixie and hurt Jamie's dad... why would he believe her? What possible reason is there for Niall to do those things other than the fact he was an asshole. *'Hey, Harry, your son is an asshole. How about you kick him out and forget he exists?'* Blood is thicker than water. The only other option, if she could face it, was to leave. To move out of the loft and wave goodbye to her career and the commitment she made to herself to succeed. Is that what Niall wanted all this time? Was he that jealous of her relationship with Harry that he was forcing her hand to run away?

The biting air stung her cheeks when she finally jumped off the bus. A light dusting of frost sparkled on the wooden fence lining the lane way snaking towards Meadow Dawn. Stones crunched underfoot, and her fingertips tingled until she slid them further up her sleeves. A flurry of white air bellowed from her mouth with every determined quick step. Close to the yard, she noted a huge glossy purple horse lorry with the name 'Ashfield' scripted along the side. Picking up pace, she jogged to the car park and opened the side door at the living quarters. "Mitch? You there?" she called. No response.

A murmur of voices suddenly drifted around the yard as she drew closer to the paddock. There he was, Mitchell Ashfield, cantering a stunning dappled grey horse around a course of jumps. Its tale flicked and swooshed when the powerful hooves hit the dirt after each effortless jump. She ambled to Harry's side, crouching down to snuggle Jackson's wiry muzzle.

"Why is Mitchell here?" She kissed the dog and stood, waving over to the handsome man who let his horse open up into a gallop at the long side of the paddock.

Harry clapped his hands. "She's a beauty, Mitch!" he said turning to face her with a broad smile. "That's his new mare. She's an ex race horse. He plans to compete on her next year. What do you think?"

"She certainly knows how to jump." Effortlessly, with grace and agility.

Mitchell walked his horse to the partition, letting the reins slacken. "Hey, Shannon, it's great to see you again. How are you getting on with Venatrix?"

"Really well, thanks. I've secured my place in the finals, so you better watch out!" She giggled.

"I knew you would, but don't expect me to back off just because there's a new kid in town," he roared with a wide toothy smile. "It's all out warfare from here." He smirked.

Mitchell was only twenty-five, a good-looking guy in his own way, with a strong square jaw and kind grey eyes. He came from money, which always surprised her because he was kind. Rumours were rife about his roguish way with the ladies, but Shannon never saw any malice in the guy. There were no sexual sparks electrifying the air between them, only competitive rivalry and taunts. She admired his riding career and aspired to reach the same level.

"You don't need to back off, Mitch, I enjoy the competition. Bring it on!" She smiled warmly.

He nodded, tilting the peak of his velvet helmet as the horse sauntered past them. "I'll drink to that. Speaking of which." He angled his torso and the horse began to loop back around. "How about you both join me at The Curragh race track tomorrow. It's the Champions Weekend? I've got a few tickets in the van."

Before she could decline, Harry answered on her behalf. "That's a great idea, Mitch. This one needs a day out." He nudged his head to the side gesturing towards her with a silly look on his face. If only he knew why she'd become a recluse and reserved.

"Brilliant. It's a fun day out, Shannon. I'll get the tickets once I've loaded Minstrel into the lorry."

Shannon groaned and her shoulders slumped subtly. She would have to plaster on a fake smile and be sociable. There was also the small issue, or rather huge issue, of an outfit... to hide the fading bruises. Champions Weekend meant elegance and style. Any outfit she picked would have to safeguard the unsightly marks.

***

It was the morning before race day. Shannon had asked Jess to help her pick out an outfit. An overcast sky darkened the streets of Belfast, matching her clouded mood. A haze of drizzle not only dampened her clothes but her already jaded energy too. Every step took effort and each thought lost its way in the brain fog. She was exhausted. Drained. Lacklustre. Simple things had become a chore. And today, the last place on earth she wanted to be, was Belfast, with Jess, in a swanky shop that sold highly priced classy clothes.

"What style are you after? Long or short? Sexy or modest?" Jess slid a coat hanger along the rack, rubbing metal to metal making a shrill screech.

Shannon laughed lightly, tucking a messy strand behind her ear. "Dunno." She shrugged without care. "I asked for your help so you could pick. I guess something young and sexy without a lot of skin on show. I'm going VIP so I need to look the part."

A wide smile stretched across Jess's face. "And what's the budget? Are you talking all out big bucks, or move on to the next shop?" she whispered, leaning close enough to

211

smell her minty chewing gum.

"Harry gave me his credit card. I didn't want to take it, but he insisted." Her smile tightened. The man had never handed over his plastic to her or anyone else. Harry was eternally frugal but clearly lavish when he wanted to be. He practically forced her to take his credit card. Apparently spending money is good for the soul and wearing nice clothes can lift the spirits. She told him it was bullshit but relented when he scowled like an angry father.

"Got yourself a sugar daddy there, Shannon?" Jess slid her a knowing glance with brows waggling.

"Wise up. It's not like that." She scowled.

Jess ran her fingers over the glamorous garments, one by one. "Oh yeah, that's right, you were shagging his son, weren't you?"

Icy chills raced down her back. "Yeah." That's all she could say on the matter.

The soft chuckle bubbling from Jess was wasted because Shannon was lost in her thoughts, recalling Niall's threats and the biting sting of his blade. "Loosen up. We're shopping, not having an ingrown toenail removed."

Ingrown toenail? Why those words snapped her away from Niall was unknown, but they did. "Why are we talking about ingrown toenails, Jess?"

Her friend's narrow shoulders bounced. "Just. My Nana has one. She said it was worse than child birth. The look on your face was a picture. Like you were thinking about killing someone."

"Maybe I was," she muttered, crossing her arms tight across her chest.

Jess strolled across the shop floor, flicking her head over her shoulder to look back. "Be prepared to get the wow factor, girlfriend. I'm going to transform you like pretty woman."

Cocking her brow, Shannon puckered her lips. "We've gone from sugar daddy to prostitution. Why did I ask for your help?"

Green fabric whirled through the air. "Because I have

style, and you, my friend, dress like a boy. Not just a boy, a drab, boring penniless boy."

"Seriously, Jess. Keep the fucking insults rolling in. Kick me while I'm still breathing." She huffed. "Just hurry up and find something that covers my boy body."

"I didn't say you had a boy body, grumpy guts. Your curves are killer, and you'll see that in the right dress." Dangling a hanger from her forefinger, she asked, "This one?"

It was short, sexy, black and sparkly. Everything she loved in a dress but her thighs would hang out the bottom, exhibiting twelve or more welts. "Nope. A bit longer."

Sooner or later, she would have to enter the dreaded changing rooms. Her ribs tightened. What if Jess saw the bruises and asked questions?

"Seriously, where do you go in that head of yours, Shannon?" She hadn't noticed Jess land beside her with an arm weighed down under reams of material the colours of the rainbow. "It's like your brain is only functioning on one percentage battery power."

Shannon traipsed behind the walking wardrobe that chatted insistently about the cut and shape versus the right material. This was why she hated shopping, being bored and the unforgiving lighting in the changing rooms.

"Ugh!" Shannon groaned when she was thrust inside the cubicle. The curtain whooshed across, and the spotlight flooded her pallid cheeks, highlighting purplish crescents under her bleary eyes. She was surprised her eyelids even had the zest to stay open. Her jeans hit the floor first, then her fiddly cardigan buttons slowly popped open. The woman staring back at her was distant, haggard and sad. Angular hip bones jutted sharply, and the lines of her ribs were more prominent than usual. A constant wave of nausea made eating unappealing. "I guess this is what heartbreak looks like," she whispered to herself, shocked by her weight loss. An unflattering paleness gave an unhealthy gaunt look, never mind the bruising that scattered her skin like dying constellations.

The curtain flung open. Jess's feline eyes bugged. "Holy fuck, Shannon. Those aren't... What the actual fuck are they? Boxer briefs? I was half joking when I said you dress like a boy..."

A nervous giggle hummed in Shannon's throat. Her cheeks flushed to a colourful raging crimson. *They're Jamie's.* "They're for riding," she lied.

This scenario wasn't meant to happen. She never imagined her friend bursting in on top of her or that Jess would have the chance to see her underwear. Crouching down, she snatched her balled cardigan and held it to her chest.

Jess's gaze wandered. Resting a hand on her hip, her face contorted. "No wonder you're single, girl. Is there something you want to tell me? Is this some fetish thing?"

Kind of... yes. A Jamie McGrath fetish.

Shannon clucked her tongue. "I'm single because I choose to be. So, leave it." Enough said.

A suspicious look flashed across Jess's scrunched face and Shannon knew only too well what was coming next. "And those bruises. I know you work with horses but, Shan, you're never gonna get a fella looking like that under your clothes." She wagged her finger back and forth and hitched up her chin.

"Like I said, I don't want a guy anytime soon. So we're good here, okay. Let's just focus on the dress and get the hell out of here. I'm tired, and I hate shopping. I'll buy you lunch as a thank you for helping me." She sounded like Jamie. His words were ingrained in her memory, his smile in her pulsating heart.

Jess cleared her throat, trailing her eyes over Shannon's bare legs. "You hate shopping and taking care of yourself. You have such potential."

Shannon clicked her fingers. "Eyes, Jess. Up here. A dress. Focus on the task at hand."

"Not until you agree to a spray tan."

"No! I don't want to look like an orange."

"You won't. I promise. My mate does a super natural

one. It'll mask those unsightly…" Her hand waved at Shannon's legs and her nose scrunched. "Those… bruises. You'll look like you've just come back from Spain. Pinkie swear."

The idea had merit, if it actually looked natural and helped disguise Niall's torture. "Fine, but if I look like I've been rolled in shit, I'll kill you with my own bare hands," she warned.

With a quirk of her lips and a fake gasp, Jess stepped back. "That's just gross, Shannon."

"Why are you still staring at me?"

Clapping her hands repeatedly, Jess grinned. "You're going to look incredible." The curtain bellowed behind her as she left Shannon alone again with only her pitiful reflection.

She released a long gust of air, puffing out her cheeks. Shannon slumped against the wall. "Please get me out of here." Her palms dragged down her face.

After an hour of arguments, they finally agreed on something. A teal figure skimming dress with foil finished bodice that felt luxurious against her achy ribs, fitting the curves and dips of her silhouette and ending at her ankles with a slit to her thigh. Luckily it was on her good side, the side that she laid on during Niall's tirade. To top it all off, a pair of delicate sheer sleeves covered her shame.

Fanning her face with her palms, Jess's eyes misted. "WOW! Just wow."

Harry was right. Money felt good. "This is it. We've found the one!"

Chapter 34

Race day arrived. Niall was still hiding out in Belfast, or wherever his scrawny ass fell after partying. The spray tan had mostly swirled down the plug hole in the shower, but the remaining layer gave her a sun kissed glow like she really had been on holiday. The dark semi circles under her eyes had faded, and the hateful marks seemed less obvious.

The fabric glided over her freshly moisturised skin and fastened at the back with a discreet zipper. She paired it with fine silver strappy sandals and a matching clutch, opting to let her hair flow freely. With a light dusting of bronzer, a swoosh of mascara and a slick of gloss, Shannon was ready.

In contrast to her sickly reflection yesterday, today she looked and felt like a million dollars. For the first time in days, she smiled. Jamie was a happy memory and best kept locked away. He'd never find out about Niall and his threats to hurt his father because it was over. George and Trixie were safe and Jamie had moved on. Everyone was happy. The slow sigh and juddered breath, threatened tears. Shannon wasn't happy. She was merely surviving.

A car horn tugged her away from the loft. The morning sun tried to poke through a misty haze, and the chilly air mocked warmth, being a degree or two milder than the past few days.

"Holy shit, Shan. Is that really you? You look like a movie star!" The creases at the corners of Harry's eyes deepened, and his smile reached his ears when he peered out from the back of the car. "You're a pretty wee thing in jodhpurs, my girl, but I have to say, you sure as hell scrub up well." The look on his face was like a father on his daughter's wedding day.

Shannon hoisted the dress to her shins and sank into the rear passenger seat beside him. "Isn't it amazing what a false tan and a few bucks can do." She winked.

"Shannon, the tan only brightens your already beautiful face. You always make me so damn proud." His voice wavered on the last word.

She glanced over. "Harry, are you crying?" she mocked playfully.

"I don't cry." His laughed wheezed from too many rolled up cigarettes. "My son is an asshole. He missed out on the best damn thing he ever had – you." The car rolled forward, and his palm covered her hand with a tight squeeze. "You deserve better than him anyway."

Apprehension prickled her scalp at the mere mention of Niall. "Hmmm." She barely acknowledged his comment.

Please don't talk about him today. Don't ruin this. Don't make me tell you.

"Right, then, brandy?" he suggested cheerfully, lightening the mood that had taken a dip. Harry reached for the crystal decanter positioned on the shelf behind the driver and poured a large measure. "I bought you a bottle of champagne. You can have the day off tomorrow."

Looking at his worn face, Shannon noted the kindness and honesty in his eyes. She exhaled softly and called upon her inner strength to get her through the day. "I'm sure I could have one day off." A light smile tugged her lips when the corked popped free.

"I'm glad you came today, Shan. Maybe you and Mitch will get together. He's always had an eye for you." Harry's bushy brows slid up.

Angling her head to the side to look him face on, she scowled. "Don't play match maker, Harry. You know my career comes first."

Harry hummed a low chuckle. "You're certainly dedicated to a fault."

Taking a sip of bubbles, her eyes rolled and her tummy flipped as the alcohol settled on her tongue. "We've worked too hard to mess it up with boyfriends and all that nonsense."

"There will come a time, Shan, when you need someone by your side. You can't walk this world alone. We all need a companion."

"Oh, Harry. Why would I need a silly boyfriend when I've got you to keep me company!" she said softly through a light laugh. "You know me better than my own parents."

"I'm an old man, Shan. You need a man your own age. Someone who will take you out and treat you like a princess."

"I don't need a guy, Harry, and I'm certainly not a princess."

"You look like one today." He smiled, clinking his glass to the side of her champagne flute. He was completely oblivious to the demons in her head and the barriers she placed around her heart.

"Have you heard from Niall?" he asked suddenly.

Shit. Why is he asking that? He knows there's no love lost between us.

"No... Do you think Niall has been acting a bit off lately?" she dared, feigning nonchalance.

Harry's breath gusted from his lungs. "Yes. I've noticed. Look, Shannon, we need to talk."

"Oh?" The pace of her pulse matched her quick breathing.

The look on his face changed. Tightened lips, deepened frown lines framed earnest eyes. "I want you to take over the yard. I'm going to train you to be my right hand, so when the time comes you can take the lead. Niall needs to find his own calling in life. Horses are my passion, not his." The intensity in his gaze slipped to sadness. "He was never interested in it. Like his mother."

"But Harry..."

Keeping his eyes on the driver he avoided contact. "I see a lot of myself in you. Your drive and determination. The care you have for those animals. I know what he's like, Shannon. I'm not blind. He'd sooner cart them off to the knacker's yard or sell them to pay for his next hit. I'd like to get you more involved in the general day to day running and the finances, if you're up for it?"

"You know about the drugs?" A wave of relief washed over her tense form.

"I've noticed the change in him over these past years. He has his mother's mean streak and addictive personality. He called me this morning to ask why I had frozen his bank account. Fuck if I'm going to let him kill himself with my money. I told him to stay away for a while, told him to check into rehab before I'd reinstate his funds. He knows you're my right hand now, not him."

"You told him that?" Her pulse jumped.

"It's better this way, Shannon. He can do his own thing without my expectations pulling him in the wrong direction."

This was the best news. Niall was in rehab for God knows how long, and she had been offered the chance to run a top-class yard... with a man who believed in her ability. Excitement surged through her veins and relief kissed her weary limbs, letting them relax. "How long will he be away for? Is the rehab clinic in Northern Ireland or over the water? How long do those sort of things last for? It could be months, right?" All her thoughts spilled out.

Taking a long gulp of brandy, Harry turned to face her, gazing into her eyes with an odd flash of something unknown. "You seem awfully interested in Niall?"

He was suspicious, she'd been too keen to find out the details of his stint in rehab. Her poker face had crumbled at the slightest mention of him leaving. "Oh, you know, just curious," she lied. "He needed help."

The limo slowed and Harry tilted the remaining drink into his open mouth. "He'll be gone for a few months. I arranged for him to attend a private rehabilitation retreat in Switzerland."

Hot air steadily left her lungs, circulating in the back of the car. This was it. Everything was falling into place. Niall would surely come back a changed man, and she had stepped up from rider, to the yard general manager.

"I don't know what to say, Harry."

"Then don't. It's written all over your face. I know what this means to you. Shannon, you deserve this. I know you'll take it all in your stride. We'll start the day after tomorrow."

A cheery driver decked out in a black suit opened the door and nodded. Shannon discarded the full glass of champagne and stepped out onto the tarmac with her sexy dress catching the winter sun. The air was fresh and clean and a feeling of freedom filled her entire being. The Belfast clouds stayed up north, letting the sun brighten the vivid green grass around them. Evidence of a recent rain shower sparkled in the sun rays as they strolled arm in arm to the VIP entrance at the marquee.

The top-level terrace was set up to serve a three-course luncheon, alongside various accompanying wines. There were circular tables, linen napkins, pretty pink flowers and reams of fabric stretched across the ceiling adding softness to the sharp lines of the rectangular white couches. It was conveniently located close to the parade ring and adjacent to the track. Mitchell was propped up at the bar with a pint of Guinness and a leggy brunette nestled to his side.

"Shannon. Harry. You made it. Drinks are on me all day. Go ahead and order. We'll catch up later." A smirk tugged his lips as they were drawn into a sultry kiss, and his eyes cut away.

"I'll get you a glass of champagne." Harry nudged her elbow. Why she was staring at Mitchell was of no consequence to how she felt about him. The sensual kiss playing out before her reminded her of what she had and what she missed. It wasn't just the kisses that she longed for, it was the text messages, the late night phone calls, the smile on Jamie's face that made her wish they could have been together.

A tall flute of pink champagne broke her reverie. "Sorry, Shannon. You're too good for Mitch."

The champagne tasted like raspberries, cooling her

throat on its way down. Today was a good day and alcohol was the best way to celebrate. A sip turned into two, that turned into a few, and she sank the whole lot. "Humm, that was good. Mitch isn't my type, Harry. Never was, never will be." She lifted the glass to a passing waiter, waggling it for a refill. "Thanks, Harry. For everything." Tipping into his face, she pressed her lips to his scruffy jaw and kissed him. "And I mean everything."

A flurry of emotions swam in his eyes. As he reached out for her elbow and squeezed, the waiter filled her glass to the top. She nodded before taking another long gulp of the refreshing fizz.

"The horses are racing today, Shannon. Not us," he said through a husky chuckle, tipping his own drink to his lips.

"I want to pick all the winners myself. The parade ring is downstairs." She wobbled. "I'll go to the toilets first." A dizzy sensation made her eyes widen.

"And I'll get you a glass of water."

Shannon loved the energy of race day, but most of all, she enjoyed the horses. Eying up the runners in the parade ring and choosing which one was her favourite to win, was the best part. The excitement of Harry's news and the bustle of the event had her happiness soaring. Her body was alive for the first time, in too long.

She passed by the occupied accessible toilet on route to the washrooms. Hitting a long queue of woman dressed in their finery, she retreated outside the door rather than be forced to talk. The champagne was having a weird floaty effect on her head. Leaning against the wall she inhaled deeply. After a few lingering seconds, the door to the engaged toilet in front of her flung open.

"Play your cards right and I'll fuck you later," cooed a woman hidden behind the firm hard physique of a tall broad male, dressed in a fitted pink shirt with snug grey trousers. Her eyes flicked up and the feelings of happiness dissipated into the electrified air.

Jamie.

Chapter 35

Jamie had moved on. Why wouldn't he? It was expected, wasn't it?

There he was, exiting a toilet after doing whatever, with another woman. That was the last thing she wanted to see, not today, not ever. The reality reached inside her chest and ripped out her vigorously beating heart. Tiny fragments of shattered hopefulness caught fire and incinerated all chances of ever being with Jamie McGrath again.

How dare he look so sexy with his shirt sleeves rolled up to his elbows and the cut of his shirt so neat, so tight to the curve of his muscular body. The same defined torso that had always reacted with goose bumps when her nails scraped his skin or when her tongue trailed his abs, the very same torso she had memorized in detail.

How dare those amber eyes of his be filled with lust and surprise, or for his sudden shift in posture to shoot off flares of sex appeal.

How dare her pulse pound so hard that sentences failed to form.

How dare that woman touch him.

Jamie swaggered free of the cubicle with his usual confident gait, checking his phone before draining the liquid in his glass. She continued to stare quietly, unsure if the dizziness was anger or lust. Then he stopped dead and looked up from the screen. The empty glass swayed just a fraction, and the satisfied wolfish grin dimpling his cheek in that roguish way, dropped with his jaw.

"Shannon…" The way he said her name, with such familiarity, all husky and stunned, made her heart skip. He stepped closer. "You're here. You look fucking amazing,

Shannon."

A fierce combination of anger and attraction reverberated aggressively within her. The urge to slap his handsome face fused with the need to taste his lips, but those delightful lips had just been all over the woman behind him.

Under the thrum of her heartbeat, she noted the muted din of ladies chatting in the corridor, glasses clinking, a man's crackled voice over a loudspeaker, announcing the next race. It all blended into white noise as her gaze fell on the woman in the background.

Jamie continued to stare, his eyes wandering all over her fitted dress. After a beat, he asked, "Who are you here with?" The scent of his cologne brought back a flood of emotion.

She wanted to speak – hell, she wanted to beg him for forgiveness after pushing him away, but shock rammed her words back down her throat. Resentment replaced sadness, and she became annoyed with herself for being so upset. It was all too easy for him.

The attractive woman reapplied her lipstick in the mirror. A floral bodice hugged her breasts upwards like big juicy melons, and her slender legs hung down from a thigh high dress. Miss Fancy Pants was her polar opposite.

It was either the tremble in Shannon's hands or the wobble of her knees that sent her clutch thudding to floor. Loose change scattered, rolling to a stop at his shoes. With his eyes still on her, Jamie crouched down on his haunches and gathered the contents. Stupefied silence was shattered by Miss Fancy Pants. "Jamie."

He didn't flinch, only stood tall and pulled back his shoulders.

Shannon looked up into his eyes, finding the kindness she once knew, feeling the draw of his wickedness, and then gave in to the unbearable twang of jealousy that crushed her lungs. She nodded curtly and snatched the bag, without saying a word. Turning on her heels, she hurried into the ladies to find sanctuary.

She retreated from his sexy dimple.

She took refuge from the lust darkening his gaze.

The reality was harsh, her actions had pushed him into the arms of another woman.

Bunking past a horde of patient woman standing in line, she raced to the mirrors, barely keeping herself upright. Her stomach began to heave as her pulse matched her breathing.

"You okay?" asked an older woman with a coral fascinator plonked on the crown of her head like flamingo vomit.

Shannon shook her head, clutching the sink for support. "The bubbles have gone to my head, and I get claustrophobic in small spaces."

"That one's free. You go ahead and take my turn, sweetheart."

"Thank you."

Shannon dove into the stall, pressing her back to the door. The idea of Jamie being with Miss Fancy Pants hurt her more than she could have ever imagined. A pain far worse than the lashes of a whip.

The past few weeks had been nothing less than horrendous. There wasn't a minute when she didn't regret telling him to back off, especially the way Niall made her do it. Until today, she had held onto a glimmer of hope. Then Harry told her Niall would be away for months, and she finally allowed herself to dream of possibilities, to indulge in a silly fleeting idea that Jamie would take her back. Now she doubted everything. Had he just been on the charm offensive all along and the gifts were part of his game. A rich man buying his way into the bedroom.

The noisy hum of gossiping stopped. Silence. A faint giggle.

"Shannon." Jamie was standing at the other side of the door.

"Go away," she said with a shaky breath.

"I need to speak with you, in private."

Her palms fanned the door, and her forehead pressed

onto the wood. "I have nothing to say."

"Please, Shan. Just five minutes. The whole time she sucked my dick, it was your cherry lips I thought about."

Anger. That's all she felt. Fury that another woman had given him pleasure and kissed his delectable lips. "Am I supposed to open the door and run into your arms now, Jamie?" Her voice strained.

"Shannon. Open the fucking door. Talk to me. You're the one who told me to back off."

He was right, but all this was so messed up, so wrong. "A jar of cherry lips wouldn't make me talk to you then, and knowing that you've just been sucked off, sure isn't gonna work either."

Thud.

All of a sudden, a female voice chirped up, "If you don't want him, I'll have him."

Water dripped from the tap.

The same female called out again. "He's gone by the way, after he punched the shit out of the vending machine. He's probably gone to find the woman who sucked him off."

Her cheeks flamed with a nasty flare of embarrassment, and her heart crashed with a surge of envy. Inhaling her misery, she opened the cubicle door to meet the gawking eyes of an audience. With a tight smile, she nudged her way to the exit, freeing herself from scrutiny.

Back in the bar, Harry was huddled in the corner with a busty brunette, who's wide brimmed hat made it almost impossible to see their touching faces, but Shannon recognised Harry's tweed jacket instantly. It was the wandering hands that crept below the draped tablecloth that made Shannon smile inwardly. He deserved a good woman, or some fun at least. Before Shannon arrived at Meadow Dawn, Harry's wife took off with her Spanish hairdresser. Harry was left holding the baby, or the monster, more like it.

Turning away, she took refuge at a neighbouring table. Her legs were shaky and her head light. It was only when she settled in the chair and poured a glass of icy water from the jug, that she found him. Jamie stood at the bar, alone. Miss Fancy Pants was nowhere in sight. His hip dipped into the bar, and his gaze fell to the golden liquid in his glass. She wanted to look away, but her gaze was drawn to him just like her body. It was impossible to stop herself from staring. The sight of him invoked pleasure and pain, memories of intimacy and trust. Niall had taken it all away from her. But the cruellest realisation was that her devastation was just that, hers. Jamie had been able to wear the next female as easily as she had worn his boxer briefs.

From the corner of her eye, Miss Fancy Pants approached the bar with a slinky strut. She was all bouncy curls, lacquered nails and white teeth. Fingertips walked up his arm. Her hips angled closer, and her laugh arced across the room, stabbing her right in the heart.

In a hasty retreat, she rose from the table and stormed to the stairwell. Cold air tingled her cheeks and tears misted her eyes. The thought of Jamie with that woman was a consuming reality. It was only natural for a man like him, especially after her solid rejection. But to actually see him again, so soon, with someone else.

Breath. Just breathe. Focus on what you know. Pick a horse.

Spirited horses pranced around the parade ring. The sunlight fractured the faint clouds making her squint. She watched the glossy, well turned out race horses, circling the cordoned off paddock. They bounced like coiled springs, giving her insight into the anxious or overexcited horses that would either burn out too soon, or gallop like a demon to the finish line. Selecting the skinniest bay mare with visible ribs and lean muscles, she noted its race number.

Choosing a bookmaker with good odds, she stood in line. "Fifty quid on the nose. Number 56."

The elderly man swiped her cash and printed the ticket. "There ya go, love."

Even that simple endearment flashed Jamie's face in her subconscious. Shoving her way through the throngs of spectators, she found a space at the edge of the track just in time to witness the runners explode across the starting line. Pounding hooves flew past, spreading a thrum of adrenaline through her body. Looking to the large screens, she watched as the horses galloped around the track, all of the jockeys hoping to cross the finish line as the winner. The thrill urged her to jump up and down, screaming as if number 56 could hear her.

The winner hurtled over the white line. Shannon squealed momentarily, clapping her hands, then fisting the air. Even the win of a cool one thousand pounds couldn't brighten her heartbreak. A droplet of rain splatted the crown of her head, nestling into her scalp. Turning from the track, a display of coloured umbrella's all opened in sequence. Clouds darkened and one drip quickly turned to hundreds. Sheltering her face, she darted for cover only to slam into a rock hard form.

Raindrops bounced on the black canvas overhead, shielding her from the shower. The air carried a waft of sautéed onions from the nearby burger van mixed with a haze of sweet sodden grass rising from the track, yet the heady familiar scent of man, of Jamie, took centre stage. Her senses were attuned to him, to his confidence, to his irresistible presence. Looking up under her lashes, she met his intense amber eyes, filled with emotion akin to anger or hurt.

"Did you win?" Jamie said in a sultry timbre.

A bundle of nerves fluttered in her chest. "Uh-huh."

"I didn't expect to see you here."

"Clearly." She had no right to sound so irritated. "You looked cosy."

A flash of anger made him growl. "I've had a shit load to drink, and it seemed like the only way to stop thinking about you." His free hand brushed over her bicep. "You've always blown me away, but right now, fuck. I'm struggling here, Shannon. What went wrong?"

Arching a brow, she cocked her head. "Jamie… I..." The words stuttered. "So much has happened, Jamie. I just didn't need to see that."

The heat of his sigh was a welcomed warmth, and the pressure of his fingertips cuffing her arm only made her sway into him.

"Shannon. You told me to back off. To walk away when I wanted to be there for you."

"Jamie, I need time to explain…" Her breathing shuddered, the pain, the hurt, it was all too much. "I didn't want to say those things."

"I don't understand. Was it just a game to you, Shannon?"

"A game. No! It was never a fucking game. Not for me anyway. Maybe it was for you. I mean, look how easy it was for you to move on."

"I hardly think I was moving on. I could chase a hundred women around the world and back, Shan, and they still wouldn't be able to replace you. Truth is, I couldn't even bring myself to kiss her. I made a fucking mistake. Anyway…" His chest rose and fell in sharp bursts. "You told me to fuck off. What did you think would happen?"

She swallowed back the lump forming in her throat. "Just because I said those things, doesn't mean I meant them. It's complicated."

Her emotions were on overdrive. Anger, fear, hurt, desire. She could feel them all swirl inside, taking control. It must have been the swell in her chest and the uncertainty on her face that made his brow crease and his breath still.

"What can be so complicated?" he said with a gravelly tone.

His gaze darkened like swirling nectar while his palm drifted to her waist, drawing her neatly against his body. "I want to know how you are, Shan." His tone was commanding, reaching her insides and shaking them with lust. "I want to understand why you pushed me away." The vibrations bouncing from his body to hers was making her dizzy. "I want you back."

His handsome face tilted, his lips so close that his feathery breath caressed her cheek. Hidden beneath the oversized umbrella she felt safe and secluded, keeping intrigued faces out of view. The patter of raindrops, the spectators cheering, the booming voice echoing from the speakerphone all faded. Cursing herself, she closed her eyes briefly, anticipating the feel of his mouth. The rushed cadence announcing the final furlong chase, which matched the tempo of her racing heartbeat, and just when her eyelids drifted open, she found confusion swimming in his eyes.

"Are you fucking with me, Shannon?" The tone was strained like he was in unchartered territory, begging for a lifeline.

"No," was all she could whisper, silently begging to taste him.

"I'm not fucking with you either." When his lips finally landed, they clung lightly, softly, with a hint of hesitancy.

Their kisses shared before had been obsessive, fierce and fuelled with hunger, but this one felt different, so very passionate and tender. Dipping his tongue into her mouth, he controlled the pace, sweeping, teasing and savouring her with a delectable pressure. Shannon's insides liquefied, melting into his strength. Lost in all things Jamie, her soft moans turned wild. His hand jerked her closer, pressing the dip of her lower back, holding her tighter. Her palms drifted higher, mapping his chest and hooking his neck. The clutch fell, only this time neither of them cared to gather up the contents.

Pulling his lips away, she just stood there, gazing up at him. Fascinated by the effect he had on her body, mind and soul.

His mouth dropped to the side of her neck. "The whole time she had her lips on my dick, I wished it was you."

Shannon swatted his bicep and clucked her tongue. Jamie lifted his face, sporting his signature oh-so-sexy dimple that made her smile every time. "What a guy," she said lightly, feeling a little perturbed by the idea of him tangled up with Miss Fancy Pants.

His eyes danced. "You look sexy when you're jealous."

A light puff of air blasted from her nose, trying to be

playful. "Jealous? As if."

"You so are. I can tell by the wide baby blues." He grinned.

Short hairs at his nape were smooth and soft to the touch as her fingertips ran up and down. "I bet you'd eat yourself if you could, Jamie."

"Shannon. If this is going to work, I need you to be honest with me. I need to know what's going on." He licked his lips, awakening tiny flutters in her chest.

Moving a hand to his mouth, she pressed her finger to his lips lightly. They were so warm, wet and inviting. "Let's not talk about it now."

A deep gravelly sound rumbled in his chest, igniting the neediest swell between her legs. His breathing was shallow, puffing through her hair. "Stay exactly where you are. The crowd is close. No one will see a thing," he whispered into the shell of her ear.

Shannon stayed perfectly still, absorbing the sensation of his electrifying touch. A reckless hand traced along the slit, sliding under her dress. The rise of his lungs nudged into her breasts, only to blast from his lips in a ragged breath when he found her heat. It was naughty and thrilling. They stood among the crowds while Jamie slipped his fingers between her thighs. She needed him, she craved him in a way that was bordering on obsessive. The featherlight kisses floating down her jugular made all the wrongs irrelevant. The slow dip in and out, teased with promises of him in ways she wanted desperately to remember. Her arm snaked his shoulders pulling her hard against him while his wrist angled with a demanding pressure.

"God, Shan, I've missed you." Just as she groaned, his mouth covered hers with a kiss that was violent and hard, fast and passionate. Pulling away, his eyes blazed like embers, his restraint hanging by a thread. Parting her legs, she gave him more access, and her forehead dropped to his shoulder. "I want to taste you again," he growled into her hair.

Every nerve ending sizzled as she rocked into his hand, getting herself off. She shuddered, opening her mouth to moan but forcing her lips against the fabric of his shirt to stave gasps. A gentle whimper was lost in the cheers of the next big winner. Shannon exploded.

Lifting her flushed face, she looked up at him with a ghost of a smile. Jamie slowly removed his hand and rectified the slit in her dress. Those sinfully wicked fingers found their way to his mouth. She took a second to calm her racing heart and to collect her thoughts. Feeling light headed, her fingers grasped his arm.

"I got off earlier by imagining that whip buried inside you. Then, as if by divine intervention, you appeared before me like my sexy little vixen, wearing this dress and hair as wild as the wind - just to fucking torture me."

The blood swooshing in her skull deafened her ears and her body drained of energy like he sucked all the life from her bones.

The whip. Niall. Trixie. George. Threats. Pain. Heartbreak.

"Shannon... Shannon?" He ducked down to meet her gaze.

Gripping his brawny biceps, her vision clouded, and her thoughts raced to an impenetrable place where fear was her master.

Immediately a strong arm shielded the uncontrollable tremors. Her legs moved without thought, propelled forward with every stride of his. She vanished into her memories and became lost in the fear.

A haze of words mumbled from the back of her mind. "Jamie, the next runner is ready. They're taking her to the parade ring now."

"Good. I want visuals of all races and a full stat report this evening. Update me on our finishing positions after each race." Jamie's voice drifted.

A deafening whirling suddenly caught her attention, slamming her back into reality. He led her by the shoulders to a black helicopter, closed the umbrella and handed it to the pilot. Assisting her into the aircraft he buckled her in and placed his lips to her temple. A warmth remained on her skin even when his mouth retreated, and he rounded the helicopter. Joining her side, Shannon clawed the crook of his arm as her head fell to his shoulder.

"I'm taking you home, love."

"Is this your chopper?" She was dazed and confused. "Please, I have to go back to the yard," she muttered.

Before he could respond, her eyelids fluttered shut and her face nestled into his warmth.

Chapter 36

Her eyelids sprung open. "Where are we?" She bolted forward but bounced back, held in place by her safety harness. "Where did you get the helicopter from?" Through the glass window she gazed out at a velvety navy sky hung high above tall trees surrounding a monster sized property. The touch of his skin grazing her palm made her flinch. She'd fallen asleep, into the nightmare of hurt. Now she was awake and anxious knots tightened her voice. "Jamie. I don't recognise this place."

"I use this thing for work." He shrugged lightly. "It's okay, we're home. At my place in Fermanagh. Wait here."

He jumped out of the helicopter and reappeared beside her, hoisting the door open and unclasping her harness. She shuffled forward, slotting her hand in his firm grasp. Instantly the skin to skin contact soothed and calmed, she felt safe with him, even though they were miles away from Meadow Dawn. Dropping down to the tarmac, he held her upright with an arm tucked tightly around her shoulders.

When she looked up at the massive building that Jamie called home, her jaw dropped in awe. There were impressive fresh white rendered walls, black window frames and crisp lines, all illuminated by floodlights because it was isolated amongst acres of woodland. This was where Jamie really lived? A mansion in the countryside? Staying silent, she eyed the modern building with wonder, letting him lead her through hefty double doors.

"You feeling okay, Shannon? Your face is so pale. What the hell happened back there?" He tapped a code into a keypad on the wall.

"Can we talk about it later?"

"You're not hiding from this, Shannon." With a click of a button, well placed lighting glowed and ambient melodies drifted out of hidden speakers. Glossy floor tiles spread like a winter's snow fall through the reception, leading them to a high beamed living space at the rear. Windows stretched the entire back wall, reflecting the inside like a mirror. Black sofas surrounded an open fire place. The smell of charred wood and sound of kindling flames crackling gave the open space a surprising homely backdrop. It was awe-inspiring and intimidating. Even the charcoal coloured kitchen looked like something from a luxury home interior magazine.

"My housekeeper left a chicken curry out of the freezer, if you're hungry?" He just stood by the standalone kitchen island, watching her assessment, as if waiting for a reaction. The living area was at least five times bigger than the loft, no doubt his larder was bigger than her bedroom. How much money did the guy really have?

The heat from the fire drew her trembling hands closer. Without his arms around her, she felt lost and isolated. "Do you really rattle around here on your own?" she asked holding out her palms to the flickering flames.

He tossed his keys and slid his mobile phone onto the worktop. "Sometimes. Marcus lives a mile down the road in the old Coach House. We wanted to have at least one house that kept us close, so I built this place last year."

She scowled. "At least one house. You have more than one?" Holy hell, how did she underestimate his wealth?

"You knew I had cash when we met. I have a villa in Italy and a penthouse in New York."

She gulped. Her brow furrowed, and her eyes darted from corner to corner, soaking up the high spec interior. This was a new side of him, an unbelievable shit storm of financial inequality. It was obvious from the get-go he had money, but the revelation of a private helicopter was completely unexpected. They had always been together in her territory, and now she was in his, it was another world entirely.

"How much does a place like this cost?" The fire spat a tiny ember into the air, and she followed it's flurried decent until the glow died.

"Does it matter?" Jamie took a few steps closer, his hands slotted under his armpits like he was defensive. For a man who was confident in every aspect of his life, he looked vulnerable like he was hanging on her reply.

"It depends…"

Jamie's brow creased, and he shifted position. "On?"

"Are you going to turn into an asshole? Or tell me that I'm number three girlfriend and introduce me to one and two?"

"Number three? Humm." His cheek dimpled. "What about four and five?"

"Asshole."

"Hey, Shan. You know you're number one, right? As in, the only one."

The flutters in her chest nearly made her faint. "I just under estimated how rich you are."

A slow smile tugged at his lips, and she could've sworn he actually sighed with relief. "It's a bit big for just me. I need a super-hot, black haired beauty to live with me. Specifically, one with amazing blue eyes, a great ass and a really cute laugh."

Her cheeks flushed, and her tummy flipped in all different ways. "I'm sure you've had plenty of girls who fit that criteria." She teased.

Crouching down she unbuckled her sandals and slipped them off. Within a heartbeat he was slap bang in front of her. "Nah. You're the only one for me. How about you take a hot shower before dinner? It'll only take a few minutes to zap the curry. I need to make a call first."

Jamie jogged to the island and lifted his mobile phone, selected call and pressed it to his ear. He paused waiting for an answer, then shrugged. "No answer. I was calling Harry to let him know that I'll have you back first thing tomorrow."

Her palm fanned her heart. Jamie actually understood. He had listened to every word she had said. "I'll text him. He gave me the day off, but I still want to ride Trixie."

Patting under her arm, it suddenly hit her, the clutch was gone. "Jamie, my bag. I don't have my bag or my phone." Her palms flew up to her cheeks.

"Shit. Look, don't worry. ''I'll call my guys at the track and see if anyone handed it in." He turned away and brought the phone back to his ear.

While he chatted, she watched his fluid movements as he strolled around the kitchen, lifting a silver container out of the fridge. The authority in his tone flicked a switch inside her, lessening the aftermath of fear and sparking volts of electricity around her muscles instead. He was handsome and powerful, kind and caring. Sure, the guy was rich, probably wealthier than she had first thought, but it didn't matter anymore. Now that Harry was training her up to take over the business, she'd be able to earn her own cash and maybe, just maybe, match him penny for penny.

Jamie ended his conversation and called out to her from across the room, breaking her haze of lust and speculation. "They found your bag and the phone was still inside. I need to grab a quick shower, then I'll heat up dinner."

A few brisk steps brought him close to her again, his gaze roaming the teal fabric all the way down to her toes. "Come on, Shan." He stared at her momentarily like he was trying to figure her out. Whatever questions that sat on his tongue, remained there, and he tugged her close instead. "Let's go upstairs."

Circling her small frame in his arms, he escorted her to a set of bone white concrete stairs that floated up the wall to the next level. Framed art work of charcoal horses followed each step.

"You like black and white. And horses." She smiled, studying the free form horse silhouettes.

"It's a contradiction. Most of the house décor is black and white but each room has an element of grey – because nothing is ever straight forward, or cut and dry. Everything worth having is in the grey."

Everything about Jamie was audacious and manly, right down to his master suite. The plush dove coloured carpet was soft and snug underfoot, whereas slate grey walls and white cornicing lead to a four-poster bed with bolster cushions and a wooden head board with a masculine bulk. This place was so left field, so out of her imagination. As she moved into the room, past the super king-sized bed, she rounded a corner to find a white couch facing a bay window. He actually had a sitting area in his bedroom, and it was bigger than the floor plan of her loft by miles.

Jamie followed behind, his lips tight and arms folded. "Do you think you'll be okay sleeping in here, with me?" he asked with a weird uncertain tone.

"Are you joking, Jamie? This room is like a hotel. What exactly do you do for a living? I know you own The Fitz Hotel with Marcus but..."

"Like I said, I buy and sell." His answer was vague, and he looked to the floor when he spoke.

"Do you deal in human organs? Because this house must be worth a fortune."

His back straightened and his eyes flashed with something unknown. "Does it matter how much it's worth? Surely the fact you like it outweighs the cost?"

Shannon had accepted the fact he was rich, but the house just seemed so vast and imposing, like no expense was spared. It had thrown her right off course. "This is how the other half live then?" Her fingertips traced the buttery leather covering the massive couch. "It's pretty awesome, Jamie, but then again so are you."

His face lit up and his arms finally unfurled. "Sweet Jesus, she actually thinks I'm awesome!"

Suddenly he lunged forward, sprinting towards her. Shannon bolted from his wide stretched arms and darted around the spacious room, jumping onto the perfectly made bed with a loud giggle. In one leap he joined her side, sinking into the mattress. "You're one unpredictable woman. That's what makes *you* so awesome."

"Sweet Jesus, he thinks *I'm* awesome," she said through a mocking laugh.

"Baby, you've known all this time that I think you're awesome." His lips pressed to the tip of her nose with a quick kiss. "More than awesome." He angled his head, and for that split second, she thought he was going to say something else, but he just sighed lightly, and the corner of his mouth curled up so his cheek dimpled.

The heat from his body evaporated when he pushed off his hand and sat up. "The shower is through there." He pointed to a door that she hadn't even noticed. "Take your time. I'll grab a shower in the guest room and then get dinner sorted."

She hated how he dragged himself off the bed, away from her. For a beat, he stood at the bed post with those amber eyes of his swirling. Then he smiled tightly and left. He seemed different. Emotions roiled, his expression unreadable. His irresistible charm was still overpowering, but it was natural, authentic, real.

Entering the adjoining bathroom, no different in proportions to the bedroom, she sighed feeling uncertain. It was obvious there was a huge financial gap between them. A gaping hole of a difference. After stripping off her sexy dress, she stepped into the massive shower. Even the shampoo was luxurious, the expense mere pocket change. Lathering the suds over her scalp, she thought about the events of the day and how tired her body had become. She was always tired these days. A manifestation of stress. The daily endurance that held her under a cloud of fear and vexation.

Jamie wanted answers and tonight she was going to tell him everything. How would he react? Would he look at her with pity, like she was pathetic for letting a man like Niall get the better of her. Tears gathered, swelling up from below the surface of her forced strength. Her juddered gasp swirled in the steamy shower. Water sluiced over her curves, splashing her face. A mass of white foam slid down her forehead, covering her eyes like a mask. Snapping them shut, a second too late brought about stinging and biting. She pressed the pads of her fingers to closed eyelids, stumbling into the glass door. It slammed against the wall as she toppled out. A whimper broke free, plastic bottles toppled, fingertips searched blindly. Locating the sink, she traced the square lines, feeling for the tap.

"Fuck!" she yelped as the burning intensified.

She heard the bathroom door swing open. "Shannon?" The worry in his voice startled her. "What's wrong?"

"Suds. Suds in my eyes." She was crumpled over the sink, naked and shivering.

Large hands latched her arms, and she was yanked away from the basin. In a few steps she was propelled back into the shower with Jamie close to her side. Cupping her jaw, he nudged her head back, forcing water jets down onto her closed eyes. "Keep your head back." He ordered.

Even if she wanted to move her head, it was impossible. His fingers dug into her cheeks, his body crushed against hers. The water flowed down her face, removing all traces of the villainous soapy residue. After what felt like a minute, he released her head. "Open up," he commanded. "Slowly."

Standing back, she blinked and let her lids lift. There was steam swirling, heat rising and a wet Jamie inches from her chest. He was dressed in a white tee with track pants, both of which were now drenched. The tee clung to his skin like a wet tee shirt fantasy, hinting flesh and muscles and sex.

His brow furrowed. "Can you see?"

"Yes…" She panted, holding back the urge to peel off his clothes.

A slow smirk lifted his lips, and he just gazed at her naked body with an intense glow to his wandering eyes. "So the shower wasn't quite as relaxing as it could've been."

Her head shook, words not forming as her libido shot through the ceiling.

"You're one of a kind, Shannon Colter." Dragging a

hand over his darkened hair, his biceps flexed and beads of water slid over his sexy dimple. "Let's get you dried off and fed. It's been a long day."

That was the last thing on her mind as she ate up the site of him, but her legs were shaky to match her breathing. When he peeled off his tee and stepped out of his sopping wet track pants, she wrapped a fluffy towel around her chest. He was right there, with a pair of snug boxer briefs and his tanned chest on full display.

"I can't believe that just happened." Embarrassment shaded her cheeks with a rosy glow.

When he glanced over at her with thick black lashes framing his eyes and a hint of amusement on his lips, her heart bucked.

"You're not having much luck today."

"Maybe my luck has changed."

"Oh, really, what makes you think that?" His sexy swagger brought him closer, breaching the damp air.

"Being here with you. Maybe you can kiss it all better." Her words came out in little gasps.

The pad of his forefinger tilted her chin upwards. "I don't want you to push me away again. So, for the first time in my life I'm going to take things nice and slow. I've left out one of my tees and a pair of track pants. When you're ready, come downstairs for dinner. I guarantee you it will knock your socks off." His eyes flickered when he said the last few words, both of them knowing what he'd already done with a pair of knee length socks.

She folded her arms over her stomach. "Is that what you really want, to take things down a notch?" Her soft tone was tainted with disappointment.

"I feel like I should, Shannon. It's like I can see straight into the darkness hidden in your eyes. Like you're broken and lonely, and I have this crazy fucking need to find all the scattered fragments and piece you back together, stronger and happier. I want you to smile from the second your eyes open, to the second I kiss them closed."

He angled his head and lightly kissed the corner of her

mouth. Their bodies didn't meet, his distance an obvious method of restraint. The heat of his delicate peck stayed on her skin, like a featherlight promise of protection.

In that moment, she realised, maybe he needed that promise just as much as she did. After all, she was the one who kept pushing him away. "Jamie, I don't want to take it slow. I don't want you to treat me like I'm broken china, like something you need to tip top around in case I cut you. I'm here, with you and there's nowhere else I'd rather be. What I need right now, is you. All of you."

Jamie didn't answer, he just held her gaze. It was a look of uncertainty, an internal war raging behind his eyes. She didn't know if he was planning to kiss her again or walk away. After a beat, he took a step closer until his chest pressed into her breasts and his mouth crashed down with such force that she groaned.

Jamie was a thrill, a powerhouse of adrenaline that grew in magnitude, surpassing even the rush she felt in the saddle. Her passion for riding was rivalled by a man, by him. The commanding and fervent kiss was broken with a tug of her lower lip. "Don't push me away this time."

She smiled up at him, her lashes fluttering. "I won't."

He tucked a clump of dishevelled hair behind her ear. "You're going to tell me what happened, or this ends here. I need to know why the hell you fainted earlier and who hurt you. No more secrets."

Shannon's fingers trailed through his thick damp hair. "I'll tell you everything, I promise." Knowing she had to say the words out loud, weighed her down. Palpitations of anxiety pulsed in her chest. "We'll have something to eat, and then I'll tell you all about it. That was the first time I fainted. I've been really tired lately."

Chapter 37

His jaw clenched and his fists balled as he sat there and listened to the pain cracking her voice, feeling the tremble of hatred vibrate from her body and watch the flush of shame veil her face. The truth was brutal, her secret was a fucking whirlwind of being beaten into submission, knowing the life of her beloved horse hung in the balance and worse still, his own father was brought into the mix.

Her words were rushed and shaky, and, in that moment, he saw the vulnerability she so desperately tried to hide. Jamie finally understood the reason why she had cut him off. When the explanation finished, he reached out and nudged her body into his, holding her so close he could feel her pulse thrum in the dip of her throat. Shannon was a tough girl who didn't need pity. She deserved his strength and revenge.

Pulling back from his tight embrace, she looked up at him with those glacial blue eyes that sucked him under every time. "Jamie, please, say something. I didn't want to keep it from you, but now Niall is in rehab, everything will be okay. Trixie will be safe and your dad too. We can be together, if that's something you want?"

The hope in her voice speared his heart. If only she knew how much he'd missed her. How he woke every morning and wondered if he should drop by Coffee Kicks just to see if she was working. He needed time to process the fucked up information that had just unfolded, but mostly, he needed to ensure that Marcus had a security detail on their father. After that he would set up eyes on Niall. Jamie would give the guy some time and then hit the bastard when he least expected it. He wouldn't kill him, but he sure as hell would let him know not to threaten the McGrath's, and that included Shannon.

Her mouth parted. "Please, Jamie. Say something. Anything."

Pressing his forehead to hers he growled with a low murmur. "All I can think about is the pain he caused you. The fucking whip we used for fun. I want to kill him, Shan."

A sharp burst of air expelled from her lungs. "Don't do anything stupid, Jamie. He'll not be around for months and when he comes back, things will be different." The tone of her voice was stressed, and her eyes were pleading. "Don't get yourself in trouble over him. Promise me."

Nothing will have changed. Niall will still be a self-righteous asshole who beat her with a whip and held her at knife point, and Jamie would still have fire and revenge running through his veins. "Don't worry. It's okay." It was far from okay. His anger was spinning his world off course. He was pissed it had taken her this long to tell him, he was furious that Niall had been given a get out jail free card and he was enraged that he couldn't get to the bastard right that second.

Pushing the curry around his plate, he made himself a whispered promise to find Niall the day and hour he returns to Belfast and have a quiet chat with his fists.

Regardless of her honesty, Jamie knew the time would come when he would have to own up to his billionaire status. He was reluctant to discuss the pounds and pence crammed into his many bank accounts like zillions of ants hoarding leftovers. Did he want to go head first into that conversation with a woman who had issues with rich men? Or more precisely, with the only woman who mattered. No, tonight wasn't the time to enlighten her.

Earlier, he purposely held back from telling her about the hundreds of properties he leased out, and only focused on the homes he lived in. Maybe the best way to tell her about his wealth would be to show her Unity, his pet project that was also a big earner. "I'd like to take you somewhere tomorrow, once you've finished up at Meadow Dawn."

She sat back on the leather sofa with the flames dancing in her eyes. "I can't eat anymore." Her hand drifted to her belly. "Where are we going?"

"It's a surprise."

"Hmmm..." The soft sound was filled with uncertainty. A low murmur that was unsettling, like she was standing at a crossroads unsure which road would lead to him.

His eyes narrowed. "What's wrong?"

She exhaled slowly, pulling her knees to her chest. "You and I are clearly from different worlds." Drawing in her lower lip with light nips, she stared at him with a look he couldn't decipher.

"We'll work something out. I promise." He thumbed her cheek. "Thank you for telling me everything." His head shook lightly. "You've saved my father for the second time."

A fine mist covered her big blue eyes. "I didn't really."

"You did," he said firmly. "So, let me think about this. You saved him the first time and I bought you lunch. The second time deserves something more..." He knew exactly how he wanted to repay her, and the fact her pupils flared meant she wanted it to.

"How about we go to bed now, Shan." It wasn't a suggestion, and she didn't put up a fight.

Her pouty lips curved to a soft smile, and her contented sigh shot straight to his dick. Wrapping her arms around his neck, he scooped her up.

Marcus hadn't prepared him for this. Whatever this was. Since meeting Shannon, he had lived and breathed a multitude of emotions, all fighting for supremacy. Their very first kiss had been fascinating, intriguing and full of eagerness. She gave him a taste, a bite of the apple, making him covet the one thing he'd never had - a connection. What actually was the connection he craved? Was it an alternative name for love?

She lay on the bed, swamped in feather filled pillows,

hair fanning the bedspread and that look of temptation in her eyes. A dreamy smile was followed by a light giggle, that same little sound that gave away her nerves. Stepping out of his shorts he quickly covered his hardness with a thin veil of rubber, ready to take back what was his. He dragged off the baggy track pants covering her lean legs and watched as she slowly revealed her braless chest. Her usual porcelain glow hinted warmth like she'd spent the summer months under the hot sun in nothing but a skimpy bikini. Bending over her, he tipped down to those cherry red lips that were so inviting, those perfect lips that haunted his thoughts.

The need to watch her unravel filled him and the desire to feel their connection burn in his chest. His palms glided, sensually mapping every curve of her perfect body. The sensation of her skin was like a fine silk that he craved to wear. His lips found hers, covering them in a surge of lust. She responded with a hunger that drove him wild, teeth nipping, lips parting, nails scraping. Her sweet moans whispered in the air, and her hot breath tingled down his spine. Angling his hips, he held her prisoner beneath him. Pulling back from her hungry mouth, Jamie looked into the eyes that had successfully pulled him under the surface of sanity.

"I'm not going to let you go this time," he growled, holding his stare with fervent intensity. "No matter what happens, you are mine, Shannon. I'll protect you."

He noted the quiver and watched as tiny prickles of gooseflesh rocketed across her skin in a wave. With each brush of his fingertips, he could feel the tiny hairs lift from her body like they were drawn to him.

His breath hissed when she nudged her hips with desperation. The pounding pulse in his throat only made his possessive kisses more rabid, distracting him from the anger locked away in his heart.

In one beat he pinned her wrists to the mattress, in two beats he ripped away his lips and locked their heated gaze and in three beats he thrust deep inside her. So tight, so warm, so wild. He watched a swirl of emotions surge through her mind, keeping their gaze welded together until she lost herself in a powerful orgasm and he chased his own.

Chapter 38

Shannon sipped her coffee and stared out at the low mist seeping out from the dense woodland behind Jamie's Fermanagh home. When she arrived, darkness had stolen the breath-taking view, and now she caught a glimpse of the Lough behind a clearing in the trees.

Perched on a bar stool, his large tee ended mid-thigh, her hair was swept back in a low ponytail and her hands clamped a hot mug. As much as she revelled in their all night sexploits, between her legs felt swollen and used. The thought of sitting in a saddle for hours was not the most inviting. She could almost hear Harry laughing if she slid over Trixie's neck to the sand below when her focus flipped. Grinning happily, she eyed Jamie as he rounded the long kitchen island with just a towel wrapped around his amazing ass, his rippled wash board abs on display.

"Are you ready to go back?" His hands rested on her waist, and his head dropped, pressing his lips to the back of her neck with a chaste kiss.

She inhaled slowly, indulging in his touch. "Yes, I'm ready. Thanks for bringing me here. A break from the monotony was good for me."

He swivelled the stool round so she faced him. "You'll be coming back here once you're finished up. I have something I want to show you. There're a few things we need to discuss. The chopper will be at your service to take you back and forth."

Sucking in her lower lip, her brow pulled together. "What do we need to talk about?"

His mouth quirked with a half-smile, but there was an inkling of hesitancy behind it. "All in good time." His eyes

247

flashed like a secret was begging to be revealed. Jamie cleared his throat. "With the comps coming up, you should leave Coffee Kicks, that way we can spend the evenings together, here," he said with confident persuasiveness.

Only a rich guy would suggest such a thing. "Jamie, I've been given a promotion at the yard. Yes, I'll have to hand in my notice at Coffee Kicks, but taking over the running of the business is an amazing opportunity. I'm going to have to shadow Harry even more than I do already. This is everything I've worked for. I've got bills to pay, a job to learn and a reputation to build," she scolded.

"Stay here, with me. Leave the loft. Use the chopper whenever you want. That way you won't have to worry about the bills." His shoulders met his peppered jawline.

Her eyes narrowed to a harsh glare. "Are you serious?" The stern tone of her voice plummeted to zero. A niggle of his expectations irked her to the core.

Shannon reached back and banged the coffee cup on the counter. "You know I've worked so hard to be in the position I am today. Don't think for one minute you can entice me to give it all up with a wave of your money. I'm not about to throw away my morals, or my dreams to hang off your coat tails. And what exactly will I do when you decide to move on to the next damsel in distress? I'll be fucking homeless, Jamie. You just don't get it, do you?"

His cheek dimpled with the subtle curve of his lips. "Baby, you're no damsel in distress. You do want to spend time with me, right? I'm just trying to find a solution. Stay here with me and focus on the yard. Let me take care of you."

"I'm serious, Jamie. I'm not a fucking pet. Stop throwing money around like you have too much. One day, I'll wake up and this dream will be over." Her breath juddered from her lungs, even the suggestion of it being over hurt.

Jamie smoothed his palms over her fists. "That's not going to happen, Shannon."

"Well, I'm not prepared to take that risk," she said

flatly, sitting upright. "We do this on my terms."

His eyes dropped to their linked fingers. "What difference does it make if I have a bit of extra cash? It's my right to spend it how I want." His voice rumbled in his chest.

Her shoulders crept up to her ears. "Money can't buy everything, and the more you throw around, the more it feels like you're trying to buy me."

"Not 'buy' you, Shannon - care for you."

A puff of air shot down her nostrils. "And then you dump me back to squalor, leaving me broken hearted and penniless. I don't need anyone else's money. I can make my own. If this is going to work between us then we need to be equals, and that means financially too."

An odd look washed over his face, and he momentarily stared at her in silence. "You would be heartbroken?" His expression softened, masking uncertainty lurking behind his eyes.

Looking up under hooded lids, her lashes fluttered. "Yes, Jamie. I'd be heartbroken," she said softly feeling a wave of fear prickle her skin.

Gently leaning down, he pressed his lips to her mouth in a deep sensual kiss that rekindled the swell between her thighs. Pulling back, a faint smile brushed his mouth. "So would I, Shan. Please, stay here when you can. A compromise?" Their eyes locked, emotions swirling in dark wisps of fear and desire.

Bringing her hands to his bare chest, she traced the outline of the black tattoo sprawled across his bulging bicep. "Why three wolves?" she whispered, feeling the deepest urge to lick his golden flesh and bite his pebbled nipples.

"Wolves hunt in packs. Marcus and I are a team, brothers – a pack." His beautiful smile faded. "And my dad, of course. So how about it – will you stay?"

Shannon's mind ran out of control with possibilities, allowing the idea of Jamie McGrath being hers. "I'll think about it," she said playfully.

A quick burst of air shot out of his mouth. "I expected nothing less."

***

A cold breeze disturbed loose hay scattering it around the yard like tumble weeds. It was eerily quiet for a weekend. There was always a clatter of hooves and a bustle of activity as staff groomed horses, skipped out stables and cleaned the leather tack. Now there was just a flurry of birds gathered around creaking weather vein.

Shannon peeked over Trixie's stable door, to find it empty - all the stalls were unoccupied.

That's weird.

"Shan!" a raspy voice called from behind. Bucky stopped in the middle of the yard, shoulders slumped, hands in pockets. "I tried to call you." He was always a man of few words, but this time his tone was almost regretful.

"Why are the horses out?" she asked. "I've got a lesson with Harry in an hour."

"I put them out in the fields. The staff have left for a few days." He looked to his dusty boots. "I couldn't reach you, Shan. There was an accident." Bucky rubbed his hands over his weathered face.

Her heart clenched. Something was wrong. "Bucky?"

"Harry…" The weakness to his voice scattered chills down her spine, chasing her pulsating heartbeat.

"Bucky, where's Harry?" Her words drifted out almost echoing around them.

"Shan…" Bucky held his breathe like he was struggling to speak. "He died this morning."

"What… no?" Her brain shook and her stomach flipped. "Who died, Bucky. Who fucking died?" It can't be Harry. It can't.

"Harry was in an accident. He died in the hospital just after 3 a.m. this morning."

Her hand slid to her stomach, and she bent over, holding back the ragged breathes that fought to escape. "Please, no…" Silent sobs rattled her lungs, and her knees buckled, bringing her to the cold damp cobbles in a heap. "This can't be real, this can't be happening. Please, Bucky, please tell me it's a mistake."

Bucky's voice was distant, masking his own grief with the facts he knew. "He was in a car accident, Shan. The car was T-boned by a forty-foot lorry at a junction. The woman he was with died too."

Scrambling to a stand, her legs shook and her mind raced. This had to be a dream, a nightmare she could escape from. Looking past the stables, her bleary gaze searched for the house.

He's up there sleeping, in his chair, with Jackson curled up at his feet.

She started to run, her legs moved without thought. Tears pooled behind her eyes, but she swept them away with determination.

He's not dead.

Harry always left the back door unlocked. The stove was stone cold, the kitchen still and dark. "Harry!" Her voice trembled.

"Harry!" she called into the silence. Walking through the rooms, her heartbeat thrummed in her skull.

The familiar smoky aroma of tobacco laced the sitting room, and a musty smell of charred wood lingered in the air. She was frozen in time, gazing at his leather wing back chair, indented with the grooves of his thighs after years of sitting in the same seat. Finding herself at the crystal decanter, she poured the burgundy liquor into a glass and lifted it to her nose. Inhaling the sweet scent, she released a deep breath filled with memories. The proud smiles, the warm comforting arm when she fell from the saddle, the nights spent chatting about tactics around the dining table.

The rim of the glass rested on her lips. She took a slow sip and felt the liquid burn a path down her throat. It blended with the pain in her heart, the crushing weight of loss.

A sudden clank startled her. "Harry?" she gasped, only to watch Jackson trot into the room with searching sniffs.

He stopped at her feet, sat down and lowered his head. Crouching down, Shannon buried her face in the dog's furry shoulder.

That moment shared between them was acknowledgment of each other's heartache. "It's just you and me, boy, you stick with me." She sobbed, supping the brandy. "I'll take care of you. I promise."

Death cloaked the room with an icy chill, his low chuckle echoed in her mind. Rising to a stand, she noted a packet of his cigarettes on the side board. She fumbled with the carton, selecting one of the small rolls of tobacco and brought it to her lips. Flicking the lid on a silver lighter, a flame danced, and she torched the tip, just like she'd watched Harry do a thousand times over. The small inhalation made her cough and splutter, the smoke choked her lungs but the smell - that freshly lit smell evoked his presence in the room. Placing the cigarette on the ashtray with a plume of smoke filtering into the air, Shannon clambered onto Harry's seat and drew in her knees. The pain was just too real. No amount of time could erase the cataclysm of his fatality.

The worn leather, cold and lifeless, held a reminder of his essence, ingrained after years of use. Clawing at Jamie's cosy sweat top, she tugged the hood over her head trying to hide from the truth. Jackson curled up on the rug and she dragged the cuff over her face, wiping away all of her tears. They both knew he was gone, and life would never be the same. Harry was in her heart and always would be. She just had to accept the loneliness that his death would bring.

***

The brandy had numbed her pain, the glass empty, held close to her chest. Her eyelids blinked open when Jackson shifted, his name tag tinkling. Swallowing hard, she licked her lips, dehydrated from too many tears. Her breath caught. Jamie sat across from her. His body tense, his hair mussed up and his smile warm. All the emotions playing behind his eyes made his voice thick and raspy. "Hey."

Harry was dead. It all flooded back. Her chest heaved and the sobs shuddered her lungs. In a stride Jamie was crouched down on his haunches, gathering her trembling body and jerking her into his arms. He held her while she cried, he wiped the burning tears from her streaked cheeks, he watched her world crumble around them and gently whispered how they would rebuild it together.

His warm lips soothed and comforted as he kissed her temple and promised her that everything would be okay.

Chapter 39

The weeks came and went, and there was still no sign of Niall. Shannon was quietly relieved that he stayed hidden like a dusty old skeleton in the closet. After Harry's funeral, it was agreed that Bucky and Shannon would run the yard together, given the will had yet to be heard. One thing they did know, was Harry's ashes would be scattered in the fields, near the house. He'd spoken about it in the past, but the whole ceremony was at a standstill until Niall found his way back from Switzerland.

"You don't need to do the stables, Jamie." Shannon propped her hip against the wooden frame. His jumper was slung over the stable door, leaving only a black tee draping his tight mucky jeans. "Manual labour looks good on you."

Jamie jabbed the prongs into the fresh bedding and rested his forearm on the handle. His eyes were almost black in the shadowed stall as they drifted from her dusty boots to her messy tresses. A light dusting of scruff covered his angular jaw, giving him a sexy masculine edge and disguising his dimple.

"I'm helping you. It's been a shit few weeks, and I want you to know that I'm here."

The back of his hand swiped his forehead, mopping up minuscule beads of perspiration that glistened on his brow. She swallowed back the urge to reach out and touch him, but the slow wicked smile that curled his lips gave away his own intentions.

"It's dirty work. I didn't think a pretty boy like you would appreciate getting covered in filth?" She swallowed a giggle and bit her lip.

"I'm used to getting down and dirty, Shannon." His

lazy grin lit up the darkness in her heart. "Anyway, all this has taken its toll on you. Even if you don't want to admit it, you need me."

Her brows snapped up. "I need you?"

"You need me." He smirked. In two strides he had her close to his chest and his fingers raking through her hair. The intoxicating smell of Jamie filled her lungs. His woodsy smell was intensified by the heat radiating from his body, a manly sexy aroma that made her weak at the knees.

A flash of sadness suddenly burst into her heart. "I miss him." The waves of remorse came and went, sometimes they just hit her out of nowhere.

"I know." He threaded the lengths of her hair, holding her chest close to his heart. "Once we get finished up here, we'll take the chopper home."

Home. She could get used to calling his place, home. Whether it was his house in Fermanagh or a shack on the beach, it didn't matter, because her heart knew that wherever he was would always feel like her home.

She nodded into his chest, squeezing tighter. Over the past four weeks, Jamie had helped out at the yard with clients and finances. He was more than hands on with the horses too. The whole set up between them just flowed, like they were meant to be together, yet she was scared to admit that her feelings had escalated to the next level. After Harry's sudden death, she had been waiting for the other shoe to fall, for something else cataclysmic to happen, for Jamie to get bored.

For now, they followed the routine, taking his helicopter back to Fermanagh every evening with Jackson by her side. The big dog sat on the leather seats and peered out the window like he was accustomed to the high life. She didn't argue with Jamie about staying at his place because that's where she wanted to be – with him. It didn't matter that she had given up her independence because the loft had lost its appeal. It was filled with painful memories, and the yard was empty without Harry's usual banter. Being with Jamie was like safety and sex and sustenance.

"Thank you," she whispered. "I couldn't do all this without you."

"Come on, love, let's go home now. Bucky can finish up," he ordered, running his nails under her top, tickling her spine.

Her eyelids were heavy as she trudged wearily at his side, leaning into him for support. She was reluctant to tell him that between running the yard and going back and forth to his place, she was close to burn out. Every day a fog of exhaustion drained away every ounce of her energy. Functioning had become a struggle, and missing Harry had become almost too much to deal with.

Jamie had seamlessly placed himself in her life, and it was becoming increasingly difficult to consider a future without him.

"How much does it cost to use the helicopter? Wouldn't it be cheaper to take a car?" she asked as they clambered in the aircraft.

His answer was short, almost like he was being frugal with the truth. "It's a tax thing. Don't worry about the small stuff."

If she was truly honest with herself, the convenience of the chopper was an added bonus, even if she couldn't comprehend how it was always available. It cut down the journey time from Meadow Dawn to Fermanagh, leaving more hours to spend with Jamie.

"You look tired, Shan," he announced once she was buckled in.

Her gaze remained outside of the small aircraft, watching the propellers whiz around in the cloudy sky. "I'm exhausted, Jamie. I feel really drained."

His fingers searched her face, pulling her gaze to meet his. "Then tonight we'll eat and sleep. I promise."

A glimmer of a smile crossed her lips. "Don't make promises you can't keep, Jamie."

His brow furrowed. "Shannon, I'm not going to do anything that makes you unhappy, or even ill. You're sickly pale. I can control myself until you feel better," he said in a raspy serious tone. "Tonight, you can have a long bath before dinner. No fucking sudsy showers." He chuckled. "Then an early night. I have work to do anyway, so I'll join you later. You won't even know I'm there."

"Then I may as well stay at the loft." She suggested flippantly, without giving it consideration because it was never going to happen, and she knew it.

"No!" The word shot out like she scalded him with hot water. "You'll have a better night's sleep at my place. Knowing you're in my bed, waiting for me, gives me a reason to stop working."

"Okay." That little bit of confirmation made her smile. Dropping her head onto his shoulder she inhaled everything about him. "Maybe in the morning you can do that thing with the rope again."

Jamie's grasp locked her thigh with a tight squeeze. "Fuck, Shannon. Behave yourself. If you keep talking like that, I won't be able to keep my promise."

That evening Jamie was true to his word, after a soothing lavender bath, she indulged in an oversized bowl of Irish Stew, mopped up with crusty bread. Heaped stodgy potatoes and thick gravy reminded her of Harry. Jamie's housekeeper, who was only around when they weren't, happily tried to follow Harry's family recipe, but it lacked a certain something, maybe a hint of brandy - it just didn't taste the same. The idea of the accompanying wine made her stomach churn, so she washed it down with a cold glass of raspberry fizz instead.

Once she was well and truly stuffed, Jamie carried her to bed, propped her back with pillows so she didn't get a tummy ache and clicked on the television. He lay beside her, holding her hand like they were a happily married couple, minus the vows.

When they weren't together, she found herself looking for him. Her heart ached until the moment her senses felt the rush of his proximity. An overwhelming burst of emotion would swell in her chest like a tidal wave obliterating the shore, surging around her body with so much rapture that her poor heart was ready to combust.

She wanted to tell him the truth, to lay her cards on the table and put her heart on the line. Was this love? Was it the swell of her heart, the persistent flutters in her chest, the yearning to be near him every second of the day, the desire to be worshipped by *him?* Were all those emotions just the principles of lust, or was it truly love? Glancing at his handsome side profile, drifting her eyes to his large hand curled around hers, she nodded lightly to herself.

Yeah this is it. This is earth shattering, life changing love. I love him. I'm in love with Jamie McGrath.

Chapter 40

Half way through the sitcom, Shannon dozed off with her cheek pressed to his heart and Jackson huddled along the length of her legs. Carefully sliding out from under her head, he lowered her face to the pillow. This wasn't the first time he had taken a moment to breath her in and watch her lashes flitter against her cheek. Women like her were rare. It wasn't just her stunning looks and priceless body but her vulnerability that she locked away from the world, yet gave him permission to see.

He patted Jackson's warm head and whispered, "Watch her for me, mate." Then he crept out of the bedroom, looking back over his shoulder at the perfect woman asleep in his bed. It was really weird how happy he felt, even though they hadn't had sex that evening. The emotions swirling inside his chest were like the sex after glow, times a hundred – scrap that – times a fucking million. He was floating on clouds of cotton candy and chewing up every sweet and tasty morsel. With Shannon, it wasn't just about the whips and ropes and rip-your-clothes off sex, albeit he craved to hear her sexy little groans all day every day. It all boiled down to the secret glances, featherlight touches, sweet and sexy smiles and how they could talk about a rubber band and still never grow tired of each other.

He had a mountain of work to get through. Business was always the priority, but lately Shannon had become a huge distraction, making it virtually impossible to get anything done. Marcus had already called him out on it. Now he had to play catch up. He happily helped out at the yard, running the day to day business, leaving Shannon to deal with the horses. It worried him that Niall would wonder back to the yard under the pretence of being a changed man. No amount of rehab would rip evil from a person's soul. It had to be her decision to leave Meadow Dawn permanently, and he was going to do everything in his power to entice her.

Watching her on the back of a muscular horse, jumping courses at Meadow Dawn had quickly become one of his favourite past times – she was fearless in the saddle, yet so defenceless in his bed. Shannon was a perplexing contradiction.

When he eventually pulled back the sheets and sank into bed at 2 a.m., seductive soft moans filled him with limitless contentment. She was curled up like a cute kitty, her warm and inviting body absorbed his touch, anchoring him to the idea of forever. Her eyelids twitched when his fingertips ran through her hair. He was ready to commit to more, if this was monogamy, then he was ready to tackle it head on. Slipping his arm under her petite frame, he nestled closer. All the money in the world couldn't replace the surge of emotions that ran through his veins. He could never delete the memories of her kisses, they were his to think upon, his to crave, each and every one. Right by her side was 'that' place, where lust and love joined forces.

Shannon had quickly become the most important factor in his life now, yet a persistent niggle ate away at him every single day, to drop the billionaire bomb into the mix.

He was fucked if she found out before he could tell her, and the chances of that happening were rising, fast. In fact, he was surprised she hadn't looked him up on the internet already. It was all there for the world to see, and the finer details were being hunted down by the press, each one scavenging for scraps about his life. The fact she had issues with rich men was a massive problem - he was rich beyond comprehension, and realistically, she would never match his wealth.

The time would come. Shannon wouldn't run from him would she?

Chapter 41

Jamie sat alongside Bucky in the viewing gallery, watching Shannon canter Trixie around the arrangement of colourful fences in the indoor school at Meadow Dawn. Even though she had conked out for over ten hours the night before, her body was verging on limp.

Shannon threw her leg over Trixie's back and slid down to the ground, almost toppling over as her legs hit the sand, they shook, and her knees buckled. Black dots danced across her eyes blotting out the floodlights. Her fingers curled around the stirrup leather to stop herself from swaying. A thud from landing boots came from behind and a firm hand pressed into the small of her back. Jamie's intoxicating presence still affected her, and right now it was adding to the quickened gallop of her heart.

"Shannon?"

Drawing a deep breath, she turned her head to meet his narrow eyes, filled with concern. "I'm okay, Jamie. Don't worry about it."

He glanced at Jackson when he let out a low growl. "I'm taking you back with me. We'll spend the weekend together eating pizza and drinking beer on the sofa. You need rest."

"I don't know, Jamie." Her head was spinning, and a dull ache in her belly made her feel like vomiting.

Bucky took the reins and lead Trixie away. "I'll take care of the yard, Shannon," he called over his shoulder. "Get some rest."

She sighed heavily. "I'll be back tomorrow, Bucky."

Jamie stepped closer, his minty fresh breath and woodsy aroma lingered between them. "No, you won't. A weekend off equals your sexy ass in bed, with me... just resting." He pressed a light kiss on her temple.

"I do need a few days off, but there's so much to sort out on the yard. I have a new customer arriving tomorrow, they're dropping off their horse, so I need to be here in person."

"I'm ordering you to take a break, Shannon stubborn Colter. I've helped you, haven't I, so let me arrange for someone else to greet the new horse. I won't take no for an answer."

She fisted the fabric of his jacket and pulled herself up on tip toes, kissing his pouted lips. "I think you're right, but I'm not taking a break because you're ordering me to. Got it?" Her forefinger prodded his hard chest. "A few days off, in bed with a certain good-looking guy would be fun... To rest, of course." Her smile ached her cheeks when he grinned down at her. "I'll grab some stuff from the loft. Meet you at the helicopter." She tilted into his chest, leaning on his strength.

His eyes danced. "That's why you like me – isn't it? Because I order you about."

The safety clip fell away, and she tugged her helmet from her head. "Hmm... Do I like you?" Her cheeks puffed out, releasing a slow steady breath playfully like she was thinking long and hard about her answer. "I'll admit it. I do like you, Jamie. A lot actually, but don't let it go to that big head of yours." She blinked up at him with fluttery lashes and an impish grin. "I'll see you in five."

She broke away from his teasing dimple and wandered to the barn doors, feeling a surge of relief for a whole weekend off, to rest, relax and more importantly, to be with him.

"Hey!" he called out. "I kinda like you a lot too. Don't let it go to *your* head. You should count yourself lucky that you tied me up with your fucking lasso."

Her stomach flipped over like a silly puppy doing tricks. Jamie McGrath was amazing on all levels - from fantasy to surreal, and oddly enough he was into her – the plain little country girl who stank of horse shit most of the time and came with a wheel barrow of drama.

"Lasso, Jamie? Is that another one of your fantasies?"

"Yes, ma'am." He smirked. "I never did get to see that Stetson."

"Later, big guy." She winked, tossing her hair over her shoulder and flashing him her best sexy come-hither look. "I'll make sure I pack it now."

An icy chill scattered her scalp when the loft door swung open. So much had changed since the days she curled up all alone. Jamie had given her life and Harry had lost his. Glancing at the couch, a ghost of a smile held her lips, memories of Jamie pushed through the hell. It was odd how the loft felt cramped and unwelcoming after she'd made it her home for many years. Now it felt empty, soulless, just a place to store her things.

Dread burrowed deep in her chest. What would happen when Jamie finally becomes bored of her drama? She would end up back here, facing her demons alone. In a matter of weeks, she felt more at home, safe and content with him in Fermanagh than she ever dreamed possible.

The deal was done, her heart was signed, sealed and sent by courier to Jamie – to do with as he pleased.

The bed sheets were neatly tucked and draped just as she left them. A faint scent of her perfume lingered in the still air, but it was the open drawers that caught her attention. They sat all wonky, hanging precariously, ready to crash to the floor. Her clothes were crumpled which wouldn't normally be an odd thing as she hated ironing, but it looked as though they had been disturbed by searching hands.

A click echoed down the galley kitchen, like the front door had closed. Grabbing her favourite trainers, she tossed them in a tote bag and reached for a photograph. Harry's chirpy face beamed, and his arm wrapped her shoulder as she grinned at the sight of her winning rosette.

"I'm nearly ready!" she called, snatching her perfume from the dresser.

Silence.

Footsteps followed the flow of the loft stopping at the bedroom door.

"I told you, I don't need any hel...." Her words trailed off when the smug face of Niall Ross met her startled gaze. Her heart dropped like an elevator, bringing her warm smile down with it.

Leaning against the frame, he folded his arms across his pale blue shirt. "Moving out, Shan?"

Shit. Where's Jamie?

"Why are you here? Does anyone else know you're back?" Her words tumbled out in rush of air.

Niall unfurled his arms and rubbed his palms together quickly with an odd look of joy plastered across his pale face. "Just, Bucky." The friction swipes stopped, and he slipped a hand into his jeans pocket. "I always hated that asshole, but today he's a legend." His hand drew out into the open. "He was so happy so see me that he gave me this." A small bag of white powder dangled from his fingers. "I couldn't be bothered with rehab. Amsterdam was a better retreat," he said through a chuckle.

A jangle of keys sounded as he tugged a bunch free from the opposite pocket. With a nip of his teeth the clear pouch opened, and he scooped out a mound of powder, resting it on the length of the key. In one long inhalation he hoovered up every trace of the cocaine.

"What the hell do you want?" she hissed. He was blocking the doorway; the only way out was through him. With a nasal passage full of drugs, she'd have no problem ramming him like a skittle. If only she wasn't so damn weak and weary.

"You didn't keep your promise, Shan. Gracie told me you haven't been staying here and that McGrath has been sniffing around my yard, trying to replace my father. She's been keeping a close eye on you."

"Has she been in here... going through my stuff? Fucking with my head?" she hissed.

Niall shrugged. "I paid her well. So, Jamie? In my

fucking yard, after I warned you."

"He's been helping me. This place doesn't run on its own, you know? The money for that shit up your nose comes from hard work. Something you know nothing about." Her patience was fraying. "Jesus, Niall. We've been waiting for you to come back so we can scatter Harry's ashes."

Hair flopped over his forehead covering his brows, and his constant need to sniff was driving her nuts. "He's dead, Shannon. I don't give a fuck what happens to his ashes." Narrow shoulders bobbed upwards. The guy didn't care about anyone other than himself.

"You're sick in the head."

"Gracie is quite the little good girl. She's been keeping an eye on you for ages now. She likes the party life as much as I do. Maybe I'll let her share this later." Another key full of powder was snuffed up. He pinched the bridge of his nose as his eyes watered. "Wow, this is some shit. I didn't realise Bucky had fingers in all the right pies."

"Your father's ashes, Niall. We need to honour his wishes. You don't seem to give a shit? Was it you? Did you ram the limo?" A sudden rise of fear made her heart pound.

Niall clucked his tongue. "Oh, you'd like to believe that. Wouldn't you? Seriously, why would I do that? The man was my main source of income, why the fuck would I want to take him out. You really are dumb." Another trail of powder vanished up his nostrils. "What part of stay away from McGrath did you not understand?"

Her hands balled and a whirl of fury scorched through her veins. "Go to hell, Niall. You're fucked up," she spat. "I think the problem here is that you're jealous of him."

She hated how his slow smile made her jaw visibly tick. He knew he was getting to her. "Ya reckon? Jealous of the guy who's tapping your ass. I've already been there, Shannon. I got there first."

"You're pathetic, Niall."

If there was ever an ounce of goodness in his soul, it had run away from the evil lurking behind his eyes. He just stared at her with a furrowed brow. "You do know the horses are all mine now, including Venatrix. I can do whatever the hell I want to them, because I can. Trixie isn't up for sale." He ran his tongue across his gums. "Well okay, she is up for sale, but I'll never sell her to you or your billionaire boyfriend."

Her jaw slackened, and she sucked in a gust of air. "Billionaire? What? Really? He would've told me, wouldn't he?"

"What's wrong? Surely you knew he was filthy rich? Oops! Have I planted a bomb in your pretty little relationship?" He cackled, wiping his nose with the back of his hand.

"Fuck you," she blasted.

Niall slinked closer, the stench of his overpowering cologne stuck in her nostrils. She was fuming mad that he knew something about Jamie that she didn't.

"And before you offer me your condolences, I know my dad wanted to hand this place over to his protégé. The great fucking, Shannon Colter." A slithery smile split his lips, and his eyes darted from her mouth to her chest. "It's a shame he never got the opportunity to amend his will. Don't worry, I have an idea." He stepped closer with prominent dark crescents under his bloodshot eyes, cracked lips and a dusting of white powder gathered in his nostril hair. "You run the yard for me, and I'll let you stay here." A slight tremble to his hand matched wide pupils that flickered back and forth. "You can be with Trixie, on one condition. Jamie McGrath gets the big elbow. I don't want to see his ugly face around here, and you won't be running off to his place either. You work here. You live here. My rules."

She inched back. "No fucking chance," she gritted out.

One large stride brought him inches from her face, trapping her between his body and the open drawers. "Fine. Get the fuck of my property." His sleeked smirk fuelled her wrath.

With all her effort she shunted him away, watching as

he staggered back. "I can't believe a good man like Harry had a mega prick like you for a son," she snarled.

His mouth tightened to a firm line as he stuffed the powder into his jeans. "My dad thought I was a looser, Shannon. He never looked at me the way he looked at you. You were everything that I wasn't. I just reminded him of that bitch who left him, and the fact I hated horses made it even worse. I tried for years to pretend riding was my thing. But you know what? I fucking hate horses, just as much as I hate you. I'm glad he's dead. I'm going to sell this shit hole and move on."

The words burned her ears like a swarm of wasps. The yard meant everything to Harry – it was his life's work. Her gut twisted at the thought of Trixie being sold off to the highest bidder.

"I wish Harry really thought you were a looser, that way he wouldn't have left this place to you or funded your addiction." She lunged forward, diving into his narrow chest with her shoulder. Niall toppled to the floor. "I hate you!" she screamed.

The tone of menacing chuckle only fed her rage. "Do you want to play rough, little Shannon?"

Taking the opportunity while he was crouched on his knees, she flicked out her foot and booted him in the ribs, the very act she had seen him do countless time before to the horses. As he lurched forward letting out a howl, she launched an attack with her fists.

In one swoop, Niall smashed his hands into the back of her knees, forcing her legs to buckle. She hit the floor with a thud, banging her head on the drawers on the way down. His movements became sluggish, grunts and sighs followed a scramble closer. Her head ached, and she couldn't tell if she was concussed or if he was on slow mo because of the drugs.

Niall clambered on top. She thumped her fists into his chest. The weight of his body weighed heavily on her pelvis, only making her hips buck more furiously. Exhaustion slowed her efforts.

A sudden slap stung her cheek. "Don't make me mark the places people can see, Shannon. I'll put that horse in the ground if you don't play ball."

She spat in his face only to feel his fingers dig into her throat. Her strained screech was barely audible beneath his wicked laugh. Tapping nails carried Jackson into the bedroom, skidding to a halt. His teeth bared, his head lowered and low warning growls turned to fierce barking.

Her head spun. The barking was so loud. Her nails dragged down his cheeks. Then she saw him. Jamie ran into the bedroom with a look on his face that was terrifying. He grabbed Niall buy the armpits, slinging him effortlessly to the wall and pinning him in place as his prisoner. A deafening crack of bone pierced through the barking when Jamie threw a punch, directing it on Niall's nose.

"I've finally got the motherfucker who beat Shannon and left twenty-three unforgivable bruises on her perfect body. Well guess what, asshole, I'm gonna make sure I break at least twenty-three of your bones. One down, twenty-two left!" he snarled, his handsome face contorted.

"Wait!" Niall roared. "I'll give her the horse if you fuck off and never come back here again."

"No way, dickhead. You think I'm gonna let you get away with hurting her? You're scum, Ross, and you need to find out what happens to scum. They get wiped out."

"Jamie!" Shannon lifted to her knees, unable to stand but determined to speak. "Please, he'll let me have Trixie. That's all I want. Let him go. You'll only get in trouble if you hurt him."

"No, Shannon. He hurt you and he threaten my dad. I can't let him get away with it," he spat with his palm curled around the fabric of Niall's jumper.

"You heard her, McGrath. You hurt me, and I'll make sure that fucking horse is dead by the time you leave Meadow Dawn." Niall smirked, his eyes danced like he'd won an epic battle.

Reluctantly Jamie's hold dropped. Niall slumped down the wall, blood trickling onto his shirt. He scuttled out of the bedroom, and when he got to the front door he yelled, "The horse won't survive the night, and you, McGrath, can't do a thing about it."

Jamie's eyes flashed with fury. His muscles were tight and his shoulders stiff. "Fucking, asshole," he gritted out. In one stride he was gone, running after Niall.

Shannon scrambled behind, her head thumping and her eyes filled with tears. "Please, Jamie, don't do anything stupid. He's not worth it," she yelled after him.

When she reached the cold damp air outside, Jamie was chasing Niall down the steps. She watched the manic tussle, gasping when Niall struck out his boot and kicked Jamie in the back. But it was the sucker punch that landed on Niall's face that forced him to stagger and fall. His head hung, and the wind left his lungs in a mighty gust. Raising on all fours, he wobbled, gasped loudly, slapped his palm to his sternum and slumped down. He just lay there, motionless.

Bucky appeared. His fingers searched Niall's throat for a pulse. His head shook. Jamie's hands flew up to the crown of his head, his elbows jutting out.

"He's dead." Bucky's words were like a knife slashing through their happiness, tearing through the world they had created and cutting off the future.

Jamie turned away from the lifeless body at his feet. His eyes were wide, gazing up the stone steps where she folded to her knees. "I've killed him." Was a distant murmur. Chopper blades cut through the silence, men with ear pieces arrived out of nowhere. The pulsating in her throat quickened until she was panting for air.

Jamie's face was suddenly so close, his palms cradling her head as she stared up at his pale cheeks, drained with shock. "I'm sorry, Shannon." His slow murmur drifted away, lost beneath the loud voices calling for him.

She blinked, desperately trying to banish the black blobs tracing her sight. Her head lowered, his hands retreated and he was gone.

Chapter 42

"Shannon?"

"Yes?" She looked up at the stunning blonde gliding towards her.

"I'm Lana. I've come to take you home. Marcus is with Jamie."

When she heard his name, the deep ache in her chest splintered. Shannon glanced back at the nurse and nodded. "Thanks. I'll be off now," she said softly with a ghost of a smile.

The nurse reached out and squeezed her wrist. "You need to tell someone, sweetheart. Your friend here seems like she'll be able to help you."

Shannon nodded. "I'll see you in a few weeks."

"Shannon, why are coming back to the hospital?" Concern pooled in Lana's big blue eyes, framed by long black lashes. She wore knee length leather boots, tight black jeans and a streamlined camel coloured coat made from the softest fine knit wool. The woman was gorgeous and exactly the type of female Shannon expected the McGrath men to settle down with.

"Where is he?" She changed the subject. Jamie's well-being was priority for now. Shannon hadn't seen him since he left her at Meadow Dawn. The female body guard hadn't said much when she escorted Shannon to the hospital. Apparently, the brothers had set up teams of security.

Lana slipped her hand in the crook of Shannon's elbow, tugging her closer like they'd known each other for years. "He's with Marcus and the police. Jamie has requested that you wait for him at my place in Fermanagh.

He doesn't want you to be alone."

"Okay," she said tightly. There was nowhere else to go. "I need to speak to him."

Lana nodded to the smartly dressed female discreetly following behind. Her arm tightened as they approached the helipad to the rear of the hospital. "Marcus will bring him home, Shannon. I promise you."

"I need to see him... before... I have to tell him something." The thought of Jamie rotting away in prison because of Niall, because of her. It was all too much to deal with, especially now, Shannon knew why she had struggled with exhaustion. A serious looking doctor just gave her some news. She needed time to process everything that had happened and everything still to come.

Clambering into helicopters had quickly become the norm. She didn't think twice about sliding on the lightweight headset or buckling herself in. It felt odd to look at the blonde woman beside her, and not find Jamie in the same seat.

"Lana, are they really billionaires?"

The helicopter lifted to the sky. Lana adjusted her headset, moving the arm of the microphone closer to her blood red lips. "The fact you're asking leads me to believe that you didn't know. Yes, the boys recently signed a deal that changed their lives."

"He left that part out."

"Is it a problem?"

"He should've told me."

Lana fell silent, gazing out at the birds-eye view of the city as they headed west. "Does it matter?" Her words were crystal clear, drifting into the cushions hugging Shannon's ears. "I mean, surely a woman will know that a man loves her when he spends all of his time with her, not just when he spends all his money on her. I don't know why he didn't tell you, Shannon, but I know his heart is breaking right now. He thinks you'll look at him differently."

"He lied to me about money, when I told him we needed to be equal. He had every opportunity to tell me,"

She gulped back the lump in her throat. The reality was, she didn't give a rat's ass about his money now. She just wanted to hold him, protect him and take away the memory of what happened. She cursed all the things that had kept them apart for so long. Maybe they just weren't meant to be together. Had the signs been there all this time? "The fact Niall is dead… well that's irrelevant to me. It was an accident. The guy won't be missed. Jamie didn't set out to kill him. It's just Niall's fucked up way of getting the last word in. I'm in love with Jamie, Lana. I need to know that I won't have to face this on my own. I've lost everything. My mentor, my home, my horse, Jamie and now my career."

"You haven't lost him. Marcus always comes through, Shannon."

"He killed Niall. They'll lock him up and through away the key." A ragged sob bubbled from her chest. "I need him now, more than ever."

"Marcus will bring him home to you. I promise you."

"If he doesn't then I'll…" Her palm pressed to her belly. She titled forward, holding herself tightly like a vulnerable child.

Lana's hand rested on her shoulder. "Shannon, why have you got another hospital appointment?"

"I'm pregnant. I'm having his baby."

Chapter 43

He didn't want to leave Shannon on the doorstep with shock breaking her shaky voice. The newly appointed security detail had dragged him away from the fucked up scene of death, and tore him away from her. That was the hardest part, even more devastating than walking past that bastard's dead body. A not so tough guy who tried to break his woman.

Marcus was already waiting at the police station when he arrived. Together they spent the night with a legal team, detectives and a coroner, thrashing out the whole mess. Now he was a free man, with a clear conscience.

They landed just in time to witness the burning orange sun sink behind Marcus's home in Fermanagh. Turning to his brother, he gripped Marcus's arm. "Marcus. I owe you, mate."

"You always owe me. I'm your big brother, saving your ass goes with the territory," Marcus replied with a light hearted chuckle.

Jamie squeezed his arm tighter. "I mean it. I love you, bro."

Marcus stared at him for a second and then smirked. "Toughen up, kid. You're talking like a woman. You should have said something like, 'Marcus, you're a fucking god,' or 'Marcus, you're my hero.'"

"Fuck you, Marcus." Jamie scowled, worry still creasing the corners of his tired eyes. "I can't believe Bucky switched up the cocaine with tranquillisers. It's just as well the security guys saw the transaction."

They exited the helicopter. "And I can't believe you lost your shit, Jamie. It was a stroke of luck that the asshole

273

had a heart attack so they couldn't pin anything on you," Marcus said over his shoulder.

The welcoming smell of home cooking wafted through the Coach House. Jamie had spent many a night in his brother's home, but this time, as he stood in the entrance hall, his nerves jumped, and a dull pain ached in his heart. Shannon was here, waiting for him. "What if she thinks I'm a monster. She didn't need to see that. The guy was a dick, but he didn't deserve to die, not like Carl Reed."

A flash of anger darkened his brother's eyes. The memory of how Carl had tried to kill Lana and Marcus was still so fresh for them both. "Niall had a heart attack. The guy was on his way out, long before you punched him. If anything, she'll be relieved that you're back." Marcus's eyes softened. "I'll do anything to keep my family safe, you know that, right." His hand curled behind Jamie's neck drawing his head closer. "I love you too, Jamie. This is our family now. You, Dad, me and Lana... and Shan." He jerked Jamie into a hug and slapped his back. "I could still take you down, even though you think you're Rocky Balboa now. You know word will get out that you killed a man, in a bare knuckle fight, with one punch, even though it's bullshit and your big brother had to save your ass." Pulling apart, Marcus's eyes gleamed.

"Marcus!" Lana's sweet voice came from behind. Her arms flew around Jamie, and she held him tight. "I'm so glad you're here. She's in bed resting."

His brows snapped together. "Is she okay? Did the hospital run tests? Is she sick?"

Lana's hands slipped down his chest and found their way to Marcus. "I'll let her talk to you."

Jamie's heart skidded to a halt. "About what?" Before waiting for an answer, he spun around and marched in the direction of the guest bedroom. Consumed by emotion, need and desire, his legs carried him with speed until he reached the closed door. He held a deep breath and entered. A prickle of fear burst over his skin, goose bumps scattered over his scalp. His heart stilled, suspended in his chest, waiting to drop. There she was, with red eyes and a blotchy face, curled up on the bed hugging a pillow.

"Did he hurt you?" His steps accelerated until he was by her side.

Words seemed to stick in her throat like dry toast as she gulped, sobs heaved from her chest. Dragging his hands through his hair, he waited, hoping and pleading silently that she was okay.

"Lana told me you didn't kill him and that Bucky mixed horse tranquiliser with the cocaine. It wouldn't have mattered if you had of killed him, Jamie, because I love you, no matter what. You were trying to protect me. I love you so much." Her words strained with stress and fortitude.

She loves me.

The emotion swimming in her eyes reached right inside his heart and tugged. Her puffy lids blinked rapidly as she fiddled with the pillow case, openly declaring her love for him. Before he could round up his relief and gather the words to reply, she shuffled closer. "We would have waited for you." Reaching forward, her soft little hand grasped his. It was so warm and inviting, so delicate yet strong. She guided his palm to her belly and let it rest on her abdomen. "We're having a baby, Jamie."

His eyes widened, blood swooshed around his body like he just injected himself with caffeine. "Holy fuck! A baby? You just said a baby, right?" He knew exactly what she had said. That one little word 'baby' meant so much. It was pieces of him mixed with pieces of her, parts of the amazing woman staring back at him. "I thought you were my soul mate when you made me a bacon sandwich, but this? What the fuck? I didn't think you could top that feeling, Shannon."

She had just gifted him with the one thing he cherished the most, family. He was going to have his own perfect little family with the woman he worshipped. As his fingers moved around her bump, his eyes misted with pride.

"You're okay with it then? With our little bacon bits growing inside me?"

"Okay with it? I'm more than fucking okay with it." He gulped back the emotion swelling in his throat. "How?" he gasped. "I mean, I know how it happened, clearly because it was fucking awesome, but we used protection."

She nodded. "It can happen even using condoms, you know? On the date of the competitions I'll be over five months pregnant. I can't ride now, not until after I've had the baby. It would be too dangerous, in case I fell off. I'm giving it all up for us, for the baby."

Time stood still in a momentary loop with the word, baby, fluttering around in the thick silence. Her belly felt soft when the pads of his fingers lightly prodded and pressed. "You're having our kid?"

"Yes." A light smile graced her dry lips.

"I won't let you give up on your dreams, Shan." He perched on the edge of the bed. "We'll work it out." This was it. Time to spill the billion pound bank balance out in the open. "I'll support your career, Shannon. Once you've had the baby you can get back on track." A light sigh left his chest when he said baby out loud. "I need to tell you something. Here me out, okay?"

She nodded lightly and rested her hand over his, holding their combined heat over the little person growing inside the slight bulge.

"Marcus and I recently signed a business deal that made us billionaires. I didn't tell you because at first, I didn't know if you were like the rest of them. Deep down, I knew you were special from the second you refused to take my money. I've had my share of women sniffing around, not just for sex but for the money. I know that's hard to believe because I'm the full package, right? A good-looking rich guy." He smirked, watching her face brighten. "Then you told me that all wealthy guys were assholes, which was perfect and a disaster all at the same time. I was going to tell you, until all this happened."

Her lip wobbled, and she sucked in a sob. "I knew you had money, I accepted that fact when I realised I was in love with you - for the man you are, not for the size of your bank account. Although it never occurred to me that you were that wealthy."

"Shannon. We've had this crazy connection from the day we met." His hands moved to her face, cupping her cheeks with strands of hair all at the same time. She stared back at him with so much emotion behind her eyes, emphasising her feelings. "We've been through a lot together, and I still look at your mouth and wish it was on mine, I still think about the softness of your skin, I still hope you'll look at me with those piercing blue eyes and return all the feelings I have for you." Soft breaths flurried over his face making his lips find the salty tears rolling down her cheek. "I love you, Shannon. I always have."

Those powerful sparks rocketed through his core when their lips met with tenderness and hunger. Her sweet moans vibrated inside his whole body, and he knew. He knew she was the missing connection that he had craved all this time. Shannon was his, and he had to make sure it stayed that way.

Chapter 44

"Why are we going in here?" she asked, when the Mustang slowed down. There were acres of green fields stretching as far as she could see, horses scattered in every direction, sectioned in fenced paddocks and a large sweeping wall at the entrance of Unity equine facilities.

"I own this place," he said as the car turned in.

"You're kidding me? You own Unity? One of the most prestigious racing yards in Europe? I didn't even know there was one in Fermanagh."

"It's called Unity because we have facilities all over Europe, providing the utmost service and high-end services. Anyone who is anyone stables their race horses with us for training. Together each site forms one brand – Unity. This is where it all started."

The car crept up the lengthy lane, leading to a stone barn conversion to the front and a handful of large barns and out buildings at the rear.

"Jamie… This is crazy. All this time… You kept this from me."

His fingers gripped the wheel. "Shannon, our very first encounter involved me trying to give you money. You made it perfectly clear you didn't want to be owned, or bought, or whatever you thought I was trying to do. I never expected you to meet my salary. You're the one who put that stipulation on the table. Even I can't get used to the big fat zeroes at the end of the bank balance. Our finances have only recently rocketed off the charts. You fell for me without all this."

"Who said I fell for you?" she said playfully.

His eyes cut to hers.

"I like you, a bit. There's a difference." Her fingertips covered an obvious smirk, watching his showstopping dimple dent his cheek.

"I like you a little bit too."

She glanced out the window. "It's so much to take in. Life has been a whirlwind since we met. I know you said Trixie was in good hands, but I'd like to see all the horses at Meadow Dawn before they're all sold. I'm scared that they'll take her away from me."

"Don't be scared." His thumb dragged over her lips, and his palm drifted down to her belly, holding it there quietly. The intimacy of his touch was all she needed to sooth her tumbling thoughts. His large hand often found its way to her bump. It was comforting and so was the subtle smile that tugged at his lips every time. "Do you trust me, Shannon." Those words had meant so much in the past, and now they meant even more.

"Yes."

"So you won't be angry with me when I tell you that I'm in the process of acquiring Meadow Dawn, and all the horses in it," he said with a shy smile.

"What? I don't understand?"

"When we were at the police station, I thought I was going to be arrested for manslaughter. I wanted you to have something of your own. The very thing that you've worked so hard for. Even if I was locked up, you would still have your career, and I would know you were happy doing what you do best. I have my legal team working around the clock to make sure you get the yard, for yourself and to carry on Harry's legacy."

A mist covered her eyes. "Jamie, you're more important to me than Meadow Dawn, or even my career. I don't know how I would've survived without you."

"That's why I love you, because your strong, you would've been okay. You're mine, Shannon, and all this belongs to you too."

"What about, Trixie? Is she okay? I need to go to Meadow Dawn to see, her."

He flung open the car door and leapt out. "I have a surprise for you." Jamie rounded the car and appeared at the passenger door. "Take my hand."

She slotted her hand into his, instantly evoking that delightful shiver that only he could bring.

Together they walked through the bustling office. Phones rang, voices mumbled, staff waved at Jamie, acknowledging the big boss.

"Everything in order?" Jamie asked a small guy with thick glasses and a goatee.

"Yes, sir. The vet is ready."

Leaving the office through a back door, she gazed at the row of white rendered stables with a corrugated roof sprawled wide with no less than ten thoroughbreds peering out.

"How big is this place?" she asked, filled with disbelief that the man she was having a child with was super rich and into horses, in a big way.

"It's only 58 odd acres. The smallest yard we own, but it's my favourite – even more now that we've made some important modifications. Let me show you the rest of the place. We've got a hydro pool, round pen, walker, gallops and an onsite veterinary clinic. We recently enlisted a guy who maps out the horse's bones on the outside and monitors alignment for both horse and rider. He'll come in handy when you're training your horses at Meadow Dawn."

Her eyes widened, her fingers buzzed in his firm hold.

"There's a horse getting the once over in the veterinary facility, if you want to have a look?"

They crossed over a large concrete yard filled with staff cars and a horse transportation lorry.

"In here." He opened the door wafting a clinical smell of antiseptic up her nose.

As soon as the door opened her lungs exploded. There stood the first love of her life – Trixie. Safe and sound, undergoing an inspection by a young male in a white coat.

"She's not hurt, is she?" Shannon lunged forward,

caressing Trixie's warm muscular neck, kissing her silky smooth coat. She exhaled loudly as the vet confirmed the horse was as fit as a fiddle.

"Does this mean she's yours now, Jamie?"

"I don't own her Shannon and the owner would never sell her."

"What? No? Who owns her?" Shannon's lip wobbled.

"You do. She was always yours. Harry put your name as the owner on her documents the day she was born."

"She was mine all along? Why didn't Harry tell me?"

"Perhaps he was waiting for the right time." Jamie scratched the white star between Trixie's eyes. "The dust needs to settle at Meadow Dawn before you can go back. I want to update the place for you, so it mirror's Unity. All this belongs to us, Shannon. In the meantime, I thought you would want her close by."

"All this is yours, Jamie, not mine."

His mouth tightened to a firm line but he carried on stroking Trixie without saying a word.

"It's such a shame I can't ride her."

"I know, that's why Mitchell Ashfield is going to ride her on your behalf, with you named as the owner and trainer. He's agreed already but wants to chat with you about a way forward."

Shannon's head swirled. Too much information to take in. Her heart was racing and her stomach was in knots. Trixie was finally hers, she was safe, but Harry was dead.

Jamie shifted. A sudden wash of something unknown swam in his eyes, and his shoulders looked stiff from stress. "Walk with me. I'll show you her stall."

He led her out of the clinic, across the yard and into a large barn lined with open air stables. His presence was a constant, his hand fixed between her shoulder blades. After they passed three of the unoccupied stalls, Jamie stopped. On the stable door a small name plaque had been recently attached with the name Venatrix Meadow Dawn etched into the metal. Slung over the door was a dark leather saddle bag.

"The stable is for your horse, and the saddle bag is for you."

"You do know I was taunted at school and called saddle bags?"

His smile widened. "Yeah, I know, they were assholes. Go on, open it."

Shannon cautiously lifted the flap and peered inside. A small velvet box sat at the bottom.

No way.

No way.

No way.

Her hands shook, flipping open the lid to reveal a delicate smoky grey diamond ring, surrounded with dazzling black and white diamonds flowing down the platinum band at either side.

"I had it made by a designer in New York. I want to marry you, Shannon."

It was a stunningly heavy ring, enchanting and completely unexpected. "Are you asking me to marry you because I'm pregnant?"

His sexy low chuckle drew her closer. "I'm good, love, but I'm not that good. The ring was ordered a few days ago and expedited – before we found out. I'm in love with you. I can't wait to meet the little guy." His palm settled on her belly. She treasured how his eyes sparkled every time he touched her there. "But I'm shit scared that all this will tumble down because of my money. Whether you like it or not, if you agree to marry me, all this will be yours too. The whole fucking lot, Shannon."

Her hands brushed his washboard abs, hidden beneath the fabric of his polo shirt. "You love me, right? And I think we both know that I like you a little bit. Everything will be okay now, Jamie. We're a family already with or without marriage."

Jamie's head dropped, resting on her forehead. "How can I impress you, so that little bit turns into a whole fucking lot." The heat from his growl fired up the synapses in her brain.

"I have a few suggestions, most of them will have to wait until we get home." She nipped his lower lip with her teeth. "Yes, Jamie. I'll marry you. But I'm marrying your heart and soul, not your money. I'd be honoured to become 'The First Mrs. Jamie McGrath' and the last woman to give you a blow job." Her lips curled to a sassy smile. "I don't just like you a little bit, I love you more than my heart can take."

"I've always known you wanted me, for me. It means more to me than all the money I've earned." His eyes gleamed. "I hope you like this too?" He waved his hands, gesturing towards his body.

"Nah, the body is over rated. It's this thing I love...." She grabbed the front of his jeans, rubbing his hardness against the palm of her hand.

"Get in the stable. Drop to your knees!" he ordered, slipping the ring on her finger. "I want to see my ring on your hand while you suck my dick with that perfect mouth."

"Jamie."

"Shannon?"

"Thank you."

"Show me how thankful you are, Shannon." His eyes twinkled.

Touching his lips with teasing pressure, she wrapped her arms around his neck, tugging his head down. "I'll do anything for you, Jamie. You've already done so much for me."

A smirk graced his lips. "Anything indeed. Well then how about you get that rope and…"

His words were muffled as she tugged his mouth down to meet her hungry lips. Her heart rate rocketed as she kissed him with everything she had, with passion, with heat, with rawness and with all her soul.

Horses whinnied and nickered in the background, buffering the sound of his zipper sliding down.

Eighteen month later…

"Let me help you, mate."

"No, Jamie, this is my thing now, apparently," Marcus said with a light sigh of disbelief.

A small hand tugged his jeans. When he looked down, big blue eyes stared back at him. The same ocean blue eyes that his wife used to get whatever she wanted from him. Which was usually just him, all to herself for a few minutes while their son slept. "Harry, where's Mummy?"

The boy with wispy black hair pointed to the long table where George sipped whiskey and chatted to Shannon about horses. His father had recognised her the second they were reintroduced. It was like he knew all along that she was family. Shannon traced her nails over her protruding tummy. She was pregnant again, something about having all the kids in close succession so she could focus on riding once they were all born. There was talk of three or four small people, which scared the hell out of him after witnessing Harry's birth. Sweet Jesus, he almost fainted when the little guy appeared, like a messy miracle. He relented to her persuasive tactics because, let's face it, he enjoyed making love to his woman. As long as he woke up looking into Shannon's happy eyes every morning, he was a happy man.

"Marcus, did you actually listen to Freddy?" Lana brushed her small hand down his brother's back, nudging into his side with her round tummy. She was a month away from having their first child and Marcus wouldn't let her out of his sight. "You're kinda hacking your way through that thing." She laughed as her arms circled his waist.

Jamie scooped up his son and swiped a piece of turkey from the oval platter. "Tastes good, even if it looks like road kill."

"Are you two competing for laughs? I never thought I'd see the day when my wife took sides with my kid brother." His head shook but a slight smile curved his lips. "Once you put gravy over it, you'll not care what it looks like. I've never carved a fucking monster bird before. This shit is stressful."

Shannon appeared by his side with a huge grin on her pretty face. The sound of her voice, soothing and husky, never failed to make Jamie's heart buck. "Here ya go, Marcus." She winked, holding out a glass of whiskey. "I'll quite happily eat roadkill, I'm starving."

Marcus took a long gulp of the amber liquid. "Lana McGrath, you have a lot to answer for. I can't believe you roped me into cooking the Christmas turkey this year. Why the hell isn't Freddy here to do it?"

"But you're so good in the kitchen, Marcus." Lana pinched a stray piece of meat and popped it into her mouth. "And other areas."

Jamie looked at his brother who pretended to huff with the woman who had him wrapped around her little finger, a hundred times over. He noted how the touch of her hand softened his eyes, those bright green eyes of his that were clearly undressing his wife in one sweep.

"Are you okay?" Shannon stroked Harry's hair, but her gaze was fully focused on Jamie.

"I'm more than okay. I love you, Shannon."

A little hand ruffled his hair. "Dadda…" Soft tiny lips pressed against his ear, and his son's head dropped to his shoulder.

"I think he's tired." Shannon tipped forward and brushed a lock of hair from their son's face. "I'll put him to bed."

As much as Jamie wanted to lie beside his son and watch him sleep, he also wanted something else. "Hold the turkey. We're putting Harry down for a nap." He grabbed Shannon by the wrist and dished out a knowing look. "Let's go. Now."

Marcus sighed and Lana giggled. Just as he was about to trail his wife to the bedroom, his father appeared in the doorway. "Jamie."

"I'll be back in a few minutes, Dad. Marcus will get you another drink."

The old man lifted his glass and nodded. "I'm proud of you, son."

"I love you, Dad."

Shannon curled her hand around Jamie's arm, and Harry nestled into the crook of his neck.

The billions in their bank accounts meant nothing, not when his life was fully enriched and complete with his wife, his children and his family.

The End

Dear reader,

Thank you for reading Venatus.

Look out for more books coming soon!

***

I'd like to throw love around like confetti - all over my editors, Allison (@excessivereader), Pam (@love2readromance) and my cover designer, Becca. Every author needs a supportive team.

You guys are my A Team!

Lastly, thank you reader for taking the time to read my books. I hope they have touched your heart in some way.

If you've enjoyed the series, please take the time to let me know what you think!
A five-star review would mean the world to me.

SIGN UP

to my newsletter for updates on upcoming releases and secret info!

www.autumnarcher.com

ABOUT THE AUTHOR

A Northern Irish Contemporary Romance & Romantic Suspense Author who thrives on gin and the written word. She's a mother to two cool kids and two cute dogs and has a fluffle of wild rabbits in the back garden. Between working in the city during the day, entertaining the brood, feeding the husband and cuddling with the pups, she somehow manages to write romance.

She delves into the darker element of life at times giving her romantic suspense books a curious edge, with alpha men who have to work hard to win over strong women. That being said, she also loves to write sweet and swoony books that make you fall hard. The stories always have a heap of sexy scenarios that are best enjoyed by adults.

VENATUS